T0246674

# KREE

A UNIVOCAL BOOK
*Drew Burk, Consulting Editor*

Univocal Publishing was founded by Jason Wagner and Drew Burk as an independent publishing house specializing in artisanal editions and translations of texts spanning the areas of cultural theory, media archeology, continental philosophy, aesthetics, anthropology, and more. In May 2017, Univocal ceased operations as an independent publishing house and became a series with its publishing partner, the University of Minnesota Press.

*Univocal authors include:*

Miguel Abensour
Judith Balso
Roger Bartra
Jean Baudrillard
Philippe Beck
Simon Critchley
Fernand Deligny
Jacques Derrida
Vinciane Despret
Georges Didi-Huberman
Manuela Draeger
Jean Epstein
Vilém Flusser
Barbara Glowczewski
Évelyne Grossman
Félix Guattari
Olivier Haralambon
David Lapoujade
François Laruelle
David Link

Sylvère Lotringer
Jean Malaurie
Michael Marder
Serge Margel
Quentin Meillassoux
Friedrich Nietzsche
Peter Pál Pelbart
Jacques Rancière
Lionel Ruffel
Felwine Sarr
Michel Serres
Gilbert Simondon
Étienne Souriau
Isabelle Stengers
Sylvain Tesson
Eugene Thacker
Antoine Volodine
Elisabeth von Samsonow
Siegfried Zielinski

# KREE

*Manuela Draeger*

TRANSLATED BY
Lia Swope Mitchell

UNIVOCAL

University of Minnesota Press
Minneapolis
London

The University of Minnesota Press gratefully acknowledges financial support for the publication of this book from the Centre national du livre.

Originally published in French as *Kree.* Copyright 2020 by Editions de l'Olivier.

Translation copyright 2024 by the Regents of the University of Minnesota

All rights reserved. No part of this publication may be reproduced, stored in a retrieval system, or transmitted, in any form or by any means, electronic, mechanical, photocopying, recording, or otherwise, without the prior written permission of the publisher.

Published by the University of Minnesota Press
111 Third Avenue South, Suite 290
Minneapolis, MN 55401-2520
http://www.upress.umn.edu

ISBN 978-1-5179-1512-4 (pb)

A Cataloging-in-Publication record for this book is available from the Library of Congress.

Printed in the United States of America on acid-free paper

The University of Minnesota is an equal-opportunity educator and employer.

33 32 31 30 29 28 27 26 25 24          10 9 8 7 6 5 4 3 2 1

This translation is dedicated to my mother,
who taught me to read and write.
—*Lia Swope Mitchell*

*T*he guy swung his head slowly from to side. That was his way of showing he was thinking. He had the mug of a half-asleep giant, a red baseball cap over his forehead, pulled down to the eyes, if you could call them eyes, those two little gray dots glinting above his nose, moist with sleep and wine, so close together they were nearly lost in his enormous face. He widened them as best he could, in a questioning expression from which the gods had shorn any sign of intelligence. An idiot concentrating on an answer that wasn't coming, a great upright ape confronting the unknown, standing before a woman dressed like a soldier. His corpulence was impressive, the stature of a carnival wrestler, with a salty drop sliding down the length of one cheek. He'd just come out, the door behind him banged shut on a heavy, noxious atmosphere, darkness, odors of grilled meat, grimy skin, and alcohol. He was wearing bermuda shorts in a Hawaiian floral pattern, and on his torso an undershirt that might, a few months before, have been white. Everything else, fat here, muscle there, was naked.

Kree repeated her question.

"Loka, I said. Do you know how she died? Was it you who killed her?"

The guy continued moving his fat face from left shoulder to right shoulder, back and forth. He didn't seem to understand the

*3*

language being spoken to him. Slender or skinny before him, dressed in fatigues that were worn but still far from ragged, Kree clarified:

"Did you eat her?"

The night was dense, the street silent.

"Yes? No?" Kree went on.

It was three o'clock in the morning and it was hot. Though there were stars in the sky, they illuminated nothing. The spot where Kree and the giant were standing had been crudely covered in boards for the bad season, the time of year when mud made it too difficult to walk on the sidewalk and access the houses. The now-superfluous boards in front of the shack cracked at every step. They accentuated the theatrical nature of the scene: two immobile characters, a laborious dialogue, a wooden set, a miserly light with shadowy effects.

The giant was positioned stolidly in front of the shack door, and if he was preparing any response, he was having trouble getting it out of his mouth. The slow nodding of his head spread throughout his entire massive body, down to his massive legs, and even though he was not shifting his weight from one foot to the other, now and then the boards cracked.

A theatrical scene almost without words, with sound effects.

Three minutes earlier, Kree had knocked on the shack's door and hailed its occupants, whose names she'd just learned from an informant. Two brothers: the Grodons. Marcus and Dourdoul. In the nocturnal silence she'd called them with authority. Her fist beating against the door, the ridiculous shouted names. Marcus Grodon! Dourdoul Grodon! She wanted to catch them by surprise in their beds, in an alcoholic stupor and the black of night. For what she wanted to do, it would work better, in their drunkenness the men would be less alert. The informant had described the two brothers. You couldn't confuse them. An obese brute and an almost puny crank. So it was Dourdoul, the younger one, the fat one, who came to the threshold to see what the visitor wanted. He'd dragged himself out of sleep too quickly, which, in combination with the wine fermenting within him, did not favor the emergence of clear thought. He stared at Kree in stupefaction, and she was unable to draw him into anything resembling conversation.

From within the shack came the phlegmy voice of a drunk. An interjection from Marcus, Dourdoul's elder brother.

"What's she want?"

As if his brother's question pushed him out of his apathy, the giant let loose an almost human bawl toward the door, toward the stinking shadows that constituted the space beyond the door, and the brothers ran through an exchange:

"She's asking about her dog."

"What dog?" the other rasped.

"Dunno," the giant said. "Named Loka."

"So, what's she want?"

"Wants to know who it was who ate it."

There was a warm breeze through the street. Ten or twelve seconds of rumbling, then nothing. Often morning entered in this manner, but morning was still immeasurably far off. The wind rushed through the deserted street, stirred up the black dust and the nocturnal heat, renewed the veil of humidity that clung to Kree's cheek. And again the street was silent, full of scents: wood, earth, empty houses, the deserted city. Again the spectatorless theater scene, a scantily clad bruiser and a woman-soldier hiding her anger, again the creaking boards and the door, opening into darkness and stench. And above, a moonless sky, ten thousand stars not really shining or twinkling, perhaps due to trails of soot up on high.

Kree's nostrils filled with a vile haze of increasing strength, consisting of unaired bedding, unclean bodies, wine, and meat.

"You are the Grodon brothers, right? No mistake?" Kree verified.

"You got a problem with us?" asked the giant, suddenly loquacious.

"Someone they told me what one of the Grodon brothers he trapped Loka and he ate her. My dog, Loka."

The giant lifted his round, red baseball cap and scratched his scalp, introducing a little more disorder into his oily hair, then replaced his head-covering, smashing it down as far as possible over his forehead. His porcine eyes were now completely hidden under the visor. Then his arms dropped down again to hang alongside his torso.

He had not managed to construct a response for Kree and preferred not to open his mouth while waiting.

A few sounds came from inside the shack, the elder Grodon's hacking cough, then his voice. A sound of rustling straw. Marcus Grodon was still in bed, participating in the conversation from his mattress.

"What did she look like, this dog?"

Kree wasn't in a hurry to answer. First she took off the bag that she'd been wearing slung over her shoulder. She set it on the ground, on the boards. It was an army backpack, left open so she could plunge her hand in without wasting any time on pulling the zipper. She was having trouble containing her rage, feigning tranquility before this mountain of idiot flesh, before this shabby house, inhabited by two men she planned to kill—as retaliation for the death of her dog.

She touched something metallic that clicked softly under her fingertips. A chain, its musical fluidity. She stirred it for a second but did not take it up. She wanted to make sure her weapon was within reach and, at the same time, to confuse the giant with movements that he did not understand. She stood up, empty-handed, unthreatening. She made an effort not to look like any cause for concern. The giant wondered heavily over her, and in his gaze, behind the shadows and slitted eyelids, she made out a gluey stupor. He did not understand her attitude, her calm; he did not understand what she was asking, and he was not entirely sure whether she was afraid of him, with his large stature, his strength.

Finally she answered the question the elder Grodon had asked.

"A beautiful black dog," she said. "Shiny fur, brown eyes. Affectionate, but very independent."

"Loka, you said?" Dourdoul Grodon confirmed.

He had reactivated the oscillation of his colossal head. He was thinking, powerfully and in all directions or, at least, from left to right.

"She broke her paw in a trap," rasped the elder Grodon from inside the shack.

Then he made a brief hawking noise and spat.

As if in concert with the younger Grodon's head movements, Kree slowly shook her head, and again bent down toward her bag, then stood. And now she was holding a weapon. When she'd arrived at the Grodon place, she'd thought she could manage with a knife, but she'd changed her mind at the sight of the one called Dourdoul Grodon. Significantly more hippopatamesque than she'd expected. A knife would be inappropriate. The fat would get in the way. The blade would go astray, it might not reach the heart or arteries on the first cut. She would have to use something better suited.

Now a tangle of metal murmured almost harmoniously between her hands. Dourdoul Grodon did not make out what she was holding; he saw a mess of iron entrails, an odd chain, nothing he perceived as dangerous. Since she had spoken of her dog, maybe she wanted to show them the metal leash she used to tie it up at night. Due to the darkness and his lack of imagination, the big imbecile didn't see anything else.

Kree stood facing him and kept her voice neutral, peaceful, as if she were only interested in the information.

"Did you eat her?" she asked.

She addressed both brothers, but more particularly the one clearing his throat inside the shack, whose intelligence seemed a bit livelier.

"Well, yeah," answered the elder, the hawker, as the younger one, still standing in the doorway, attempted to weigh the terms of the question and the correct response.

There was a dead silence.

It didn't last excessively long. Prodded by some mysterious internal force, the younger Grodon, Dourdoul, the passive giant, thought best to add his two cents.

"That's what you wanted to know?" he said.

"Yes," Kree said.

"Well, yeah, we ate the dog," Dourdoul Grodon confirmed. "What's the problem?"

Kree examined him for a second. His head and hands moved mechanically, as if his brain was in the process of getting started, giving its first routine instructions to its organism so as to verify that everything was functioning, that communication between neurons was uninterrupted. A great oaf, bumbling between drunkenness and sleepwalking, not even on the defensive, when meanwhile, right in front of him, an unknown woman was manipulating an odd chain.

"Oh, no problem," Kree said, to reassure him one more second. "I just wanted to know."

An odd chain. With two ends that Dourdoul hadn't noticed. One end was armed with a lead sphere, the size of a closed fist, while the other end was armed with a sharp hook, rather like a machete.

Kree gave it an initial throw and soon had a meter of chain spinning at high speed, on an oblique plane at first, then above her head. No more than three seconds. Dourdoul Grodon had realized that she was waving around an object that could hurt him, but his brain did not successfully analyze the danger, gave him no indication regarding what he should do to protect himself. He started to take a step back. The boards creaked in complaint. Once the three seconds were up, Kree waited another half of a fourth second and then threw the chain forward. It wrapped around the Grodon brother's throat, strangling him. The lead sphere struck the base of his skull just below the right ear. In the same movement, without allowing him any time to react, Kree rushed him. With the machete on the chain's other end, which she'd kept enclosed in her hand until then, she sliced through everything under Dourdoul Grodon's chin. Skin, tallow, cartilage, tubes, veins, arteries. A perfect swordswoman's gesture. Then she fell back. She tugged the chain, which got a bit tangled in the cuts at first, but then swiftly and docilely returned to her. She took one, then two steps back, then a third. The boards whined. Meanwhile the giant had already raised his hands to the gaping wound between his shoulders. He made no sound, no gargle; he was incredibly still. A statue of lard taken by surprise, with no idea how to manage his distress, a wrestler in shorts, ridiculous and slaughtered, still balanced on his massive legs.

Then Dourdoul let out a hiccup, wavered, and crumpled noisily forward. First his knees folded, his torso perfectly straight, then he arced downward in a half circle. Kree avoided the monstrous body's crash and, as soon as the boards were quiet, she returned to plant the machete in the nape of his neck. She lingered over the base of his skull as she sawed through the spinal column. Her blade, spectacularly sharpened, moved as if there were nothing to resist.

Now Kree watched the street that looked like a wide empty hallway.

She had pulled back the machete, she'd wiped it on the giant's cotton undershirt, she'd fallen back and, before taking care of Marcus Grodon, she watched the street.

A series of dark, unoccupied houses, built low, rarely more than one floor. Boards set onto the ground in places where the potholes must become impassible in the rainy seasons. Uninterrupted darkness past two hundred meters. Kree had been staying here for a few weeks, and she knew what the town looked like. A small town with its mediocre population of survivors, the dead and the paupers passing through, with its neighborhoods in decay, a culture of survival, a culture at the end of the world for most of the people who had escaped it. Exactly the type of place you ended up after the war and after death. No city lights: that went without saying. The streetlamps hadn't worked since the end of electricity, fifteen decades earlier in this region as elsewhere. Only the sky took on the work of shedding light, and that, when there was no moon, it did badly.

"Dourdoul?" asked the older brother from the bedroom.

Kree had no intention of wasting time near her victim. Several times in the course of her life, priests had recommended that she should always dedicate a few moments, however brief, to a prayer, so that the dead person could begin their voyage in good condition. She had registered the advice, but she hadn't always respected it. She didn't see what consolation she could give to someone she had just killed. She believed in the afterlife, or rather from experience she knew that the afterlife existed, but she didn't think her voice could influence the forces that governed the world. Besides, she considered the moment of pronouncing a prayer to be a moment when vigilance was relaxed, when on the contrary, in the minutes after an execution, she needed to stay on her guard.

"Dourdoul?" Marcus Grodon repeated. "Did you snuff that cunt?"

The elder Grodon was moving around in the house. He was getting off the mattress, placing his feet on the floor, getting up. Boards creaking, a grumble, steps.

She drew back into invisibility on the other side of the street. The man was going to come out, lean over his brother and try to help him, or to examine the wounds, or to find out whether the wounded man was only passed out or already dead. He would take a minute to figure it out, or at least a good handful of seconds. She would wait with the chain for his turn. She already had it well in hand, with the lead ball swinging gently before her. She would not need much time to throw it and get it moving at a lethal speed.

The elder Grodon was cautious, however, and, no doubt after taking a glance out the open door, he closed it brusquely and locked it. He had seen enough. He said nothing more.

Kree stuck herself in a corner, against the wall on the facing house. This Marcus Grodon wasn't as stupid as his younger brother. He had swiftly realized that he had better not underestimate the criminal competence of this mysterious cunt with the dog who had come to attack them, him and his brother. He had seen Dourdoul Grodon laid out beyond the threshold, and he had concluded that the best thing for him to do was to stay in his house, out of the murderer's reach. Kree, for her part, regretted that she hadn't made a plan of attack that would take care of both brothers at once. Killing Dourdoul Grodon was only an incomplete vengeance, and now the situation was difficult to manage. Skilled in the martial arts though she was, she ruled out bursting into the shack to finish off the second brother, breaking down the door and entering a shadowy and asphyxiating space whose configuration she did not know. Her opponent was not trained in hand-to-hand combat as she was; he was nothing but a drunk trapper, a dog-eating scumbag, but he might be able to defend himself with some courage, or trickery, and no doubt he had some crude weapons at hand that he would use for killing, butchering, gutting, and cutting up the dogs he captured—knives, cutting boards, a club studded with nails. He would have that near at hand. In the dark.

Better to wait until morning. In the light of day, Marcus Grodon would be much more vulnerable.

She crouched down, rolled up the chain and put it back inside her bag. The machete's blade was sticky; she rubbed it against a rag she'd brought for that purpose, for cleaning her weapons after the enemy was dead.

The elder Grodon was coming and going inside the hovel. The wooden floor creaked under his feet. From time to time, all was silent, then, once again, his steps could be heard as he walked on the boards, stopped, walked again, stood still. He was not muttering, or he was muttering so low that Kree couldn't make anything out. She imagined him brimming with bile and fear, trying in vain to find a way to counter the next attack from this madwoman who had taken down his enormous brother, all over a dog. Behind the door, behind the shutters on the small window, she imagined his consternation as he chose the knives that later, when the darkness lifted, would offer only laughable defenses against her.

"Marcus Grodon!" she called out in the silence of the street. "Your life it's over! You'll go with your brother when I want. Me, Kree Toronto, I have come for you!"

She liked this old saying out of the depths of time, this address that brought to mind ancient duels, this challenge from humanity's very first wars. She repeated her threat, then she caught her breath in order to follow it up with a malediction on the connoisseurs of canine meat in general. She took a step forward and cupped her hands like a bullhorn.

This was a mistake. Up until then, she could not be located in the shadows. And suddenly, despite the night and the depth of the night's darkness all around her, she revealed the place where she was standing.

"My dog may she wake up in your dirty guts, may she eat your stomach from the inside," she went on shouting. "Loka may she roll underneath your liver and rip you to shreds! May she wake up and may she . . ."

At that same instant, a yellow gleam flashed from some opening in the shack, between the closed shutters and the door. The flash was accompanied by a detonation that reverberated through the street like the growl of thunder.

No, thought Kree.

A gunshot. An unimaginable event. So improbable that no fighter, here and now, even bothered to worry about it. A purely fantastical hypothesis. Firearms and their ammunition had disappeared from the landscape. In part because their enthusiastic usage during the final war, during the black wars that followed and the troubles heaped on top of those wars, had exhausted the supply and made them rare, and in part because humanity had entered a world past its death throes, because humanity was engaged in hopeless wandering, ragged wandering, and this world knew neither gunpowder, nor electricity, nor machines. Deceased humanity and its negligible survivors and remnants went barehanded in the muddy bardo.

And for Kree, the idea of being injured by a bullet was something out of folklore, almost as much a throwback as her threatening address to the enemy, her prehistoric address: I have come for you.

However extraordinary it might be, though, however unlikely, Marcus Grodon had got hold of a rifle, and he had possessed at least one cartridge. And he had just fired it at this unknown woman of calamity, at the cunt who had snuffed his brother.

Kree no longer had time to think about anything at all. She felt something incredibly violent and piercing explode within

*13*

her chest. Burning, unbearable vibrations. She was thrown backward. She had the impression she was scattering in red splashes, all the way to the sky. That spray, the urge to scream, the urge to vomit, then she felt the life leaving her.

Then she felt nothing at all.

*K*ree again. Some days later.

The sound of steel being cut in the half-light.

Some days or some weeks. Around the same year, anyway.

She was using a military-grade bolt cutter to attack the chain link fence blocking her way. The iron links gave way slowly, one at a time. A mechanical, repetitive operation, and she made use of the time to try remembering some moments that had come before. Not even the past. Just before. Nothing came to her. She dug around in her memory, and nothing came. She had already questioned herself several times. While she was walking. Or when she was resting, sitting on the ground, as if she had not slept since forever. Or while she was battling against the successive enclosures. No memories, not the slightest detail that might allow her to understand where she came from, under what circumstances she had entered this black space. An amnesia with only the slightest cracks. A night without interruption surrounded her, and this night had gotten into her head. Her brain was working, but an opaque mush flowed behind her eyes, between her eyes and the unconscious regions of her mind. She had nothing to hang onto, only illegible images, silent and very dark.

The fence had an unvaried minium-red color, and it rose so high that it disappeared into the darkness of the sky. The bolt cutter with its powerful beak bit hard into the metal trellis, link after link, with a dry sound, amplified by the surrounding void. At times the wounded fence rustled, as if some hand or even several people were shaking it in rage, as if the fence were protesting the ravages it underwent. Kree paused her work until the fence became calm again. She knew nobody was watching her, but, as on other occasions when she was on a tactical mission, she took care not to call attention to herself. The task that she'd set herself consisted of cutting out a small door, through which she could slip to the other side. A small opening at the bottom of an immense iron web that extended in all directions, to the right, the left, the sky, and soon melted into shadows.

Once she'd snipped out a rectangle large enough to pass through, she pulled it upward, pulled it out, and threw it behind her. Then she began crawling past the obstacle. The earth up close against her had a strong smell. It was damp and almost warm, and the little vegetation mixed into it took the form of a few dead twigs. The smell brushed against some unknown thing that had once been anchored deep within her, something that surged back up, almost painfully beyond her reach: inexplorable impressions, an inexplorable life. Shadowy imprints that she could not manage to reclaim. Steps in the nights, perhaps, traveling next to swamps, in mud, in muddy forests, with soldiers, with civilians, through an unknown and hostile landscape, she didn't know when. She was on watch, ready to reconstruct those stories, her own story. But the images ran into nothingness, they were deceptive, indecipherable.

For another handful of seconds she wriggled on her belly. Then she rose up and sat back on her heels as she caught her breath. The darkness had a terrible density, yet with one strange exception. Kree was not just feeling her way forward. At this moment she could make out her own dirt-covered hands and her entire body, as well as the long cutting pincer she held before her, and she could see clearly the fence behind her, fifteen or so meters of enclosure on either side of the passage. All of this benefited from illumination, although, beyond, nothing emerged from the shadows.

The silence was broken by the whistle of Kree's breath.

Maybe because she wanted to hear a voice, certainly something

other than the swelling and unswelling of her own pulmonary
sacs, Kree closed her eyes and began muttering under her breath.
She felt exhausted. At nearly forty years old, she had survived
war, famine, close combat, an incessant series of dangers, endless
years of solitude, the loss of any moral compass, and wandering
in enemy territory, but she didn't think she'd ever experienced
the sudden muscular and mental degradation that seized her in
that moment. More than once, obviously, there'd been times when
she'd lost courage, when her fatigue had brought on the desire
to give up everything, had even produced suicidal fantasies, but
she had withstood all that, without ever experiencing the feeling that gripped her now: physical turmoil, difficulty gathering
her thoughts, inertia. Her hands were trembling. Talking out
loud was a way to fight back against the void. Sitting there on
the warm ground, she began to hum out words, bits of phrases.

The black damp. No presence anywhere near. Muttering.

Some time passed. She wasn't measuring it. She took up handfuls of dirt and mechanically she crumbled them between her
fingers.

Mumblings coming from some inner place unknown to her.
Nothing coherent, at first, just pure sounds. A series of words she
could not control, arriving in her mouth like the beginnings of
a lamentation, a series of insane mutterings. Then, after a moment, something within her fell into order and images emerged.
Not specific memories, exactly, but images. Suddenly her murmur
accompanied disconnected film clips of an existence. A parade
of violent deaths, crowds, here and there gatherings of desert-
ers being set upon by masked men with clubs and scythes. A few
settings: dormitories under giant tents, squat houses, nocturnal
convoys, gatherings around fires, desolate plains. Bit by bit, she
began to play a role in this film, she began to embody her own
character. Often she felt jolts, from an arm or a shoulder, she was
stabbing with a knife, she made slicing weapons whistle through
the air. She had to kill in order to go farther into the disaster.

No chronology, jump cuts, gaps. What she saw went back to her childhood, maybe the very beginning of her adolescence. Then twenty-five years without images. As for the final days, the final weeks, they were even less accessible, infinitely far away, even farther than her early childhood.

She let out a whimper of disappointment, trying to force her mind to obey, to come closer to the past, recent or otherwise. She bit her lips, she concentrated on the disorder swirling inside her head and she fell silent. But soon whatever had, for a few instants, taken the place of her memory was extinguished. The sequences that had been revealed inside her lost their color and meaning, they froze and then they evaporated.

Again she was crushed under the amnesia.

Under the immediate reality of black soil, chain link, and darkness.

She took up her bolt cutter again and, with effort, got up. The energy of survival took over again; she thought she'd gone through a vague period of lethargy. She didn't even remember that she'd had any visions.

"Okay, let's go," she growled. "That's enough. I'm going farther."

She took five steps, seven or eight, maybe, then another dozen, and she ran into yet another fence. Identical in all respects to the one she'd passed through an hour before. She hadn't seen it getting closer, she'd almost smashed her face against it. An enclosure, abruptly distinct within the shadows, gleaming against the shadows, surrounded in absolute shadows. The minium-red lattice formed a mesh extending infinitely in both height and width. As if it divided the world in two: within and beyond.

She set to work. There was nothing else to do. Position the bolt cutter, squeeze the wire between its jaws, press the handles, cut. Place the jaws, press, force, cut. She wasn't sure of her count, she could be wrong, but it was the fourth enclosure she'd run into that night. And before—before, surely there'd been others.

Yes, before, no doubt, she'd grappled with other barriers.

*18*

"Before, who knows if what there weren't some others," she grumbled.

During other nights, during preceding nights.

"Who knows," she grumbled again.

It took her about ten minutes to cut out an opening. Always the same sounds. Click . . . clack . . . tlik . . . krid . . . klid . . . The iron wires had a thinner section, the tool for cutting them was military grade, designed to overcome more formidable barbed obstacles. Kree handled the bolt cutter easily, and she encountered no resistance. Insert the pincer at the right spot, press down, listen for the dry sound of cut metal, tlik, move on to the next link. That's what she was doing. Krid . . . clack . . . Ten minutes of work, without complications, repetitive and simple. Maybe fifteen minutes. The only difficulty came from the horizontal tension wires, which were more reluctant to give way. The severing cut was accompanied by a sharp, angry note, klangh, very short at the beginning but taken up by the reinforcing wires, in echoes that seemed to transmit their anger across the entire infinite length of the enclosure.

She took her time. Nobody was chasing her. She wasn't in a hurry.

Yes, no doubt, she had done this several times. No detailed memory, no absolutely credible image. She felt sure of it, though, because of her body, her muscle memory, the fatigue in her hands. Always the same thing. Open up a door large enough so she wouldn't scratch herself when she slipped through. Press down on the handles of the bolt cutter. Klidh . . . kalak . . . With the bolt cutter, outline an escape hatch to fit her size. Pull on the piece of fence to separate it from the enclosure, sometimes give it a shake to get it unstuck, toss it behind her. Go down on all fours, pass through to the other side, stand up again, make a few meters of progress. Sit down on the warm, fragrant, loose soil and rest. Muttering in the dark. Breathing hard. Then get up, get going again. And almost immediately, run into another fence.

The space between fences varied. Twelve steps, twenty-five steps. Never more than thirty. Sometimes it was even very small, barely ten centimeters.

Nine, ten centimeters. Like the time when Kree met the bonze.

She was just about to finish cutting out a rectangular shape in the metal mesh in front of her. Only a few links were left to undo, a few wires buried in the earth left to cut. Then she would pull open the passageway and slide through. A few additional kriks and tlacs in the humid silence. She set down her bolt cutter and gripped the piece of fence, she disentangled it from the whole and tossed it to her left. A shiver of metal against the black dirt clods, then nothing. Then suddenly a second enclosure, whose presence she had not previously noticed, appeared just before her. Separated from the first by less than a hand's width.

She let out a tired sigh.

She ran her fingers over the new fence. Same color, same interwoven metal, maybe a larger number of enforcing and tension wires, but, aside from that, it was identical to the one in which she'd just cut a door to go through.

The work would have to start over. This was unexpected but she accepted it without asking questions or cursing fate. This was the way it was. In order to go forward, she had to pass through there. She took up her tool again and attacked the first link, skrikh, a second one, klagh.

Ten minutes later, she had pulled away the second cutting, not without difficulty since it squeaked, squealed and got stuck against the first fence. Fighting to clear the passage, she had scraped both her hands. In the strange light, the drops of blood looked oily, the color of a crow's wing. Once she'd reached the other side, she sat down and rubbed damp earth on the wounds. That was when she noticed, a little ways away, a suspended brown mass, a body between earth and sky, compressed between the two fences, imprisoned with arms and legs spread out, thorax and head horribly crushed and stuck against the wire trellis. This was the bonze.

She stood up again and approached him.

The monk's eyes were open. He was looking at her.

Two characters lit from within, an oneiric phosphorescence in this inky setting. Her, stained with dirt as if she'd just come out of a cave, and him in religious rags, strangely proper in his racked position.

Like a slice of bread in a toaster, Kree thought.

Hell of a weird sandwich, she thought next.

"You're called Kree?" the bonze asked, skipping the formalities, in a soft voice that was not the slightest bit hoarse.

"How do you know my name?" Kree said, distrustful.

The bonze observed a moment of silence.

"Where do you think you are?" he said.

"Well," Kree hesitated.

She couldn't actually give the bonze any answer. The question had already occurred to her, but she had tossed it aside to avoid pain, or rather to avoid finding herself once again confronted with her own amnesia. She was walking in shadow. She didn't know for how long, she didn't know what she'd done to end up there, in that black space. In that strange, black, and unknown space. She could not answer.

"News travels fast around here," the bonze continued. "Two years ago, after they caged me, they told me that if someone ever came to free me, it would be a woman named Kree."

"Oh," Kree said.

"Kree Toronto," the bonze added.

"They knew that?"

"They told me that, and then they left me in the dark," the bonze said. "That was two years ago, but it's like it was yesterday."

Kree inhaled, then exhaled, then sighed.

"How what they knew that?" she asked.

The bonze was too tightly compressed between the two fences to make the slightest movement. Nevertheless Kree had the impression his lack of response was accompanied by a shrug.

"They couldn't know that," she muttered, furrowing her brow. A silence fell between them. The bonze broke it.

"Set me free," he said.

It was a supplication, but formulated in such a tragic voice that Kree examined the bonze's face in an effort to discern some expression of feeling there. She could make out nothing but compressed flesh, held in strict immobility under the metal crosses. After two years of catatonia within the fence's vice grip, the bonze must have unlearned any nuances of body language, how to act with the face, the play of lips.

She took her time answering.

"I'm not going to set you free," she said.

"Why?" the bonze asked, astonished.

He asked the question calmly. During the two years he'd spent in the very depths of darkness, no doubt he'd meditated on the cruelty of fate, enough to unlearn hope as well.

"I'm alone in figuring all this out," Kree explained. "I don't need a companion. I set you free, you'll be stuck on my tail. Who knows, after a while, you might get an idea in your head to have sex with me."

The bonze cackled.

"I have no desire to do that," he said.

Kree tried to meet his gaze. The bonze's face was perched too high up, it did not lean toward her when he spoke, and she didn't have enough space to fall back and see his eyes clearly. It was as if the monk had no gaze. As if these two years spent in shadow had left him blind or, as if out of wisdom, he had given up on vision.

He was dressed in a frayed robe that emitted obnoxious, animal smells, very different from the earth and metal smells hanging all around. In the early days of his ordeal he must have vomited, his intestines and bladder must have let loose. Twenty-four months earlier, or just about. The stale stench was indistinct now, but the fabric enveloping his body preserved the imprint of his physiological shipwreck. The orange of his robe had shaded toward an excremental brown. Colors have poor resistance to this sort of night.

"Anyway, I don't need you," Kree said.

"I don't need myself either," the bonze said philosophically.

He let a few seconds go by.

"Listen, Kree Toronto," he went on.

"I'm listening," Kree said.

"If you set me free, what do you think will happen? That I'll look after you? That I'll start following along behind you, like a dog or a servant?"

He paused. It wasn't easy to speak without moving his mouth.

"But I won't, nothing like that," he continued. "What will I do? . . . I'll do a few exercises to get my joints unstuck and moving again, and then I'll go along the length of the fence. I'll pray as I go."

Kree felt exhaustion overcoming her and she sat down. The situation was unpleasant for her, just as the conversation was. It had been a long time since she'd exchanged words with anyone, words had made a brutal incursion into her solitude, and to listen to someone else answering her questions, reacting to her speech, wore her out.

"Go along the length of the fence," she murmured. "There's no point in that."

Her voice was barely audible, as if she'd continued with her usual murmuring between fences.

"It's quiet," the bonze objected. "You choose your own pace. You can go at full speed or you can walk slowly. You can pray."

"I'd rather go straight," Kree said. "I have clippers. The fences they don't stop me."

"Bah," the bonze said. "After this one there'll be another. And then another. That's how it is in the worlds after death. There's no end to them."

"I'd be surprised," Kree said doubtfully.

"No, there's no end. And one day your shears won't cut anymore. And then what'll you do?"

"I'll sit on the ground," Kree murmured. "I'll pray."

Here the conversation died for a long time. They were quiet; Kree was staring at the black earth before her, then she closed her eyes. Quarters of hours went by, one after another, without a word, without number. Five or six, or several thousand. Neither of them bothered counting.

"You know how to pray?" the bonze asked abruptly.

Kree had dozed off. She had almost forgotten about the presence of the monk flattened between two iron nets.

She jumped.

"No," she lied randomly.

"Do you want to learn?" the bonze asked.

"No," Kree said.

"It's not hard," the bonze assured her.

"No," Kree said.

In truth, the question had set off an avalanche of memories inside her. Suddenly a vast quantity of magic phrases flowed chaotically through her consciousness. Fragments of prayers, beginnings of curses, supplications, bits of invocations. In the world before this one, people were constantly addressing invisible forces, demons and nature. Suddenly she remembered phrases she had pronounced long ago that, depending on the circumstances, could be used as prayers. When everything seemed lost all around her. When she was sinking into madness. When she had killed someone. When barbarians were closing in on her, wanting to rape or kill her. When the war was raging nearby. What war? Against whom, against what? She couldn't name anything, everything blurred together, a chaotic succession of images

*24*

and rumblings. The images weren't clearly linked to each other, but behind them formed a soundtrack of prayers.

She had remained seated, leaning back onto her hands that had sunken in the dirt. Now she dislodged her wrists. Her hands had stopped bleeding long before. She shook herself a little, got up, and once again stood facing the bonze. Enveloped in her rags, stained with dirt that was dry and gray, or damp and black or brown. The bolt cutter hung down alongside her right leg. A vision of wandering in the black space. Even unceremoniously flattened and compressed as he was, with interlaced metal buried in his flesh, the monk seemed better off than she did.

"I'm leaving," she announced.

The bonze let out something like a sigh of regret.

"Set me free," he said.

"Already I told you no," Kree said stubbornly.

They remained facing each other, lips closed, for two or three minutes. Perhaps the bonze was praying, or searching for arguments to convince her. Then he broke the silence.

"You have a bolt cutter," he said. "It'll cut anything. Iron wires or flesh. You could use it on me."

"What are you saying?" Kree asked.

"My body doesn't matter anymore," the bonze said. "You could make it so I could leave it behind."

"Bah." Kree grimaced.

"Lift your clippers and cut my throat," the bonze said calmly. "That will set me free."

Kree protested in an uncertain voice. She was having trouble finding words. She explained that she'd done a lot of stupid things over the course of her existence, but nothing like that. Killing a man immobilized between two metal walls. Murdering a monk.

"This has nothing to do with murder," the bonze assured her. "This would be an act of mercy. I am asking you humbly to do it."

"It's too awful," Kree said.

"It would set me free," the bonze concluded.

Kree shook her head. It was too awful.

She hesitated.

They were quiet for a moment. They had nothing more to say to each other.

She waited a little longer, time for a series of painful breaths, then she lifted her bolt cutter and directed it to the bonze's throat. The chain link made things difficult, and there was a reinforcing post a few centimeters from the spot where she wanted to start the cut. The bonze did not appear to feel any anxiety. His eyes were closed and he did not even make himself show any signs of bravery. He must have been praying. Not a quiver in his face.

She adjusted the cutting blades, at a slant because of the tension wire in the way. Then she cut at random, several times, closing her eyes as the monk did. She felt no reaction from his flesh. Skin, cartilage, muscles, trachea, arteries and veins were insignificant obstacles for a tool made for cutting iron.

The bonze's head did not move, it was too tightly pressed between fences, nor did his body move, or react, or slump.

Kree pulled back her bolt cutter, took two steps back, and soon she turned away. She turned her back to the bonze. The sensations the shears had transmitted to her hands, to her entire body, had been ghastly. The sound of the cut had added to the horror: nothing, except the voracious slide of the blades, the jaws closing together. Now Kree refused to look at the result of her awful intervention. She did not want to know whether the blood was flowing now, how fast it was, what color it was. Nor did she want to make sure that the bonze was set free, or exchange with him some semblance of farewell.

Without changing her position, keeping her back turned, she made up a prayer. The sort of thing one usually says just after killing someone with a bolt cutter. She said it without letting out any sound, she was content with moving her lips. A rather long prayer. She did not know the bonze's name, but she paid her respects to his courage, and she cursed those who had sentenced him to the ordeal of fences.

Then she began to walk.

She walked straight ahead, she trudged unhurriedly across the ground, which looked like it had recently been worked. After she had gone thirty or thirty-five steps, she smacked into a new metallic surface. Her head, her hands. She had been walking with her eyes closed. The outraged rattle of the fence filled the night, then stopped.

She had dropped her bolt cutter. She picked it back up.

The minium-red chain link extended in all directions. On the other side reigned the night.

For a moment she observed the obstacle she would have to pass. She had the feeling she was repeating an operation that she knew by heart in every detail. A fence just like the others. As soon as the passage was open, she would continue on her way. She had the bolt cutter well in hand. She kneeled down on the sticky, warm earth, and began cutting through the fence. The first tlics and tlacs seemed familiar to her. Who knows how many times I've done this before, she thought.

*T*he timber growing less and less dense. Space growing between the trees, the bald cypress, bile-sap pines, silence pines, void maples, sequoias of little virtue, potbellied larches, all these new species no one had ever studied, of which no inventory would ever be made, which had appeared since the black war and were already dying of genetic diseases, on the path to extinction like all the others. Smells of needles, mosses, the absolute calm of undergrowth, the rust soil. Never a bird's cry, never the slightest rodent's quiver. Kree had noticed that the distance between tree trunks was growing, that the smells were changing, three times already she had identified footprints left by some peasants, she knew that she was now approaching a village. Something was about to change for her. In the course of her life if you could call this a life. Soon she would leave the forest. She had been walking for an incomprehensible number of days, maybe three, maybe thirty-two, or fifteen thousand seven hundred. Numbers had no meaning. She did not care to keep those sorts of accounts.

Then she heard a brassy trumpeting in the distance, the sound unlike any other of a liturgical horn, very quickly followed by the beating of shamanic drums. She had reached the last line of trees. Lusty aspens, barren hazelnuts, madleaf plane trees. The vegetal rot was invasive, poisoning the atmosphere. She quickened her steps. Now she was coming out at the top of a grassy slope, on a prairie that descended to the valley floor. Three hundred meters away, where once a river had no doubt flowed, a small village was spread out. Leading there was a whitish road made of pebbles, with neither branches nor extensions. The village was located at the end of the road.

Everything seemed peaceful, far from the nightmares of the war. She was not trying to remain hidden, but first she spent a minute behind a bush, motionless, as she examined the space and let her eyes become accustomed to a light brighter than the light in the forest. The shirt and pants she was wearing were so dirty that she looked like some half-vegetal, half-human creature. Like some warrior witch emerging from the deepest taiga, formed through magical invocations, made of humus, dead leaves and flesh drained of blood, leaving it a mummy-like hue.

She went down the slope and reached the main street. The villagers were gathering on the central square, a large space surrounded by one-story buildings, entirely occupied on one side by what must have been a gas station or a garage, once upon a time when there were motor vehicles, farm machines to maintain and repair. Once upon a time, in a different world. The antique fuel pumps had been dismantled, but one had survived, a useless and incomprehensible monument to the past. Just behind it some scaffolding had been built, to support boards that held orators, musicians, and shamans, about a dozen of them. Apparently some ceremony or assembly was about to take place on the stage.

Already five minutes had passed since Kree had entered the village. She had no trouble blending into the sparse crowd. The peasants weren't paying any attention to her, no doubt because their outfits were no more glamorous than her own, and also because these men and women seemed worn out, enclosed in their own solitude, uninterested in those surrounding them. She came out on the square and stood still in the last row, behind a handful of middle-aged people, shepherds or cowherds or farmers, who did notice her presence. They smelled bad. Now and then they turned toward her, briefly, with eyes whose lack of expression concealed hostile questions. Kree took no offense at this. They weren't exchanging any unpleasant remarks with each other and they weren't threatening her. She could watch the shamans' meeting without staying on her guard, without fearing an attack or having to defend herself.

The meeting was both religious and political in character, with musical accompaniment. On the platform were two drummers and a flutist, all three haphazardly dressed with fur squares on their shoulders, army pants and shirts, leather hats, and dilapidated sandals. A scruffy Buddhist monk joined them, now and then puffing up his cheeks to blow a horn. The three shamans took turns giving speeches, allowing the musical ensemble to intervene at certain moments and shaking little strings of bells and clappers themselves, while their peers punctuated the instrumental highs and lows with more or less vigorous magical clamorings. The shaman currently speaking had moved forward to the edge of the stage, sometimes skirting the void and then placing a foot on the blue pump to maintain his balance. Looking as if he wanted to get closer to the crowd as it listened and pressed forward below. The other two shamans were waiting their turn, murmuring or blaring out undefined syllables. They were waving their entire shamanic arsenal, their bells and their wreaths of small carnivores, ferrets, martens, and genets, strung on metal threads by the throat.

The first speaker was dressed like a mechanic just coming back from an oil change; over his grease-stained coverall he had tied a brown leather apron, heavy with garlands of nails, small bells, and sable skulls. Although he looked like a wizard from the countryside, something about him also recalled a commissioner of the people. As was often the case, every public meeting included a representative from the Party, and he was it. He had reached the edge of the scaffolding and had his right boot propped on top of the pump as a support as he waved his arms, accentuating the rhythm of his most important phrases. A long, held note from the flute had preceded his first words, then ended in a hoarse sigh. The drumbeats did not drown out his energetic voice, which reached the last rows, which reached Kree.

After a slump, which still persisted after a considerable time, this man was saying, engineers trained by the Party had succeeded in reestablishing electricity and getting the ancient machines to function again. And one could even imagine they might invent new machines, intended to bring comfort to the survivors for all the hard work they were forced to perform today, just as people had done eight thousand years ago, as if humanity had made no progress since the very first societies of farmers and hunter-gatherers. Loyalty to the Party was indispensable, the man emphasized, even if that loyalty went along with beliefs in magic and life after death. The leaders would allow these superstitions from now on and integrate them into Marxist-Leninism. Supernatural forces governed the universe and human history; dragons, demons, and angry gods were everywhere, and although shamanism and the monks played an essential part in appeasing them and speaking to them, the Party alone could take charge of happiness for the masses currently plunged into a coal-black present with no future.

A second orator came next, less clear in his arguments, although the musicians and the Tibetan horn did their best to assist him. More talkative, more disorganized, without the slightest concern for being understood, the topic he had chosen was the successive worlds where one wanders after passing through the agonies of death. His hair escaped the shelter of his brownish wool hat and fell in a gray cascade over his shoulders. He was draped in ragged women's clothing, with an overall appearance of a scarecrow. He expressed himself in a muddled language, making asides only audible to the first few rows, the musicians and his colleagues sitting behind him on stage. His words, whether he wanted them to be or not, were not clear. First, it was difficult to tell whether he considered himself as having already experienced his own demise or if he was speculating on what awaited the living after their passage into the beyond. He refused to establish the distinction between the status of the living and the status of the deceased. In his own terms, he put them all in the same bag. This sort of assertion didn't bother Kree. She herself considered that, in principle, for a long time now, she has already been dead—the man pontificating badly on stage might well be like her. The shaman was laying out a theory on the subject that Kree, over the course of her own wanderings, had not heard. The shaman claimed that the bardo after death was one stage in an incoherent series of bardos and hells, a disorderly series that unfolded in uncontrollable and unpredictable ways. Rather than embarking on a path to reincarnation, the dead person should instead prepare to be killed or to die, over and over again. The floating worlds came one after another, you were never sure when you'd left one to enter the next, and, in summary, you were only repeating the horror of your previous existences. The shaman's voice was frenetic and hoarse. Impassioned by his topic but growing less and less intelligible, the man fiddled nervously with the little bells on the ends of his rags and grimaced. He addressed the crowd before him as if they were a bunch of idiotic, ignorant dead, who needed someone to spell everything out for them.

Once he was finished with his ramblings, the shaman made a spiteful gesture and returned to the back of the stage, pouting. There was no applause.

The monk blew into his enormous horn for half a minute, then the flute joined in, soon followed by slow, even drum beats and energetically shaken bells. They needed to reanimate the audience, whether it was dead or alive, to dissipate the lingering effect of the obscenities that had just been offered.

While she waited for a third shamanic agitator to take the stage, Kree became aware of something she had not previously noticed since she'd left the cover of the forest and moved toward the village. The way the landscape was lit up wasn't logical. In the background was an illustration of the porousness between the worlds of the living and the dead, between images out of the real and those emerging from dream spaces. The sky was nocturnal, starless, profoundly black, but down below, the earthly landscape enjoyed a natural, diurnal light. Noon and midnight blended together without contradiction. In the village, over the countryside, the grass, the rooftops, the brilliance of daylight, not the sort of dusky light that might occur, for example, when clouds hide the sun; and, overhead, an intense asphalt sky hanging heavy above the world.

For whatever reason, the third speaker decided to leave the platform behind and perched on top of the pump. The surface under his feet was slightly rounded and, in order to maintain his balance, he had to refrain from gesticulating. As he spoke he grew tense, occasionally using his arms as balancing poles. This relative inertia cost him. He would begin to move his arms and shoulders, then catch himself, reluctantly, ultimately giving the impression he was afflicted with tics, jolts, and spasms. He was a man with a deeply creased yellow face, his hair and beard the color of walnut stains, wearing a dirty tunic not overly burdened with bells and cinched at the waist with a cord that hosted three or four weasel corpses. He had the facial features of a mental patient, devoured from within. According to this mad-eyed prophet, with his gestures at once clumsy and contained, the main danger facing the dead, the deceased on their path to reincarnation, was the possibility of finding themselves trapped in the wrong womb. He exhorted the dead to take their time in choosing, not to rush haphazardly toward the first womb available. He begged them to seek out a human womb, mammalian ovaries at the very least, and most of all to avoid, like the plague, incarceration within an egg. "Never waste your fate in a shell from which there is no escape!" he cried. "Never will you be normal in your rebirth!" he bellowed. He was about to expand on his demonstration with some examples, getting ready, perhaps, to enumerate the cold-blooded animals and birds from which one must turn away at all costs, when he opened his arms wide, slipped desperately on top of the pump, lost his balance and crashed down at the feet of the villagers in the first row. They helped him get up, and he stomped over to the platform and up the steps, but upon his return to the stage he indicated he had said enough, and asked the musicians to beat their drums and play their flutes for the end of the meeting. Which they did.

On this regrettable fall, the gathering ended.

The musicians set down their drums in order to light cigarettes and chat amongst themselves; the bonze lifted his long horn and hoisted it level on his shoulder, then approached the musicians to ask for a cigarette; the shamans packed up their genets and their martens, stuffed most of their bells into a plastic bag, and began a relaxed private discussion, evidently punctuated with funny anecdotes. They were laughing together and didn't seem particularly worried whether their apocalyptic messages had gotten through to the masses.

The inhabitants of the village, for their part, had dispersed. They had been offered a politico-mystical show, they had watched it without displeasure, and now they were leaving. The ceremony had brought nothing new to their understanding of the world. It had distracted them from the dullness of their daily life, but that was all. Already they were forgetting the speeches they had just heard. The point of it all was dissolving into nothingness, the arguments about failed rebirths, deadly reincarnations inside eggs, the multiple bardos. The Party commissaries and the medicine men had always known that this would happen and had no complaints. Next time, they would not hesitate to use the same phrases and the same images, to reproduce the same performance.

Kree felt very much in harmony with the village people; she had seen the show for what it was—a moment of distraction—but she attached no importance to mystical proclamations. None had ever helped her in the slightest. She didn't believe in anything, but she had no illusions. She understood that the end of the world had been going on for centuries, with periods of slowness and even calm, and periods of acceleration, and that right in the middle of one of these periods of acceleration, she'd had the misfortune to be born. Or rather, to be reborn.

Or rather, to begin walking in the succession of black spaces.

As she was thinking about it, suddenly she wondered what had compelled her to go down to the village, to leave the forest, and even before that, to go down the road, to make her way for days and years under the trees. Answers did not come.

"Seems like I've already come once again into the world of the dead," she grumbled to herself.

She was standing alone in front of the fuel pump. The village square had emptied.

"Who knows how long what I've been in the same bag with them," she went on.

The musicians were coming down from the stage. The bonze with his horn on his shoulder, looking like an orange-robed laborer carrying a pipe on a construction site, stopped at her level and looked at her. She could smell him, the odor of a monk who hadn't performed his ablutions in a long time. He was looking at her in a slightly lascivious manner. She addressed him.

"If what I wanted to find some work around here, is there any?"

The licentious flames in the monk's eyes went out, or maybe they had never been lit; maybe it was only one of Kree's fleeting impressions, a result of his being unfamiliar and the fact that it had been a long time since she had been in contact with living beings.

"What work you looking for?" the bonze asked.

"Doesn't matter," Kree said.

The bonze thought, or made a show of thinking, and he looked over his shoulder.

"You know how to use a knife? Slaughter and skin?"

Kree took a step back, grimacing.

"People?" she asked, worried.

"Bah," the monk huffed.

"What kind of work is it?" Kree asked.

The monk nodded. His cheek touched the copper tube that he had stuck under his right ear.

"Animals," he said. "Dogs, sheep, beavers. Anything that comes through. It's for a factory."

"Not dogs," Kree said. "What factory's that?"

"Pemmican. Manufacturing pemmican."

"Bah, you do that?" Kree was surprised.

"Well, yeah, why not?"

Kree examined him severely, exactly as if she were revolted by this butchery initiated by monks, when really, at base, she didn't care. She was pretending to be horrified.

"You kill animals?" she said.

"Not necessarily us and not always animals," the bonze joked in an unclear manner.

They stood for two or three seconds, waiting. The drummers and the Party agitator were listening behind them, immobile.

"We do what we have to do for survival and the good of the masses," the bonze went on.

"For their survival and their good," the Party agitator interjected.

Kree said she was okay with working, okay to start working as soon as possible. She was agreeably surprised not to have to give her name or answer any questions about her ethnic or organic origins, or about her past.

"Come with me, it's nearby," said the Party agitator.

He introduced himself, his name was Sariyan Lov, and he brought her to a cinderblock warehouse next to the main square. He pushed the door open and unhooked a black rubber apron that he held out to Kree. Obediently she put it on over her rags.

"I'm not very clean," she confessed.

"You can take a shower at the end of the day," said Sariyan Lov, who was the factory boss.

He showed her a square room below. The door was open and there were sinks, puddles of water, an empty stall. Just next to that was a large space, arranged with hanging materials and streams that furrowed the ground, showing that here was where they carried out the first steps of butchery, the slaughter and quartering.

Kree toured the space with her eyes. In the middle of the factory proper stood a disproportionately long table, with two female workers and a man in a slaughterer's overalls busy around it. They were butchering a large animal carcass and putting small strips of meat to dry on a grill along the wall. They did not exchange a word, and they barely lifted their heads to see who was coming in. The air stank of smoked meat and bones and, above all else, the nagging stench of blood.

Sariyan Lov's voice vibrated suddenly, as energetic as when he had begun speaking with his boot on the fuel pump.

"You all tell the new person what she's supposed to do. She's starting right away. Her name is Kree Toronto."

Kree started and stood in front of him.

"How what you know my name?" she protested.

The Party representative stared at her open-mouthed. His astonishment was apparently sincere.

"Well, where is it what you think you are?" he said.

*K*ree didn't want to see the needle that Myriam Agazaki was extracting from her head. She could have examined it in the mirror, that fine brown shaft Myriam Agazaki had pinched and pulled out and twisted between her fingers. She could have. But she preferred to look elsewhere, to focus on what was happening outside the window.

But right now, in the street, just about nothing was happening. The house across the way had reached such a state of dilapidation that nobody squatted there anymore, and the Chinese pharmacy in the building next door was closed, no doubt forever. There was no movement. Leaning back against a curtain of corrugated metal, a man stood smoking. He was wearing a sailor's cap and, floating inside an infantryman's coat too warm for the season, looking like a discharged soldier up to no good. Because of her defective vision, Kree wasn't able to read his face. A recent arrival. A soldier escaped from hell. She squinted but didn't manage to make out anything more. The sun was playing hide and seek in the clouds, its light changing rapidly, and from time to time, a sudden downpour of blood came beating down and reddening the entire visible world for a few seconds. That's how it always was when Myriam Agazaki was going about her work. Flashes without color, waves of crimson. The red gleam flooded the street as well as the healer's house. The blood fell in a thick curtain, obscuring everything. Then it disappeared without a trace.

"How what you're doing, Kree?" asked Myriam Agazaki.

She was still rolling the delicate body of the needle between her thumb and index finger, trying to ease the extraction, without damage. She had to proceed millimeter by millimeter. Her operation might go on for twenty minutes, often longer. Last week, it took an hour.

"I feel like it's raining blood," Kree said.

"That happens," Myriam Agazaki remarked. "It's when what the needle touches a birth or a death."

"Pfft, a birth or a death!" Kree commented.

At just that moment, the needle clinked into the ceramic plate reserved by the healer for magical detritus, for compresses, egg white residues, hairs, scabs, bits of fat, tiny bits of skin.

Kree still didn't move. She waited to receive permission. She'd had colorful hallucinations over the past half an hour, but she had felt nothing. And, at the moment that the long ivory point piercing her brain had finally left its lodging, she had felt nothing then, either.

Now Myriam Agazaki was noisily wiping her hands on a sheet of old newspaper.

"Well, there," she said, resting the crumpled ball of paper on the plate. "There's one what won't bother you anymore. Want to see it, Kree?"

"No," Kree said.

"I'll burn it," Myriam Agazaki said.

"Can I move now?" Kree asked.

"Yes," Myriam Agazaki said. "It's done."

Plate in hand, she headed to the kitchen. She was no longer in her surgical position, her entire body hunched over the two fingers at work. Now she unwound, she rediscovered freedom in her movements. She even seemed to intentionally exaggerate the natural suddenness of her gestures. The place she occupied in space. She was a tall, anxious woman in her fifties, with a slender frame and a contrasting tendency to gain weight in the hips, and she walked with a limp, ever since someone cut her right leg at the knee when she was a teenager, during a pogrom, "to keep her from running." She rummaged around for a minute in her messy kitchen, hobbling back and forth, all the while flinging back her long witch's hair: silky and silvery, falling to mid-chest or mid-back depending on the variations in her movements. She made clinking sounds with the dishes as she moved them. Then she struck a match and stood very still. She turned her back to Kree, now a simple silhouette in a floral dress, with a rounded posterior and skinny arms. Something crackled. Throughout the apartment spread a scent of grilled fat, burning hair and gasoline.

Kree turned her head so she wouldn't see anything. The things that came out of her head disgusted her. She didn't even try to picture the needle to herself. Myriam Agazaki told her that the size varied from day to day, that some were slightly thicker than others, that the color ranged from dirty white to dark brown, and all of them were spectacularly rigid and solid. Kree made an effort to learn as little about them as possible. The needles had appeared a few years earlier, at a moment when she thought she was finally done with the abominations outside the city, when she had found refuge in the city. She always had five or six lodged in her brain, which didn't usually bother her from day to day, but when the blood rains afflicted her too frequently, they had to be pulled out. Myriam Agazaki's idea was that the needles were traces of horrors experienced in one or several previous existences, the remnants of buried remorse. To Kree, they were nothing but a filthy mutation. She tolerated it with resignation and without too many complaints. There were far worse things, in life as in death.

Once she had finished incinerating the remnants, Myriam Agazaki once again began her comings and goings. She began to make tea. The smell of butane combined with the dirty rotisserie aroma. Myriam Agazaki had an actual burner in her kitchen that worked on gas. She had explored all the empty houses in the area and gathered enough canisters to heat water until the end of her days.

Kree left her chair, went to open the window and leaned out on her elbows. The woodwork was worn, the cracked frame crumbling. She stretched her arms out over it. Powdery bits of paint stuck to her bare skin.

"How many do I still have to get out?" she asked over her shoulder.

"You know very well, Kree," said Myriam Agazaki, as she moved saucers around. "There's no point you thinking this might end someday. The ones we take out, they don't take long to come back. There's always five or six what they're there and shooting into your head."

Kree gritted her teeth.

"Five or six," she muttered.

"I'll keep taking them out one by one so it doesn't get worse," Myriam Agazaki went on. "But you'll always have a handful left. That's why you see it the blood rain. Always up to the end you'll see blood rains."

Kree huffed a noncommittal groan. Her displeasure wasn't very emphatic.

To tell the truth, this parasitic presence did not really distress her. It got in her way, but not so much that it was ruining her life. The needles grew in her head, just as other people had cysts and cancers, and so what? In her the needles brought on blood rains, and no doubt they were also responsible for her poor vision, and so what? They had never caused her any pain.

She reimmersed herself in observing the street. The Chinese pharmacy wore its yellow sign with red characters, proudly painted a hundred years before, in contrast with the rest of the setting, which was ugly and gray, with a gray ugliness to take your breath away. Here, they were in the Aniya Viett sector, where

Myriam Agazaki was one of the few inhabitants. Empty houses with broken windows, fences defiled with old posters, automobile carcasses that smelled of piss; the ambiance was no more catastrophic than anywhere else, but when new arrivals came looking for lodging, they didn't rush over to Aniya Viett, and in any case they almost never came to Julie Battambang Street, which is where Myriam Agazaki had settled down. There was no objective reason for their disinterest, if not, perhaps, precisely the fact that Myriam Agazaki lived there, and she had the reputation of being a witch.

The wanderer in the sailor cap hadn't altered his position. He went on leaning against the locked front windows of the Chinese pharmacy and he was finishing his cigarette. Kree, who suffered from an astigmatism among her other ocular afflictions, narrowed her eyes in yet another attempt to see the details of his face better. Skin tanned by life outdoors, hollow cheeks, the stubborn physiognomy of a survivor, eyes whose color she could not manage to see.

Myriam Agazaki was already coming back into the main room. She tossed whatever was in her way off the table so she could set down a Chinese teapot with an iron handle and two mismatched cups.

Kree interrupted her morose contemplation, straightened up, wiped off the bits of wood and paint stuck to her elbows, and went to sit. She let her lips touch the steaming tea and quickly put the cup down again.

"There's a guy in front of the Chinese shop," she said. "Have you seen him? He looks like he's watching us."

Myriam Agazaki sent a glance toward the outside.

"I know him," she said. "The other day he came what I examine him. He has nightmares."

"He looks solid," Kree remarked.

"Well, yeah, but the nightmares they're destroying him from the inside. They stay inside him and he can never spit them back out. That's bad for the health. It's like before death. He came last week. He's in reeducation. He has nightmares what the terrible mendicants they're beating him down with a shovel. He's got something against the Brothers weighing him down. I wouldn't be surprised if he wanted to get revenge on them before his death."

The healer shook her silvery hair from one side to the other, as young girls with long hair often do. As if she persisted in having the mannerisms of a teenager, even though she was already old.

"We all do that," Kree noted.

"What?" Myriam Agazaki asked to clarify. "What do we all do?"

"Die," Kree said. "And dream we'll have enough time to kill someone before we go."

"A terrible mendicant?" Myriam Agazaki asked in a low voice.

"Oh no, not necessarily," Kree said after a second's hesitation.

Their discussion could not have reached the man smoking in front of the corrugated metal shop front. No terrible mendicant was strolling around Aniya Viett and there were no neighbors within a kilometer in any direction. Despite all that, just as in the last hundred years, two hundred years, or thousand years, just as everyone did, they lowered their voices when they mentioned the people in power, especially when the topic involved eliminating one of them.

Myriam Agazaki grabbed her cup of tea emphatically and drank it off in one swallow.

"And besides, he's a good-looking guy," she said.

"Don't try to marry me off," Kree said.

"I'm not trying."

"I can't stand it anymore when men come at me to have sex."

"Bah," Myriam Agazaki said. "I hope you don't say that to a hundred percent of them. When it happens, it happens. We do it so we don't croak from loneliness."

"I've got no use for men," Kree insisted.

"Often they're our brothers in misery," Myriam Agazaki objected.

"Well, yeah, okay, they're our brothers," Kree said. "But me I won't stand for them raping us anymore."

They sat in silence for several seconds. Myriam Agazaki served herself another cup of tea.

"I think he'd be good for you," the healer started again. "He doesn't smell bad. And he's a handsome man."

Kree got up and went to the window to verify whether there was any basis for Myriam Agazaki's claims, but the man had just left his stationary position, and now he was walking heavily down the middle of the street and going away. Loka, Kree's dog, burst out of whatever alleyway she'd been hunting rats in and, after smelling the man's legs, she went off again to her own personal field of adventures. There were no other living beings in the area.

"He's a soldier?" Kree asked, returning to her seat.

"Yes," Myriam Agazaki said. "You could get together. He might be useful in your empty building."

"I don't need anyone," Kree said. "I have Loka. She's enough for me."

Myriam Agazaki let out a sigh.

"Bah, Loka," she said.

"She's enough for me," Kree said again. "And I don't need anyone that comes to have sex with me any time he gets the itch."

Now the tea had reached the right temperature for her.

"I won't say any more about it," Myriam Agazaki said.

"What is it, your tea?" Kree asked, setting her cup back down. The liquid had a lichen aftertaste, a hint of licorice.

Myriam Agazaki enumerated a few plants that she had gathered down by the river, near the dormitories, then she was quiet.

A silence fell.

"Anyway, I gave him your address," the healer said.

"Don't tell me that!" Kree protested.

"I didn't say which floor what you live on," Myriam Agazaki corrected, flinging her hair in all directions. "I only told him about the building."

Kree opened her eyes wide and stared at her friend in disbelief for at least eight or nine seconds.

"Just like that, you gave him my address!" she grumbled finally. "I can't even believe it!"

She was pretending to be shocked. Deep down, though, she didn't mind.

"What side did he fight on?" she asked, after a long pause between the two of them.

"I don't know. His biography, I don't know anything about four-fifths of it," the healer clarified. "But I get the impression he was cooking something up with the enemy."

"We all are, in that case," Kree noted.

"Well, yeah," Myriam Agazaki sighed.

They shared the last half cups of tea.

"A guy in reeducation," Kree said.

She didn't consider this anything especially negative, but she made a face as if she did.

"It's the usual procedure for new arrivals," Myriam Agazaki soothed her.

Outside, on the other side of the window, the street was empty, silent. The soldier had disappeared.

"Physically he's not bad," Myriam Agazaki tried again.

"I'm warning you," Kree said. "If he tries to stick it in me without any warning, I'll kill him."

"He wouldn't be the first," Myriam Agazaki observed.

"The first what?"

"The first guy you cut down."

"My place," Kree said, "is my place."

*A*fter Kree had left, Myriam Agazaki washed the cups, emptied the tea pot, and tidied up a bit. One of the large living-room windows was open; she opened the other one. The air still carried a whiff of butane and burnt skin. Outside, in the street and farther off, the day was fine. Heat and dust danced in the light. Myriam Agazaki limped here and there, nervously swinging her skinny arms, her overlong witch's hair on its way to old age, her willowy body a bit too large around the hips, and infirm. She gathered some bits of wool and feathers from the ground here, then assembled her healer's tools on a copper plate. Finally she hunted and killed two spiders, immediately apologizing to them and their superiors in the hierarchy for having taken their lives. She felt no remorse, but she knew that killing was bad and she apologized. Once her prayer was absolutely complete, she went to lean against the windowsill, tilted her head back and closed her eyes against the sun. A minute of animal pleasure. Her chest, her face dewy with heat and the blinding rays. The thousand perfumes of the near-deserted city. Scents of burning buildings, decomposing asphalt, trash long dehydrated and inoffensive. A stench had hung around during the first years of calm—the memories at times immediately identifiable and repellent, at other times soft, aching, linked to unburied cadavers. But they were no longer there.

The memories. They were no longer there.

Then she felt a cloud had just come over the sun. She opened her eyes again and observed what there was to see. The street, though very rarely frequented, was not empty. A hundred fifty meters away, a man was pulling a cart. He avoided obstacles, holes, chunks of rubble, the remains of cars, and he advanced neither quickly nor directly. She thought: This guy looks like a Tibetan.

Dark skin, a dirty scrap of blanket barring his chest diagonally, a threadbare shirt that left one shoulder uncovered, a dirty hat of beige felt.

As a little girl, she'd held in her hands a book with colored pictures that showed representatives of annihilated peoples: Somaris, Oundouks, Ishnees, Chicago Americans, Ybürs, Peuhls, Tibetans, and a few hundred others. The images were artists' renditions, which had little to do with ethnology, and between one listing and the next they became repetitive and confused, but the picture of the Tibetan had remained clearer than the others.

"Like some kind of Tibetan ragpicker," she muttered as she stood up.

She felt an urge to go to the bathroom.

Fine, I'll go pee, she thought. And make a tour of the house on the way.

"Better close the window," she muttered. "So this Tibetan he doesn't come digging his nose around in my stuff."

She lived in a small house divided in half by a hallway. On one side was the main room and the kitchen, and on the other, two bedrooms and a bathroom, with a toilet that still worked if you fed it with water. Doors opened on either end of the hallway, to the street on one side, and on the other to a small courtyard surrounded by walls. It was a fairly comfortable home, the best that Myriam Agazaki had ever had. From a security standpoint, however, it had too many points of entry. Myriam Agazaki made herself do regular rounds to make sure that no undesirable guests had taken possession of the rooms. Ten years earlier, she had gone into it by chance for a few nights, but fairly soon she had requisitioned the house and moved in permanently. Back when she first pushed the entry door open and set her canvas bag down on the tile, obviously the situation was not the same as now. Chaos reigned, the air still heavy with the gas of genocides. You didn't really know what side you were on, what conquerers were ruling you, and mostly you tried to escape death by running through the streets at random or barricading yourself in some chance shelter. Myriam Agazaki was among the very rare survivors, and at the time, she didn't even dream of sleeping under one roof for more than three or four days before being dislodged by miscreants or soldiers. She'd gone to ground there and remained for a week, then months, with less and less fear of being thrown out, watching as a few small groups of worn silhouettes arrived, followed by the terrible mendicants, and the installation of order and peace. Slowly the city had repopulated, up to something like the several hundred inhabitants that it counted today.

Attacks were rare, but they were part of Myriam Agazaki's personal history, and she was ready to defend herself; she kept a screwdriver in her skirt pocket, and she knew very well how to use it if necessary. The weapon was a comfort when, as she searched for plants, she heard something rustling behind the bushes, and it is true that often near the river one might encounter monitor lizards or dogs that had eaten rabies-carrying rats, but the only species she truly feared was the one still called human, at least in meetings, where the topic was doing something for the times to come. She feared, for example, being confronted by some starving, dejected, and insane refugee, who might seek some quarrel with her, who would take up the terrible mendicants' phraseology and accuse her, for example, of unjustly occupying a property that belonged to the sovereign working people. This had already happened. A newly arrived shouter who had poorly digested the lessons of reeducation. He'd given a hateful speech in front of her door, gesticulating there for half an hour. He'd remained in the street, and she hadn't had to brandish her cross-headed weapon as a threat. She had complained to Brother #30, who made his rounds in the Aniya Viett sector the next day. The complaint was just as effective as a stab with the screwdriver. The man never appeared again.

She closed herself briefly in the bathroom, urinated loudly, washed her hands in the bucket, then partly emptied it into the toilet. She came out and decided to verify that nothing was wrong anywhere in the house. She opened the door to the courtyard. Some flies landed on her face; she grumbled and waved them away. The flies returned, attracted to the light sweat on her forehead. Three lizards clung to the courtyard walls. She knew them. That's right, my little darlings, she thought. Swallow the flies. Swallow these stupid flies. Relieve me of these stupid flies. She closed the door again and went to inspect her bedroom, then the second bedroom, a room where she kept her stock of gas canisters and other objects she'd removed from unoccupied houses, things that that she found pretty or interesting, but which she could not use because they ran on electricity. Electricity hadn't been available since forever, not anywhere, and certainly not in the Aniya Viett sector. Piled with the gas canisters sat hairdryers, CD players, desk lamps. The space was like a storeroom, with closed shutters and a suffocating atmosphere. Somewhere in the shadows, something stank.

"Should have a look at what's rotting back there, one of these days," she muttered.

Randomly she moved around the vacuum cleaners, hand mixers, infinitely mute radio receivers, in an effort to determine where the bad smell was coming from. She didn't find anything. She pictured a rat who had slipped into the jumble and, unable to find a way out, had given up on everything, gone to sleep in a corner, and commenced decomposing.

Then she retreated back into the hallway.

On the threshold, she crushed the third spider of the day. She apologized to the spider and its divine guardians. She was not proud that she had taken its life and mutilated its cadaver under her shoe. And, just at the moment when she was finishing her prayer and lifting her head, she noticed someone looking at her from the entryway. A man. Leaning against the door he had closed behind him.

Quickly she recognized the Tibetan from a little while earlier and she put her hand in her front pocket, glad to feel the screwdriver handle under her fingers. The guy wasn't showing any particular aggression, but he had come into her home without saying anything and she had no idea what his intentions were.

"I came in since there wasn't anyone here," the man said, touching the brim of his hat with his index finger in a sort of greeting.

"What do you mean, there wasn't anyone," Myriam Agazaki said. "I'm here."

"I couldn't know," the man apologized.

He sounded drunk.

His apology isn't sincere, Myriam Agazaki thought.

"I don't want you here," Myriam Agazaki said.

The Tibetan moved his head a bit and lifted his eyes, as if calling to witness an audience located above him. He seemed exhausted in advance at having to carry on a conversation.

"You ordered a tent, right? I've come to install it."

Myriam Agazaki examined him with a suspicious air. She didn't look like she was ready to plant the screwdriver in her interlocutor's throat, but she had a firm grip on the handle and was, in fact, ready.

"The shaking tent?" she asked. "I ordered that last year. I made a request at the House of Mendicants, but nothing came of it."

"Well, here it is," the Tibetan said.

"I'd stopped believing in it," Myriam Agazaki remarked. "Are you going to install it now?"

"Well, yeah," said the Tibetan.

Myriam Agazaki softened. She let go of the screwdriver, took her hand out of her pocket and pushed her hair away from her chest and onto her back.

"I'd stopped believing in it," she repeated.

"We have been liberated from religions," the Tibetan recited in a mournful voice. "We don't have to believe."

"Bah, religions," Myriam Agazaki said.

Their eyes met, expressing no sympathy in either direction. The Tibetan looked her up and down without kindness. He looked capable of worse things.

Suddenly Myriam Agazaki wondered if she'd been right to take her hand out of her pocket.

*S*he brought the installer into the main room and reopened the windows. She'd closed them pointlessly before, since she'd done it with the idea of preventing the Tibetan from coming in or watching from the street to see what she was doing. The installer spent a few seconds sweeping a severe eye over the mess. A frown formed on his lips. Doubtful, but very clearly contemptuous. The room looked like a junkpile. Although bathed in light, it gave a sense of unpleasant tightness, narrowness, a little like being inside an egg, stuck between the yolk and the slimy avalanche of albumen. This is the comparison that went through the installer's mind, anyway, a comparison that Myriam Agazaki suddenly received telepathically and found immediately revolting.

What is with this guy, she thought. Disturbed as she felt, she almost muttered what she was thinking out loud.

Why does he see as if what he was in images of eggs?

At that same moment the installer let out a sigh, and his breath fogged over the healer's face, less than a meter away. Myriam Agazaki squinted to protect herself from the fetid smell.

They remained there without speaking, face to face, him with his frown, her with her grimace.

"What did you eat today?" asked Myriam Agazaki. "Some pemmican what was rotten?"

The installer ignored Myriam Agazaki's insolent question. He went on pushing out his lips as a sign of disapproval.

"There isn't near enough space in here for putting up a shaking tent," he said.

"I didn't ask you to put it up in here," Myriam Agazaki replied.

"I know very well it can't stay here. I'm not crazy. I want you to put it in back. In the courtyard."

The installer's frown had not disappeared. Perhaps he was a competent technician, but in the customer-service aspect of his work, he was not convincing, to say the very least. The commercial aspects. He didn't make sure to establish a friendly relationship with his clients.

He's someone what's looking for a fight, Myriam Agazaki judged.

She felt a lively antipathy for him. First because he had scared her, bursting into her home unannounced. And then there was that egg image, that dead man's breath. Nevertheless, since she had to spend some time with him while he put up the tent and explained how it worked, she decided to avoid conflict.

"Before you get out your tools, would you like a cup of tea?" she offered.

"Only if you can fluff it up with some nice frothy milk," the installer accepted.

"I don't have any of that," Myriam Agazaki said apologetically.

"In that case, I'd rather not," the installer said.

Some introductory encounters between individuals are like that, full of bitterness from the very beginning. Contact fails, the relationship gets off to a bad start and continues in mute hostility. For no reason. An irrational incompatibility appears between two beings and, no matter what they do, they will exasperate each other.

And yet. Myriam Agazaki should have felt more inclined toward her visitor. Like her, he was a member of an extinct minority. She was Ybür, he was Tibetan or something like that. Extinct or endangered minorities, existing nowhere on earth except in some idiotic books, out of print for several generations. He was a weathered man in his forties. Long, brown nomad's hands, dark arms that were almost hairless, a bare shoulder, one strangely empty plaid shirtsleeve, a scrap of covering across the chest, totally useless in this warm weather. Military pants with many pockets. An almost shapeless hat, which looked very much like a half dozen shepherds had already worn it to death. And around his neck a necklace of fat, pale blue pearls.

All together, he looked like the illustration in the little book that Myriam Agazaki had once leafed through between two campfires, between one exodus and another. He looked so much like that illustration that he could have been wearing a costume based on the same model.

"Are you from Tibet?" she asked in an interested voice, expressing a feigned yet emphatic goodwill.

"No," the man said harshly. "I'm from nowhere. Tibet doesn't exist anymore."

Myriam Agazaki frowned. They both fell silent for a few seconds, perhaps because they judged they'd exhausted their supplies of friendly sociability, perhaps also out of respect for the many countries that had disappeared and their peoples, news of whom had never come again. The healer didn't receive any more telepathic images. Neither an egg yolk seen from the inside nor the immense Tibetan peaks, erased from the map.

"I wonder how you knew what I would get a shaking tent in the shop someday," the man resumed. "It's not one of our usual products."

Myriam Agazaki made a vague gesture.

"I got the information what was marked on a poster," she said.

"I've never communicated anything on a poster," the man said.

"I'm sure I saw the word there, on a poster," Myriam Agazaki said, furrowing her eyebrows to squeeze out the doubt that assailed her. "A poster what was advertising for your shop," Myriam Agazaki insisted.

"I've never advertised my shop on any poster," the Tibetan said stubbornly.

"A yellow poster, with words what were in different languages," Myriam Agazaki specified. "It was stuck up across from the House of Mendicants."

"Maybe it was in a dream," the man suggested, shaking his head.

He wasn't frowning anymore. He touched his necklace, fiddled with one of the pearls for two seconds, then dropped his hands. As if they were a burden to him, those hard, knotty worker's hands; he hooked them on his belt by the thumbs.

"I don't know," Myriam Agazaki said. "I don't believe much in dreams. Dreams don't explain anything."

She let two more seconds go by and then finished.

"They're a burden," she said.

Now she was trying to catch the thoughts floating in the other's head, but she didn't catch anything. She wasn't a good telepath, and when she received an image, it was always completely unexpected, never on her own initiative.

The other made a small movement, took a deep breath, as if he were preparing to give his opinion on dreams, but after some hesitation, he kept his mouth shut. He was looking at her with a distinctly less roguish air than before.

"So, then, you install tents?" she asked to fill the silence.

"Not really tents. Mostly telephones," the man said. "There's a need in the city. I install maybe four or five a year there."

"That's not many," the healer observed.

"I charge a dollar every time. That makes it so I can keep going. It's not a fortune, but I can live on it."

The conversation had taken a calmer direction than in the beginning. Finally they were both making an effort. And perhaps the installer had realized that if he wanted his dollar, it was in his best interest to be less gruff.

"For the telephones, do the lines work?" the healer inquired.

"Oh, no. It hasn't been reestablished anywhere yet . . ."

"But then what," the healer interrupted.

"But that'll come," the installer went on. "The terrible mendicants promised. My clients know. They're waiting. It's enough to wait."

"I'd rather have the shaking tent myself," said Myriam Agazaki. "That's proven its worth before, for a good number of people."

"For who?"

"From before. For long-distance communication between shamans. For the Kangowés, for example. Long before the invention of telephones and the other crap."

"The Kangowés?"

"Yeah. The peoples in the Northeast."

"Northeast of what?"

"That I don't know," Myriam Agazaki admitted apologetically.

The installer showed some desire to air his sarcastic reflections, but he held back.

"Before you, nobody ever asked me for this," he said. "I don't know if there's a network, and I don't know if it's gonna work."

"I don't believe in telephones," Myriam Agazaki said.

"Telephones are the future," the installer asserted.

Impossible to tell if he was really convinced. His tone was a bit too brassy, as he flatly repeated one of the official ideology's slogans.

"I don't believe in them," she said. "I prefer methods what are already tried and tested in other places."

"Where's that?" asked the installer.

"Well, sort of everywhere," Myriam Agazaki said. "I told you. The Innus, the Yasheeks, the Kangowés, for example."

"Are you Yasheek?" the installer inquired.

"No," Myriam Agazaki said. "I'm Ybür. The Yasheeks don't exist anymore. Their territory was leveled a hundred years ago."

"I didn't know," the installer said.

"Leveled along with everything else," Myriam Agazaki clarified.

Once again they took refuge in silence. The shadows of innumerable annihilated peoples swirled around them for half a minute, then evaporated into less and less distinct clouds.

"How do you know all that?" asked the Tibetan.

"All what?"

"The Yasheeks, the Kangowés, tent communications."

"Bah," she hesitated.

"The leveling," the Tibetan went on.

Myriam Agazaki made another imprecise gesture. Her knowledge of the past was vague, and even things that concerned her directly had slipped away without a trace, leaving only a muddy swamp of information that seemed to come from nowhere. Most of the time, she no longer remembered who had taught her whatever was in her head, nor under what circumstances, nor at what point in her own existence. It was an awful feeling, as if she had always been entirely alone with nobody to care for her or teach her. Sometimes, though not always, when she was sleeping, sometimes when she wasn't dreaming, images found their way into her awareness. Those tumultuous and fragmented images were all she had to work with, to explain how she'd survived, how she'd become a witch and how she had ended up in the city of the terrible mendicants.

"How do you know all that," the Tibetan repeated.

"I don't know," she admitted sorrowfully. "It just came to me like that."

The installer shook his head, took off his hat, wiped the sweat off his forehead with his sleeve and then put the hat back. He was hot. Without asking Myriam Agazaki's permission, he took off his bit of covering and hung it over the back of a chair.

"We don't always know where it comes from, the stuff we've got in our heads," he said.

Closemouthed they remained, once again, deep in reflections leading nowhere.

"Well," the installer sighed. "Show me where it is, that courtyard what you were talking about."

Myriam Agazaki moved toward the door, had already crossed the threshold when the installer stopped her.

"Wait," he said. "My dollar. I don't do anything for free. I want my dollar right now."

*N*ow the installer was going back and forth in the hallway as he emptied his cart. He'd rearranged his shirt in the more usual manner, his two arms threaded through the two sleeves. With an apparently powerful dose of vexation, he went from the street to courtyard and back again. On his shoulder he carried birch rods, bags holding dog skins and squares of fabric. He dragged a clutch of goats' feet behind. He grumbled, he excoriated the temperature, the flies irritating the skin on his face. But he also emitted unfavorable opinions regarding the poor quality of the material he was transporting, with which he would soon have to begin wrestling in his professional role, which was perhaps worrying him a bit in advance.

"It's been sitting in stock a long time, who knows where," he muttered. "It's lost the flexibility it had at first."

"We don't know where it's from," he protested.

"Somebody must have tampered with it when it was shipped, this isn't the original material.

"Missing some pieces, no doubt, what won't make this mess any easier," he added.

He puffed his disgusting breath toward Myriam Agazaki, who was within range of his groans and sighs. She had tried unsuccessfully to lend a hand with unloading. He had dissuaded her indignantly, with an unfriendly gesture whose meaning was clear: she'd better not meddle with this, she would mess something up or break something.

Now and then he would theatrically drop his burden—which

was cumbersome but not actually heavy—and lean against the wall for half a minute, making panicky gestures of suffocation in order to catch his breath. It was hard to tell if he was pretending or if he really suffered from asthma. In any case, he frequently stopped in the middle of his efforts to pant laboriously. Myriam Agazaki was not far off. He blew noisily over her, a nauseating mix of gases issuing from his windpipe and his stomach.

This guy isn't in good health, was Myriam Agazaki's easy diagnosis as she turned away. Yeah, and it's making his mood rotten, too.

A current of air, loaded with flies and dust, whistled between the exterior door and the door to the courtyard, both standing wide open. The insects contributed their irritating notes to the wind. Panicked by all the commotion, the lizards had returned to their original cracks and holes and didn't even stick out their heads to observe the invasion of their domain. The incursions came one after another, and bit by bit, strange objects littered the ground, with its coating of lichen and bird shit. Crumpled fabric, leather squares, long pieces of wood, colored ties gathered in hanks, black ties.

The installer examined the kit spread out before him. He went looking for the covering he'd left in the main room and then returned, explaining with a dismissive gesture that he needed it for kneeling on cement. He was sweating. He took off his hat, wiped away the brine trickling down his forehead, and recapped himself. In addition to his stench of poorly digested pemmican, a damp armpit odor emitted from beneath his filthy shirt.

After an exclamation in a language Myriam Agazaki couldn't identify, he set to work. The tent's framework took shape in almost no time, but then problems arose. The ties didn't hold, poles remained unused, leaning against the lizards' wall with no discernable destination. Myriam Agazaki made another offer of help, which was tossed aside in an insulting manner. On top of everything, the flies. They were enjoying themselves mightily, and they bit. The installer waved his arms in his struggle against them and struck his left elbow against a hoop meant to hold the entire structure in place. The hoop loosened noiselessly, the tie sagged, and the structure slumped, suddenly on the verge of collapse.

"It's materials what aren't from here," the installer complained. "Must have come out of some museum basement. Not meant for here."

"You've already done the bulk of the work," Myriam Agazaki tried to reason with him. "You'll see, it'll practically finish itself now."

"It's adapted to the people what got polished off over there, I don't know what they're called. Not for here."

"The Yasheeks."

"The Yasheeks, yeah. And, besides, it's not a standard model," the installer protested further.

He was crouched near an open packet, undone to reveal ribbons, pine branches completely bereft of needles, rags and fragments of brown, rust, red ochre, and fabrics. On them ancient geometric designs were visible.

Passively he looked through the packet's contents and nodded his head. Prostration seemed to be overcoming him rapidly.

Myriam Agazaki let him decompress. She told herself that she'd been wrong to call on him, to make such an order without thinking it through. He was going to install an off-kilter shaking tent that would never work, that would remain dumbly in the courtyard for months, gradually becoming immovable and covered in guano. Already she regretted paying her dollar.

"Bah," she said after a moment. "If it's too complicated to install, you can take it back. You can give my dollar back and take off, and we won't say any more about it."

The installer did not react. He remained squatting near faded fabric, fiddling with the rags a little, and did not respond.

Several flies had landed on his hands, on his cheeks. Near his mouth. He didn't wave them off.

Myriam Agazaki stood leaning against the courtyard doorway. She was looming over the guy with all her height, a position that displeased him. Suddenly she once again had the sense of receiving the other's thought, an image. He was on his knees in the middle of a dark mound, and he was trying to extricate himself. He wasn't succeeding. The fabrics he clung to were greasy clothing. He pulled the clothes toward him, and underneath were human corpses. He was looking through the shirts, the underwear, the masses of flesh resisting within them. Far above that hell rolled black clouds, extremely black, tainting the night sky. The image lasted a half-second and then dissipated just as quickly.

I don't like that, she thought. I don't like that at all.

Who knows if that doesn't mean he has sudden attacks of anthropophagy, she thought.

Her hand was back in her pocket, gripping the screwdriver.

"What about you, do you remember your past lives?" asked the installer out of nowhere, as if they'd just starting talking about the subject an instant before.

Myriam Agazaki jumped. "Oh no," she said, and tightened her fingers around the handle of the screwdriver.

She let a few seconds go by. She observed the other's movements. He seemed more exhausted than anything. Like he was collapsing over this bag of fabric, without the slightest sign of aggression. She relaxed.

"Fortunately no," she went on. "That's not worth remembering."

The installer sighed, stood up, returned to the tent and again began knotting ties onto the hoop that linked the poles together. Again he worked quickly, with an unimpeachable professionalism. Only the flies slowed him down.

Myriam Agazaki offered to wave a towel to chase away the parasites that were harassing him, and, since he didn't refuse, she approached, but when she came within the range of his breath he turned and stared her in the face intensely. She recoiled. Her towel hung alongside her skirt, motionless. Moderately clean.

They stared into each other's eyes for three or four strangely intense seconds.

"It's not worth remembering, sure, maybe," the Tibetan said finally, breathing a heavy gust in her direction. "But sometimes you remember anyway."

*F*inally the tent stood upright. A crude cylinder with a summit narrower than its base. Certainly not a place for taking shelter in bad weather. From the inside, one would see a large opening, turned toward the sky. The tent took up too much space in the small courtyard. It disfigured the space. It was an area of her home Myriam Agazaki didn't care about much, where she made only brief appearances, without ever pausing to take in the air; she'd left it to the lizards, insects, and passing birds. But this incongruous, invasive presence suddenly bothered her. She had an urge to express her disappointment, she had something like a protest in mind, although she held it back. If he noticed any reservations in her enthusiasm, the man might rush through the finishing touches, or he might even drop everything on the spot and abandon the job. His grumbling had diminished a great deal. It was better not to get him started again.

"It's going to look nice," she commented reluctantly.

"All that's lacking is what it's ugly, besides," he said.

She didn't like that expression.

"Besides what?" she asked.

"Besides, the chances of it working aren't great," the Tibetan grumbled.

He interrupted his building operations and, after using his toe to gather together a few bits of cord and fabric that he hadn't yet figured out how to fit into the construction, he lit a cigarette. Through the smoke, Myriam Agazaki had another vision of what was passing through his head:

The top of a pit filled with mud and bodies, still two meters of wall on either side yet to be filled before they reached the level of the soil. A fine rain, silent under a coal-black sky, the dense night without vegetation, uninhabited, isolated. The Tibetan on his knees, leaning over a cadaver that looked human, in any case wrapped in clothing, rags and tatters, torn feathers wound within them in such a strange and muddled way that perhaps it was some giant avian, a barely mammalian creature, only somewhat related to the human species. He was bending down and running his hands over the largest part of the body, his hands or rather his fingers, as if trying to figure out whether the inert flesh was still living, as if probing it obscenely, without any way to indicate his intentions, whether the intentions of a healer, of a friend mad with sorrow, of a butcher. It was very dark. Around the Tibetan, there were some bodies that were clearly human, and several corpses that resembled the one he was looking over, murdered bodies next to the remains of shells, soiled with earth and blood.

The vision lasted a moment and a half before Myriam Agazaki chased it away, unable to avoid a hint of grimace. The man went on smoking. His face expressed nothing other than truculence and fatigue. Certainly he did not imagine anyone was in the middle of sharing his private abominations.

She looked away, and, since the silence was weighing on her, she made a tour of the tent. Two times she let out little grunts of satisfaction. They were forced. Then she returned to her point of departure. The Tibetan went on smoking, squinting against the sky. He was in no hurry to put out his cigarette.

"Why wouldn't this tent work?" she asked.

"I got no faith in that junk what being magic," the Tibetan said. "If what it was for me, I'd rather get me a telephone installed."

Myriam Agazaki looked at the nearly completed shaking tent, and perhaps because she already felt like its owner, she felt obligated to praise it.

"Your telephone, that's like the radio or the mixers, I have a whole pile of them in the guest room. What are never going to work again without electricity. Shaking tents have been working for everyone, the Innus and the others, for thousands and hundreds of years, they don't need an electric current. There's no reason what today the service would get interrupted."

The Tibetan threw her an ironic glance. He pulled in the last drag of his cigarette, exhaled a stream of smoke and shrugged.

"That's something from another world," he said. "That's in countries what don't exist anymore. It worked for getting together to hunt for wild cows. I don't see much use in it here."

"It also worked for shamans to talk to each other," Myriam Agazaki argued.

"Are you a shaman?" the Tibetan asked.

"I don't know if you could say that," Myriam Agazaki admitted innocently. "I don't really know. Yes and no."

"More yes or more no?"

"Well, more yes."

The Tibetan crushed the burning end of his cigarette butt against the wall and saved the remaining bits of tobacco in a small bag he'd taken out of his pocket.

"Don't ever say that in front of a terrible mendicant," he said.

He returned to his work. He had to attach some ribbons to the base and consolidate the web of rods with new ties. Every time he tied a knot, he had to say a prayer or make a call imitating a wolf or a dog. Myriam Agazaki left him to his puttering and barking and went into the bedroom with the pile of useless treasures. She tried to pretend she was looking for something. After she'd moved around two boxes full of unreadable cassette tapes and DVDs, she discovered a decomposing lizard, the source of the bad smell. She grabbed it by the tail and went to toss it into the street, beyond the cart. Then she washed her hands in the kitchen and returned to the courtyard. The Tibetan had finished setting up. He was leaning against the wall just next to the door with his eyes half closed and panting like a man sick in the lungs. Sharp notes coming from deep inside, a hoarse whistling sound.

When she came close, he made a sign not to trouble herself, that the attack would pass.

Two times Myriam Agazaki circled around the tent. She took her time, examining this and that, as if invested with expert authority.

When she had closed the circle for the second time, she stood up very straight, shook her hair and set her knotty and skeletal closed hands against her hips, which were not knotty or skeletal.

"Well, one small thing," she said. "How do you get inside it?"

The tent, in fact, did not have any openings.

Abruptly the Tibetan put a halt to his panting, and he approached the tent with the look of someone who was seeing it for the first time.

Several seconds of examination.

"Have to be inside to get it working," he said.

"I do understand what one must be inside," said Myriam Agazaki. "But how do you get in there?"

They both leaned over the roof made of leather and various impermeable fabrics, some of which had obviously been cut from old shepherds' coats. In one spot, on what one might, if forced to choose, call the front, they could make out the trace of a circular entrance.

"There." The Tibetan pointed. "That's the door. You have to cut it out, then sew it up again once you're inside."

"That's stupid," Myriam Agazaki said. "That's a stupid system."

"Have to be really closed up in there with the opening sewn shut for it to get started," explained the Tibetan, who suddenly seemed to know his business perfectly. "And then, inside, you're too scared. When you're scared, you want to run away. Once you're inside, you can't be able to run away. Like being inside an egg."

"I didn't know that," Myriam Agazaki sighed, overwhelmed.

"It's explained in the instruction manual," the Tibetan said. "It's one of the warnings."

"I haven't read the instructions yet," Myriam Agazaki said. "Did you bring a copy?"

"Of what?"

"The instruction manual."

"Oh, I can't give you that," the Tibetan apologized reluctantly. "It was a leaflet I had back at the shop, but it got mixed in with some papers I didn't need. I used them to start a fire."

"You burned the instruction manual?" Myriam Agazaki asked indignantly.

"Well, yeah," the Tibetan said.

"Well, what, then?" Myriam Agazaki exclaimed.

"Sorry. There was only one and it's not there anymore. You'll have to figure it out on the fly until you get it working."

Myriam Agazaki let out a long sigh.

"So how am I supposed to figure it out on the fly?" she said.

"You'll see," the Tibetan said. "Maybe it's easier than you think. And then I'm here. I did the installation, but I also ensure the maintenance."

Myriam Agazaki considered him silently, as if she had found herself standing before an incomprehensible phenomenon.

"For a dollar, I'll do the maintenance," the man clarified.

*S*ince the Tibetan was taking a while to get moving, Myriam Agazaki thought she might as well try again to offer him a cup of tea. Against all expectations, he accepted.

"But without any nice frothy milk," she clarified quickly, worried by this unforeseen absence of refusal.

"Have to be happy with what you're given sometimes," the Tibetan said sententiously.

He was almost done gathering up the unused debris, bits of ribbon and twigs scattered on the ground. He added to the pile his cloth covering, now more or less filthy, since he had knelt down on it several times, and now it was crusted with crow turds and dirt of all kinds. He stuffed all of this in a sack that he threw onto his cart, then he closed the doors again, the ones to the courtyard and the ones to outside, and, without removing his hat, he came and settled into one of armchairs in Myriam Agazaki's living room.

While the tea was steeping, Myriam Agazaki fluttered around him a bit while flinging her hair and accumulating useless gestures, like moving objects around or tapping her dust rag on a piece of furniture. She'd gone so far as to put saucers under the cups, which normally she never did. She was circling in all directions, obsessed with the idea of setting him at ease and showing herself in a good light. The idea had come to her in a completely unexpected manner, just after she'd poured the boiling water over the leaves and turned off the gas, and she'd allowed it to grow until soon it possessed her entirely. What's come over me? she thought. I'm acting like a little girl trying to get an adult to like me. That's not acting my age at all, and anyway, this guy? What do I want with this guy?

She debated with herself. This Tibetan stank like a game animal, he had nightmare visions of cadavers, mass graves, and eggs, he had a bad temper and bad breath. And yet, when the teapot's cover rang as she set it back into place, she had felt, within herself, a sort of click. She didn't want the guy to leave, or at least she didn't want him to leave right away. She considered him with a sort of confused repulsion, but at the same time, he did something to her. He attracted her.

She wanted to know more about him.

"Did you once live inside an egg?" she asked, pouring tea into the cup he held out.

"Yes," he said immediately. "You?"

"I don't know," she murmured. "Maybe in a dream."

"There's a bunch have done that."

"Done what?"

"Lived inside an egg."

Myriam Agazaki felt her hands trembling. The saucer that she held clinked lightly. She set the cup down before her. I shouldn't have asked that question, she thought. Maybe he's crazy.

Better to cut off this relationship, she thought.

What relationship? she thought. There's nothing to cut off. It's just that I'd better not get mixed up in that, she thought.

After that they drank their tea in silence.

She had opened the windows back up so that the room would feel less stifling. From outside, a gust of wind carried the smells of sand, cement, saltpeter-stained plaster, then the air stilled again.

The Tibetan's face was damp, his brightly lit cheeks shone, and Myriam Agazaki could not help but find him at once troubling and handsome. Not really handsome, she thought. But hard, powerful, as if sculpted in wood rather than flesh. He's sweating because of the work that he provided, she thought, and the tea that he swallowed without letting it cool, and his clothes that are too hot.

What's gotten into me, that I'm so interested in him? she thought again. I don't want to keep him here so he'll have sex with me, anyway.

I don't want or I do want? she thought again.

"It wasn't easy getting out of there," the Tibetan said suddenly.

"Getting out of where?" Myriam Agazaki said, in a sudden panic.

"The egg. Getting out of the egg," the Tibetan said, setting down his cup.

*T*he Tibetan was called Gomchen. This was the name he used when he presented himself to the terrible mendicants. The Brothers took care of the formalities of registering new arrivals in the city, and they had required an identity and biographical information from him. He'd been reluctant at first to reveal his name, and the one he provided certainly was not his birth name, his war name, or his religious name. The act of recounting his life to the inquisitorial beggars, submitting to their interrogations, disgusted him. It was like going naked and defenseless before strangers. An unacceptable act of submission. But very quickly he had recognized that the strangers in question had the power of life and death over him, and if he showed any sign of ill will during the interview he would end up unconscious underground or next to the river. The prospect of settling down in this city appealed to him, and he did not want to depart once again into the horrors that had made up his daily life since he came into the world. And so he'd swallowed his pride and told docile lies about his origins, proclaiming from that day forward his membership in an ethnic group that had not counted any proven survivors for many generations. He had chosen to call himself by a priest's name, which the terrible mendicants had accepted as an important piece of evidence that he wasn't telling lies, and then he'd made up an exemplary story, a little personal odyssey, for their pleasure. He depicted himself wandering on who knows what high, lost plateaus, where a few remnants of living beings and communists subsisted under the glacial winds. He improvised this, taking inspiration from stories he'd heard from the mouth of a real Tibetan he'd met long ago on the roads of disaster, for that one, at least, had miraculously survived. He described the fine layer of frost that covered everything ten months out of twelve, the storms with neither rain nor snow, the dying nomads, the columns of refugees leaving for nowhere, the stench of dead yak exhaling from improbable pastures. From that moment onward he was forced to cling to the Tibetan version of his existence. He adorned himself in excessively ethnic accoutrements, but due to ignorance, nobody could accuse him of overdoing his presentation. The terrible mendicants did not ask themselves the question of belief or disbelief. His words corresponded to the ones they liked to hear, all the more so because he claimed that he had always been an egalitarian at heart. This was a point in his favor, in addition to the fact that he belonged to a people that had been completely annihilated for a century. A certain Brother #27 made a peaceful gesture as he finished rereading the file in a soft voice, a movement that might have passed for a gesture of forgiveness even though there was nothing to forgive, and he had registered Gomchen on the list of proletarians and soldiers liberated from the yoke of imperialism.

His registration among the proletarians and soldiers meant he needed only five reeducation sessions. Gomchen had realized that, on that afternoon, the day of his autobiography, he had been very lucky. He had been judged by Brother #27, no doubt the most tolerant of the group. And Gomchen also understood that it would be better not to get himself noticed during the weeks, months, and then years of exposure under the Brothers' vigilant gaze. Vigilant, and much less benevolent than that of Brother #27. For this reason, he attended the solemn meetings and rallies regularly, of his own accord. Once his reeducation was completed, as a sympathizer of the regime he received the freedom to come and go, to choose a lodging, to go about his business. He had opened a small shop, a chance business that gambled on the reappearance of telephonic communications in the near future. An initiative based in faith in the future, which repeated the official language and could not displease the Brothers. Twice a year, he went to the House of Mendicants and spent an afternoon getting himself re-reeducated as a free auditor. He left his dormitory in the Mariya Kahn sector and requisitioned an apartment adjacent to the shop, a little dark, but clean and with running water. All in all, he considered himself satisfied with his lot.

To Myriam Agazaki, even after their conversations became intimate, he did not confide much about himself. He did not tell her anything about his previous life, the existence he had led before arriving in the city. In the beginning she harassed him about it a great deal, she accused him of lying, she resented his silences. She reproached him for his lack of trust in her. Several times she brought up the question of the egg, his time inside an egg, and thus she also brought up the images of piled cadavers, the form, difficultly human, that he had been handling. She saw that the subject bothered him, but he remained evasive. He would admit that nightmares came to him, admit this with an irritated cackle and then, almost immediately, fall silent. Most of the time, his mood darkened and he fell silent. During public reeducation sessions, even if he was there as a free auditor, he was obligated to dig around in his past out loud. He did not hide himself, he spoke in the appropriately mournful tone, and to some very convenient and perfectly insipid self-criticisms he added a few little fibs that Myriam Agazaki would then try to decode, with or without his help, pure fantasies. Finally she was satisfied. Onto these dubious elements, she grafted the telepathic visions that she continued to receive occasionally from him. She used them to construct a realistic story. She understood how painful it was and no longer even tried to learn the most painful parts.

Leaving aside these dark voids that remained unfilled between them, they had, rather astonishingly, found the equilibrium of an elderly couple, since the very beginning of their relationship. That first day, he left after drinking his tea, but the next day and the following afternoons he returned under the pretext of making sure the shaking tent was installed correctly and helping her figure out how it might be activated. Neither she nor he had given up on making it into a functional means of communication. He no longer stank like a wild animal, and he chewed on the scented leaves that she gave him, leaves of little-star-anson that she'd found in one of the vacant fields encircling the city. He had taken up the project again, adding finishing touches that were never finished. In the little courtyard, she'd recommenced flinging her silky hair around in all directions, to the right, to the left, from her chest to her shoulder blades and back again. She fluttered around him even more, fanning him as he knelt to retighten a knot on the tent, or she quenched his thirst with a variety of scented teas, or she offered him concoctions of her own invention to counteract physical fatigue, for she often saw him leaning against a wall to catch his breath. And, finally, they had sex.

The event went off without a hitch and even with a certain joyful calm. Yet Myriam Agazaki was breaking a period of over fifteen years of abstinence, and until the very last second she'd hesitated to lie down beside him. The Tibetan, for his part, showed an extraordinary gentleness. He caressed her and cosetted her for a long time. He waited until she reached a state of sleepy languor, even until she was transformed into a floating holy woman, and only at that moment did he introduce his cock into her loins and flood into her. Very different from the brutal practices that, for Kree Toronto, provoked such disgust and condemnation. Far from that repugnant male violence. And even if there was an element of shock in this intrusion of his organ into herself, Myriam Agazaki had drawn pleasure from it. A certain physical satisfaction, anyway. When she thought about it again afterwards, she let out a sigh of contentment, and she could not stop herself from smiling.

She attributed this immediate romantic harmony to a common history, a passion that had reunited them in a previous existence, and sometimes she hypothesized out loud, as she cuddled against him, especially when they lay awake in the night, when they were caressing each other and she wanted to speak of happiness and magic.

She struggled to hide her shamanic-romantic exaltation.

"Maybe we were lovers in another time," she whispered. "In another world. We got separated. By death or something else. And now we've found each other again."

"That's just silly talk, Agazaki," he said, his fingers gliding through her hair, between her hair and her nape. "There's no good in you thinking like that. Go back to sleep."

She did not dare describe her dreams to him for fear of ridicule, when they were rosy, sentimental dreams, but sometimes she just could not hold back from speaking, especially when she'd just emerged from an assault of terrifying visions and it became difficult for her to fight the insomnia that soon washed over her. Then, in the damp darkness of the bedroom, one might hear conversations of this sort:

"Hold me close, Gomchen. I had that dream again, where you were praying over a corpse."

"Who was it?"

"I couldn't see very well. The dead person, you couldn't tell if it was a man or a woman or some kind of animal. You were praying over it."

"That's just silly talk, Agazaki."

"There were other dead people around you. There was nothing but night and rain. You were saying something, I don't know what words or what language. I didn't understand. I think it was a prayer."

"Well, you say enough prayers over the spiders what you crush them."

"How can you compare it. They're different things. In this they were human corpses. Some kind of human corpses."

"That's only a difference in size. Go back to sleep, Agazaki.

They're just visions of nothing. Dreams don't mean anything. Go back to sleep."

"But sometimes they mean something. This one, it was like a memory coming back to me. A memory of you what was coming back into my head."

"I don't remember ever praying over corpses of dead people."

"But it still happened what you prayed over them anyway? Maybe it happened anyway, even what you don't remember?"

"I was in a world of death. We all came from there. Maybe it happened I was in the middle of a bunch of corpses. Maybe I was praying to give thanks that I was standing above them instead of lying down below them. Or maybe I was praying because I knew one of those corpses."

"I wonder why we pray. Often we don't believe in anything."

"We all pray because of that. We're thankful we're not lying there down below."

"It made me think that the corpse, you had just killed the person and so you were praying for them. It scared me."

"Forget about that, Agazaki. You didn't see it right. These are just stupid dreams. Go back to sleep."

"It looked like the corpse of a big bird. A bird as big as a man. Or a woman."

"These are just visions of the night in your head, Agazaki. I never killed any bird carcasses. They don't exist. Try to sleep."

*T*he memories of those years were so dark that most survivors, when they talked about it, seemed to have bathed in perpetual darkness. They had traveled across exclusively nocturnal landscapes, cities plunged in blackness, without ever knowing the illumination of daylight. Neither sun nor noon existed. Noon crawled alongside them like a naphtha cloud.

After the roar and the rush came a silence, and this silence lasted. It was the most difficult period of the winter.

At the animal-processing plant, there was a woman cutting meat scraps whose hands became so frozen that she cut off her finger without noticing. On the conveyor belt the carpal advanced onward amid the foul meat debris, in the direction of the grinder, and either nobody took the trouble to grab it, or everyone was too absorbed in their tasks to notice a foreign object among the other bits and pieces rolling by.

A shaman crazed with despair has set upon her head a helmet with holes in it. Two long carpenter's nails have been inserted in the holes. They stick out like the sinister antennae of an insect. Once tap with a rock or a hammer was all it would take for the nails to penetrate the shaman's skull, piercing through her brain all the way to her mouth. The shaman comes and goes among the faithful who have gathered in the street. She offers her death to whoever is willing to take it. The faithful sob, overwhelmed by this mark of abnegation and trust. A long time goes by before someone comes forth to take that death.

Kree examines her benefactor from head to foot. He is lying down in the dimly lit room, and, even though he looks as though he were plunged deep in sleep, he knows she is looking at him. Many times she has heard him say that one must always sleep this way, on the defensive, and he has confided in her a few tricks so she can train herself to do likewise, to rest and dream even as she keeps watch for whatever might happen nearby. According to him, the samurais in Japan possessed this skill a thousand years before. Their country has disappeared. She trains. She gets no result at all.

At a certain point, Kree no longer has any idea how old she is. When she absolutely must give her age, when she's about to be recruited into an army unit, for example, or when a camp has some semblance of government and demands identifying details before they're willing to hand out soap and rations, she makes something up. Something plausible for her listeners. They believe her. Soon enough she starts to believe it herself, whatever they have written in her file.

For a very long time Kree has been so brutal and distrustful in the presence of men who approach her that she has remained a virgin. When some try to push beyond her reticence, they regret it for a handful of seconds, and then die.

Several times Kree participates in sweat lodge ceremonies. One time, she is part of a gathering that surrounds a shaking tent, where a witch has been enclosed to invoke the spirits of the beasts that have fled far from man, beasts that are not there to hunt. The shaking tent is nonfunctional. The gathering disperses, unsatisfied, after one fruitless insomniac night.

All ethnic groups are represented in the procession of refugees, in the beginning. The number of survivors diminishes over the years, and some ethnic groups go missing. Then most are extinguished.

Rumors move from one devastated continent to the next. According to some, birds the size of humans are taking the place of humanity, little by little. The birds appear on the surfaces of mass graves. Their eggs hold the cadavers of predestined victims and offer them rebirth.

Near the mass graves are soldiers who break the eggs that rise to the surface. The Party has assigned them the work of fighting this monstrosity. When the Party ceases to exist, monks take over for the soldiers. They are affiliated with no religion, but they feel themselves invested with this sacred task, to kill the birds that rise from mass graves.

One day, after years of calm skies, three late fighter jets appear on the horizon. They aren't flying in the direction of the place where Kree is hidden. They graze the earth and then glide beneath the clouds. The rumbling is distant, almost imperceptible. These are the last airplanes that Kree ever sees.

Golgolian takes care of the little girl who accompanies him. He protects her, he raises her. He teaches her the basics of reading and writing, even though he is convinced that the time of written culture has passed. Kree learns quickly. Never does she disappoint Golgolian. He also teaches her combat skills in case of emergency, nasty and deadly techniques that leave the aggressor no chance of getting away.

When they pass by mass graves, they stop to pray. When they are part of a group that includes a priest, they adapt to the ritual the priest improvises. When they are alone, they mix everything together when they pray. They pray that those who are piled up and rotting down below may know, somewhere, a better fate than the one they have left behind.

Everybody prays, there are innumerable rituals, superstitions accumulate, but in truth, nobody believes in anything anymore. And especially not in a supreme power who gives order to the world and guides it toward a comprehensible future. Through inertia and popular tradition, people still place some faith in the Party, but not much, just a little.

Kree and Golgolian never saw any giant eggs or giant birds near the mass graves or the cadaver-filled trenches.

According to unverifiable whispers, there is no longer any safe haven anywhere.

The years she spent in an army corps were not the best of Kree's life, among other reasons because she had to lose herself in the collective violence, whereas before and after she knew only individual violence, but it was a time in her life when she perfected her knowledge of the martial arts, various pidgins, and basic first aid. She also learned to manage her sexual relations with men and with women.

When she thinks back to those last airplanes she saw as they grazed the horizon, Kree wonders sometimes if they were really planes or if they were gigantic birds. She knows that gigantic birds exist only in dreams or in the worlds after death, but she wonders.

She has made it a rule of survival never to feel any remorse, but sometimes she does find herself regretting that she killed Golgolian even when he did not yet entirely deserve it.

For a month, the sky is so dark both night and day that the water ceaselessly trickling over the black earth looks more intensely opaque than ink.

Inside an egg everything is horribly dark and, despite what the stories say, there is no future. Whether you're stuck to the yolk or the white, or you're wedged in between them, no future. Or even if you combine with the embryo and stay with it from one end of gestation to the other. No future.

Shelter isn't much of a problem. In the ruins, you just have to avoid leaving things to chance, you have to examine the place according to logical criteria. You have to choose a place where the main parts have already crumbled, so you won't get buried in your sleep.

As for food, Golgolian had established the taboo against cannibalism. Kree respected that taboo from the beginning to the end of her existence. There were a few exceptions, but on the whole, she respected it, that taboo.

The permanent blackness of the sky and the warmth. Like death, according to some commentators. Like in the worlds you move through after death. Blackness and warmth.

A sort of discipline reigned over the army corps in which Kree was a soldier for four years, a military but also a moral discipline, to the extent that the authorities in charge were linked to the Party or what was left of it. A good number of the abuses often practiced by other groups were forbidden and subject to special punishment. But over time the discipline degraded and links to the Party became overly tenuous, so by the time Kree deserted it was hard to see much difference between her company and a vulgar troop of thugs.

It took a few decades for firearms to become rare, then they disappeared from circulation almost completely. Arsenals and arms of all calibers had been pillaged, torched, or destroyed during the very first phase of the successive conflicts, well before the generalized civil war and the final black war. People wandered around with guns but no ammunition, and gunshots became unusual. It was as if there were no more war. Flocks of displaced people, unable to settle anywhere, one hot night twenty-four hours a day, communities diminishing more and more, but no more war.

The last generation with a normal academic and university education soon gave way to a procession of derelicts not even aware that they represented the death throes of humanity, with no other culture than the hustle, physical superiority, and fear of the other.

Among the most notable basic knowledge of the hustle, no doubt reading and writing counted for as much as knowing knife-play backward and forward. Kree possessed that knowledge to perfection, and the art of the blade most of all.

From time to time she put her talents as a killer to use in service of one patron or another.

The confection of dried meat required remaining in one place for over a week, as well as vigilance at all hours, since wanderers prowled everywhere and thefts were frequent. You had to hide away in a shelter stinking of smoke and flesh. It was best to get far away from inhabited areas, to choose some inaccessible vale deep in an unburnt section of forest, but there the wanderers you might encounter were more formidable than the urban vagrants.

When Kree was making her dried meat, she slept so little that she was assailed by hallucinations and started to talk to herself, even though she was not, by nature, very talkative.

No point in making a list of what animals are available. They are fewer and fewer. One wonders how the collective pemmican preparation shops managed to gather enough basic ingredients. It was becoming more and more complicated to make your own dried meat provisions, now that there was a lack of meat on the hoof. And yet human predators were not abundant. You could cross through entire cities without meeting a single one. You could travel the countryside for days without seeing a single living soul or beast.

Walking for eight months in a region that ancient maps called inhabited and industrial, walking under a sky either desperately gray as clay or black as a crow's wing, walking almost on tiptoe through the silent, leveled metropolis, Kree said that she had done it, and she added that, in total, over the course of those eight months, she had met a total of four people and twenty dogs.

Next to a mass grave, a guard waited, watching the inchoate mass for the emergence of watches, gold jewelry, eggs. He was sitting on a folding chair like a fisherman, and he had a box at his feet. The box was empty.

The stories claimed that the men and women who came out of eggs, the hatched men and women, looked like normal humans in every detail, like soldiers male and female, like masculine and feminine wanderers. When they escaped being killed by the monks, they blended easily into the gatherings of survivors. But, according to the stories, their deaths were always different. They were different and mysterious, in the sense that nobody was ever there to see.

A stench of slaughter and death hung over the countryside for years, it infiltrated every space, and this nauseating wind breathed even in the hearts of forests, far from the pits. No place was spared, as if the world were forever slimed with a noxious substance that generated it, that smell, then it diminished, or perhaps the survivors just got so accustomed to it that they no longer recognized it.

Although Kree refused to lead the groups she joined, which changed rather frequently since as a rule she never stayed too long among the hordes that accepted her, Kree was respected as a powerful and exceptional person. It was her choice alone not to take the lead. Leaders were not jealous of her, did not maneuver to have her killed, knowing that she wasn't interested in taking their position. Instead they sought her opinions and they tended to consider her as an official representative of the Party. Often she also assumed the function of gang consultant.

Self-anointed shamans proliferated. There were some good doctors among them, hiding their talents behind magic rituals that meant nothing at first, but which gradually became second nature. The more the doctors practiced shamanism, the less remarkable their therapeutic effectiveness became, and the greater their reputations grew.

After a preliminary period of frenetic movement, murders grew rare. Suddenly killing your neighbor became a whole business. When people didn't get along, they kept their distance rather than killing each other.

Cannibalism ebbed as well, although there were still horrifying times when it dominated as a rule. Generally, the cannibals recoiled from eating shamanic flesh, which was one reason that period saw the emergence of so many shamans, monks issued from improbable sects, seers, magicians, and so-called wizards.

Some army corps tried to make up for the absence of weapons by training attack animals, mostly dogs, sometimes polecats, wildcats, wolfchildren. Training was difficult, and trainers often gave up or abandoned their beasts before they were able to finish their conditioning, and during confrontations the results were hardly convincing. For the most part, the husbandry of attack animals evolved and transformed into meat husbandry.

Kree did her best to remain alone for as long as possible. She joined a group only when she sensed that solitude was threatening to send her reeling into madness.

Hygiene was an area where Kree was especially careful. For Kree, finding places where she could clean up was just as crucial as finding shelter for the night or a means to obtain food. Golgolian had taught her to keep herself clean, to keep herself rigorously clean regardless of the circumstances, and later she had not forgotten his lessons and, on the contrary, had improved on them.

Although she felt no remorse over the murder of Golgolian, Kree nevertheless wondered if she couldn't have waited a bit longer before killing him.

The foul smells emitting from others' bodies, whether male or female, never prevented Kree from grappling with attackers and defeating them. On the other hand, these smells were certainly at the base of her lack of attraction to sexual activity.

When shamans made reference to a sacred book, it was more out of tradition and as one fantastical magic spell among others, for most of them were illiterate and had never held a book in their hands.

Books were some of the objects from before that had been burned along with all the rest, but they were so numerous that it was still possible to hunt one up without any great effort. It was still possible to learn to read. The activity was not, however, a priority. Books remained untouched for decades, deteriorating bit by bit under the ashes and mud. The gesture of opening a book has lost all meaning, and for most it's a matter of chance whether they open it the right way, not a sign of any aptitude at reading.

The world is so oneiric and tenebrous that now there is no one who can tell the difference between the night of day and the night of dreams.

*K*ree was twelve years old, then she turned thirteen.

When she was a very small girl, only six, she got picked up on the road by a taciturn man with great physical strength and great competence in everything he undertook. Sometimes he made reference to his own childhood, mentioning colonels from the Party who taught him to overcome hardship; without getting lost in any long descriptions he evoked the landscapes of megacities and forests in flames, high plateaus, and he said that he had Ybür origins, but he told her this with so many exaggerations and obviously mendacious details that his story was impossible to believe. The goal of this theater of falsehood was to maintain his air of secrecy, even as he pretended to confide in the little girl growing up at his side. He said little about the past in general, like all adults of his generation. The survivors lowered an iron curtain in front of their memories, a curtain they strove to lift as little as possible in order to avoid sinking into madness or depression. Oblivion was salvation. And some had survived for that very reason, because they had buried their memories under layers of heavy, unfathomable semi-consciousness, or under unconsciousness, or because they had transformed their memories into phantasmagoria.

This man was called Golgolian.

Kree's feelings about him were mixed. She was torn between a silent, affectionate, filial loyalty and a fear that sometimes became intense, due to Golgolian's impressive size and, most of all, his implacable severity as an instructor. He did not beat her; he did not yell at her like the mothers in her first foster families. He watched to make sure she was washed and fed, she slept in decent conditions, she wore clean clothes. It is true that he managed to ensure this comfort for her, which was not a basic thing in the chaos that the world had become, through banditry—that is, by stealing, threatening and killing. He was at ease in this role, he felt no remorse about unburdening people who possessed what he needed, he knew how to inspire fear when necessary and he was skilled in eliminating in a few seconds anyone who opposed him. When confronted, he was a man capable of terrible violence, very sure of his movements, someone who never lost his cool and always won. Very quickly he initiated Kree in the most awful skills of war, cruel tricks that assured victory even against seemingly unbeatable adversaries. He treated her with the demanding manner of a martial arts master. He took into account her abilities, her age, her size, but still he constantly pushed her to surpass herself. Giving her no respite in her apprenticeship. Forcing her to practice day and night. She progressed with great speed, she was talented, she trusted her instructor entirely. She obeyed him during training without complaint, without even a second's thought of complaining, but as soon as the exercise was finished, inside she felt that mixture of love and fear that she could not manage to control. Fear surged at some moments, without any obvious reason, in contact with his drunken tenderness, for example, or his silences, or when she lay awake and listened to the whistling noises he let out in his sleep.

He taught her methods of close combat that a little girl could easily apply to aggressors four or five times her size, and among these methods he emphasized what he called "dirty techniques" and "demon skills." There was no lack of occasion for her to try them out. Golgolian watched her in action, and intervened immediately if he saw she was getting in any trouble, but it was rare that she was. She knew when and where to stick a blade by surprise, how to disengage from a grip, a choke hold, or an armlock, and how to respond in a way that was immediately very painful and soon lethal. When she bit or pinched, she didn't do it like a crazed little girl but like a harpy that anyone would regret encountering.

At nine-ten years old she was a budding killer, at twelve-thirteen she could already be called a war-hardened killer. Golgolian was proud of his student, and although he wasn't effusive in his praise for her quality as a fighter, he repeated to her with an appreciative smirk, almost a smile, that she'd made a lot of progress over the last few years.

Golgolian and Kree got along well and almost never argued, but Kree began to feel more and more like he was hiding something. Often he made her uncomfortable, even his mere presence close by set her heart beating fast and troubled her. She got the sense there was a part of him that was dark, a secret domain that he tried not to show and that remained mysterious under a heavy layer of silence. She imagined that this territory hidden within him was linked to his sexuality. Linked to sex, to a desire to have sex with her. When she was a girl whose body was getting ready to change, she had an instinctive knowledge, enriched with information and fantasies from the other little girls she met briefly, mostly in encampments, refugee barracks, and provisional schools. The other children were just as lost as she was, and very often they had been mistreated by the adults traveling with them. She was aware that she was lucky. She found herself adopted by a person who protected her, educated her, respected her, and did everything he could to help her overcome later trouble, the murderers and blows of fate. All in all, she had no cause to reproach him. Nevertheless, the crude stories and obscenities she heard from other girls and boys inspired her to mistrust her adult companion when it came to sex. Unlike her, all of them had been abused, raped, and mistreated. Now she became suspicious, and she feared the moment when her turn would come. She felt more comforted than jealous when, on the occasion of a halt, in a temporary camp or gathering center, for example, Golgolian got together with some woman, a refugee or a soldier. Such relationships were always fleeting, but for Kree, they became a reassuring sign. Later, though, when the two of them were once again traveling apart from everyone and everything, as if they were alone in the world of death-scented landscapes, under the black sky, in the damp humidity of disaster, once again she began to observe Golgolian, reading unclean intentions into all his acts and movements. With suspicion she analyzed the way he addressed her or, on the contrary, ignored her existence or, when he was teaching her new demon skills of which she had not been physically capable before, his way of guiding her hands, her arms, her hips, of manipulating her body so that her movements would be even faster, so she could achieve the terrifying annihilation of her enemy with even less effort.

Months went by and, at least on her side, their relationship evolved. She continued to feel a deep affection for him, had no desire to leave him, did not wish to see him disappear from her life; she was forever grateful to him for everything he'd done for her over all those years. At the same time, though, changes were taking place within her, new perceptions, a strange waiting, a bubbling in her blood that bothered her to the extreme. She was not at all impatient to become pubescent, and she had heard enough from the girls she met on the road to extinguish, almost entirely, any curiosity she might have felt or that might have obsessed her, to feel between her thighs, inside her body, against her skin, anything concretely resembling the sexual act, the sexual encounter with a man. She had no appetite whatsoever for discovery and experience of that kind. And yet, unless she lost a fight and got raped on the road one day when Golgolian wasn't there to come to her aid, she feared that it was only logical that the sexual encounter in question, her first copulation, would take place between Golgolian and herself. A prospect that absolutely did not attract her. That frightened her. And disgusted her in advance.

Golgolian did not speak of such things and did not seem near the point of trying to have sex with her; he did not appear to be waiting restlessly until she got a little older in order to force her, one fine day, to become his female. She watched him constantly, but when it came down to it, she did not discern any signs of animal frustration in him, nothing that recalled the rutting desire described by her young friends, most of whom had been victims. Nothing that might indicate he considered her prey to be conquered so he could knock her down and penetrate her, whether sooner or later.

Nothing. But her discomfort grew unabated.

She hid it, and she hid it well, for he had taught her to hide things, to maintain a tranquil demeanor and a mask of calm even when a situation was growing critical, and never to reveal her intentions at any moment, not even a microsecond before action. Golgolian had taught her this regarding combat, and she applied it to her existence and her everyday ways of being.

Then she had her first period and, since she assumed that this, which could not have escaped Golgolian's notice, would be the trigger for an impending attack, a few days later she took advantage of her companion's especially sound sleep to thrust a dagger in his temple up to the hilt, and then, although no doubt he was already dead, she slit his throat.

*K*ree knew how to neutralize attack dogs. Some breeds were more fearsome than others, but most of them were about the same size, descended from shepherd dogs. Kree had learned to turn them aside from their primary target, which was to bite the throat, rather than the hand holding the knife. She had trained dogs herself; you asked them not to pay attention to the knife but to leap into the face of whomever they were attacking without fear of taking a stab in the flanks. If their bite landed correctly from the first, their adversary would be immediately rendered incapable of harm. Kree took advantage of this weakness in the animals' education, the lack of variation in their attack. She blocked the dog's attack and left it snapping its jaws shut at the wrong height, on a body part protected by thick clothing or in empty space, and, in the same movement, she attacked the dog. She attacked with extreme violence, and she disposed of the dog quickly enough to take care of a second animal if necessary.

After incessant rains, a landscape of lakes. Lakes of mud.

Over the decades the armed gangs have fewer and fewer arms, but more importantly they've gone from having fifty-some members down to an average of around ten. At ten they stabilize. These groups can no longer maintain their internal stability when they count more than ten individuals.

The weakest shamans offer a pathetic spectacle, fleabitten wanderers begging for acceptance in some community or group, although they'd be better off gathering the handful of people likely to trust them, instead. These idiotic shamans do not know how to choose their audience, which is how they often end up in bowls of soup, held by the warriors they hoped to accompany in the future.

Though it's true that it's been years since the rivers carried corpses, their waters continue to have a strong taste of rotted blood.

According to some unverified rumors, the Party still has some teams capable of analyzing the situation and planning decisive actions to ameliorate it. Kree doesn't put much stock in it, but she remains ready and waiting. Golgolian was waiting for it, too; he heard the same rumors, he remained ready, too.

Some of the mud lakes do not dry, never dry, as if a terrible humidity is rising ceaselessly from their entrails. Under the light of the asphalt sky, they constitute a landscape the wanderers avoid, for fear of losing all courage and sitting down on the ground rather than continuing their wandering.

The humidity is more stifling in the summer, but July is generally no brighter than the depths of winter.

Now and then some monk or shaman claims to have received instructions from the Party. Since nothing in his practice changes and he transmits no useful advice for better survival, nobody listens.

One night, three pseudo-monks infiltrate Kree's house to grab her things or rape her. They try to immobilize her. She kills the most aggressive one with a knife slash under the chin, immediately followed by a stab in the ear. She gets up and kills the second one. The third monk runs. She tosses the bodies over the threshold, then goes back to bed, and when morning comes, she follows the trail of the third. She finds him and, even though he's brandishing an axe, she gets close to him and kills him.

A man says that next to a pit he saw a monk who was dedicated to breaking enormous eggs. Based on this testimony the rumors revive, claiming that giant birds are secretly dominating the world and attempting to repopulate it with creatures that they plant among the corpses. Nobody believes this nonsense, but almost everyone spreads it.

No seasons anymore, not really, a dark and dreadful sky swirling high above, months of rain alternating with periods of stifling humidity, sometimes with glacial years when pulmonary diseases became widespread and eliminated more survivors than the endemic battles did. These were also the times of raids led by generals who came out of nowhere, arising from the devastated earth to reestablish order on what they thought might be less unlivable continents. When confronted with reality, the generals swiftly renounced their epic ambitions; they slipped into rags that were easier to wear, becoming simple gang leaders. And soon they were extinguished in their turn by disease, small-scale mutinies, and suicidal moods.

After the army, Kree made it her habit to kill only selectively.

Some of the shamans, taking up an ancient tradition, bragged of being sculptors and painters, primarily of landscapes. A few clever wits called them "artists of the mud and foot" and, before putting them to death, forced them to erase their frescos or miniatures, which were, in all truth, aesthetically indefensible.

A few hundred Hinduists from the Indian subcontinent gathered in processions heading toward the Great East, which, according to legend, was less poisoned than other parts of the globe. They brought color to the hordes, with rags that were intended to run the entire chromatic spectrum, in the hope that they could show the beauty of the world, its inhabitants and its gods. These men and women cast a brief spell over the survivors' eyes, even over their dreams, and then they ended up blending into the surrounding grayness; they were absorbed into the ambient horror and disappeared.

Regarding the eggs, the stories are contradictory. According to some, giant birds hatch from the eggs taking shape in the mass graves, then go to hide in uninhabited territories, waiting for humanity's extinction to become complete before they make their appearance in the sky. According to others, after countless years of gestation, the being that finally hatches, that finally comes out of the aged shell in the mass graves, is a person, already adult-sized, possessed of a muddled memory but capable of blending into the first group of survivors that he encounters, without really feeling like a stranger to the human race.

Immense mass graves, everywhere. Cities so devastated they can be mistaken for countryside. A stench of ashes and death that persists for decades. A sky as dense as pitch. No more seasons. Never a motor, neither vrooming nor idling. Sometimes, birds with insane wingspans on the horizon. The sounds of feet crushing through mud or dust. A few wanderers. Love stories next to campfires. Legends. Assurance that the Party is watching. Shamanic chants. Assurance that a page has been turned, the worst is past, and the Party is watching.

In thirty years of uninterrupted wandering, Kree never ran into a single Party representative. Which did not call into question her loyalty to the principles of egalitarianism, or at least what she had understood of them when she listened to the lessons Golgolian taught her.

Dried meat, pemmican, grilled bits, flours milled from the surviving grasses, teas concocted with magic herbs, in the regions where magic herbs still grew and where old women, whether witches or not, had time to transmit their knowledge to the younger ones.

For such transmission was happening, finally, but in the old way, as it had happened twelve or thirteen thousand years before, and only when a group managed to remain in the same place for a long time. No group could settle in a lasting manner. But some actually spent a good amount of time in the same place, up until everything went bad and they had to leave again.

Kree adopted several young girls over the course of her life. She tried to reproduce the life she'd lived with Golgolian. Akshaya, Pari, Sora, Angelina, Oshalee. The girls stayed with her a few months then disappeared, whether they were ground down by illness or malnutrition, or they preferred to seek out a less exacting instructor. Kree experienced some sorrow whenever she lost a girl, but the pain passed quickly. For a long time she had known how to fight against grief and absence, or against ingratitude, or against puerile stupidity.

In her nightmares sometimes she found herself fighting Golgolian barehanded. She had grown up; she was skilled and much faster than she had been fifteen years before. The fight was less unequal than it would have been when she was still a kid. Nevertheless, in her dreams, she always lost.

Fighting with a giant bird. She thought about it sometimes; she wondered what grip she would take, where to land the first blow, the decisive blow. She wasn't sure she could block a blow from a giant wing. She wasn't ready.

One day Kree meets a shaman who sinks needles and nails into a little statue. The shaman is a woman, rather young. She is insane. She answer questions only in an evasive manner, or by stringing together some words bursting out of her delirium, or in an invented language with guttural sounds that make Kree cringe. For unknown reasons the shaman gets attached to Kree, she follows Kree, and for a few days the two women share their wandering. In exchange for the food that Kree gives her, the shaman holds out a little statue. In an attempt to establish contact with her comrade in disaster, Kree in her turn sticks needles into the wooden head. The shaman screams and pronounces curses. She throws herself at Kree. Kree pushes her away, but when the shaman tries to attack her with a hammer, Kree disarms her, kills her, and leaves.

Through a rip in the sky, one night, an avalanche of stars, and then the darkness seams back together.

Curiously, after countless episodes of violent barbarism, a greater calm settles over the survivors. Apathy has won them, with a greater mutual understanding, the acceptance of a few communal rules. Of course there's been no end to cannibalism, nor to gratuitous cruelty, murderous madness, the constant appeal to a more definitive self-destruction. Of course. But a greater calm has come to reign among the last representatives of the species.

In some places where there is no sign of danger, the sensation that you're drying up, that your skin is stretching, is about to split, even though the heat is humid, the air gorged with water, and you're not sweating any differently than usual. A poisonous zone. If you haven't been walking in it for too long, you might get out. If not, might as well lie down on the ground and wait.

The fast-talking horny ones are easier to overcome than the quiet ones who pretend not to see you.

No more nonreligious music, not ever, nothing but drums and sometimes flutes so the lamas or the shamans can maintain the rhythm of the chant. The few instruments that can be dug out of the ruins are sometimes taken up by children or simple souls who pick them up for a few days, blow inside or tap the top or pinch the strings without getting any definite sounds out of them, and then abandon them in the mud.

A simple observation: there are fewer and fewer children, and then one day it becomes apparent that there are no more at all.

Every one or two thousand kilometers, completely by chance, one might happen across a verdant, growing valley. While some enjoyed this kind of landscape at first, it no longer attracts them. Partly because it is much too different from what they've become used to during the years of walking through black lands, and partly because the spot is always swarming with venomous reptiles and other nasty surviving beasts.

The confrontations between gangs and army corps lost their intensity after the first twenty or thirty or maybe hundred and fifty hard years. The leaders no longer had any clear objectives and territorial issues no longer arose, since no territory possessed enough quality to be worth claiming and defending for more than a few months. The soldiers, both men and women, were fed up with gutting each other over religious trifles, the fanatics set the law for a while but then grew tired of it themselves, and, since they could not manage to surround themselves with viable communities, one by one they rejoined the ordinary processions, the hordes with no ideology other than the will not to devour each other immediately.

For an entire year, Kree lived near a mass grave that stretched more than a kilometer in length. The sky was the color of charcoal, of crows' wings, China ink, naphtha, licorice, shoe polish, death. The land was deserted, there was water, inaccessible shelters in labyrinths, and enough wood and books to keep a campfire going for an eternity. A few easy-to-kill ruminants grazed in a nearby valley. From time to time, shamans came to see her. They claimed they were guardians of the site and said that they walked up and down the length of the pit to make sure no one emerged from it.

Incongruous and ephemeral sects, religious remnants without reference, rituals inherited, transmitted, reinvented, but, mostly, underneath a thick layer of superstition, no belief. Kree kept in mind what she had been told, that there were successive hells, inserted within death itself, leaving no respite to either the dead or the reincarnated, but she did not really understand what that meant, how the system worked, and she didn't much care.

Although the atmosphere is often unbreathable and unhealthy in the hardened shelters, which are everywhere, the survivors prefer them to camping under the stars. Walls offer better protection against attacks, which are still possible. Of course it was necessary to make sure there were emergency exits, trenches, or hallways where one could run if necessary, in case of an attack with multiple assailants or in case of an attack by fire.

One of the greatest dangers is sinking into lethargy and depression, and there is no way to guard against it. The mind loses courage and then dies out. The body follows. Around the mass graves one can often observe new bodies, people who have lain themselves on the ground, who are waiting for the world to loose its grip on them or who have already joined the infinite masses of the departed.

Even though she is among the people who have lasted the longest, no legend follows Kree, and in any case Kree considers that discretion and self-effacement are one way to ensure survival.

One day Kree lies down next to a mass grave, in the mud because it's raining. She doesn't want to live anymore. A monk prowls around her. He prowls for two days, then he attacks. Kree defends herself. Reflexively she stands up, she evades him, she kills him. Suddenly, with no more personal belongings at her disposal, clothed in dripping rags, heavy with earth, in the din of rain, with the defeated monk's corpse lying before her, she wants to live again, to know what will come afterward, when she will begin walking again. She shoves the monk's remains toward the grave and she does not lie back down beside it.

Kree has had some difficult fights and she recalls them with disgust, for she is not proud that she didn't finish the business in the first instant by using one of the military techniques she perfected while wandering with her army corps, or one of the dirty techniques that Golgolian taught her when she was very small, but she is even less proud because she has had recourse to some very, very foul improvisations to ensure her superiority over her adversary or adversaries.

You must not get hurt, or at least not much, otherwise after a little while you die, from infection, septicemia, gangrene. And sometimes you simply die of fright.

No doubt because they don't really know what to say, the monks have the survivors they're speaking with talk about their dreams. These stories circulate and persist in the form of echoes, rumors, legends. They become established facts in the collective memory. Yet this memory is unstable, and very soon the oneiric information that for months or years was considered as vitally important is completely erased. They are replaced by other deformed dreams.

Two half-settled communities observe each other from eighty kilometers apart. They watch each other in the black of day, in the dark of starless nights, in the damp, in hunger. Inevitably, if one of them doesn't take to the road, there will be a war. A miserable war without a victor, and in the aftermath the communities will disperse.

In a few places more hospitable to their existence, mollusks. Snails, slugs of great size. Some people gather them and eat them in broth with herbs. The majority of wanderers look at them with stubborn revulsion and consume them only when nothing else is available.

The sea coasts are not attractive. The graves near the beaches seem to be moving in permanent agitation, as if permanently swollen with ghosts or bubbles of putrefaction, even though they are forty or fifty years old. The sea teems with dead fish, the crustaceans distill juices that cause diarrhea.

Under the soot-heavy sky, the ocean offers a repellent spectacle, the waves look like a pelt bristling with threads of sweat and drool, an unpredictable animal skin. The worst stories come from the sea. No one has gone near it for decades.

A large part of the world is inaccessible. People say: "over there." For a long time now they have not sought to know more.

Sometimes a herd of buffalo seems to get comfortable in a swamp. A few intrepid hunters decide to retrieve one for the group waiting on the shore. The hunt is long and difficult. Their weapons aren't suited to such large beasts. The buffalo get farther and farther away, the hunters lose ground. Those who keep going end up sucked into the voids of mud.

The dog that accompanied Kree before her death was named Loka.

Although Kree ordered her life according to a rather strict code, she happened to steal some provisions from a hiding place she had just discovered, and, when the owner showed up unexpectedly and opposed her, she fought and killed him.

With no more powers to overthrow and nothing more to build, for some time people fought between themselves without any goals for the future. No one knows how a good number of survivors hung on, even after that period of miserable chaos, to the idea of a powerful egalitarianism that would benefit everyone, and a fraternal transition, intelligently ordered by the Party. The idea that, in spite of everything, it would happen someday.

For a long time, the accounting of days, of years. Then the calendars get mixed up and calculations of time's passage are made in an approximate way. People start to measure time in relation to personal events. It was when I was traveling with a company of women who knew how to heal using mushrooms and sawdust. It was when I broke my teeth on a cement curb. It was when there was a rain of falling stars. It was a long time ago. It was once upon a time.

Up until her death, Kree has the advantage of an excellent memory. She does not, however, keep a mental count of seasons and years, and, like almost all survivors, she situates the past in a long-lost time without landmarks or importance. Her memories are organized in chronological order, but they are undated.

It's not true that Kree never cries. But almost no one has ever seen her with tears streaming down her cheeks.

Even if the sky does not change at all, there are still some differences between day and night. The lighting is not the same. At night, sounds take on a mysterious quality. Smells get stronger. And then it is, very simply, the time of day when people sleep while feeling more troubled and vigilant than at noon.

Several times a year the sun pierces through, the stars pierce through. Nothing that provokes much enthusiasm among the survivors, whose world is in twilight, shadow, darkness, and the absence of joy.

Army corps welcome fighters of both sexes. Men and women do not seek to perform any heroic acts so as to claim that one sex is superior to the other. The male soldiers are less effective than the female ones in most areas, but they pretend not to realize it.

For a few months, Kree shared her meals and wandering with a monk, who carried a bag full of hundreds of charms and amulets, which he exchanged for food after ceremonies or prophecies. One day, the monk's bag was stolen. He and Kree followed the thieves' trail for a week. The gang was small and easy to spot, but they moved fast. Then the thieves dispersed, no doubt after an argument. Kree gave up the hunt. The monk continued stubbornly following one or another of the criminals by chance, he didn't know which one anymore. Then he ended up entering a region that was totally unfamiliar to him. He was a solid man, and one might suppose that he succeeded in retrieving his goods, but Kree never heard any news of him again.

We know more or less what happens inside an egg for twenty-eight days, and also during longer gestations, such as nine months, for example. But what happens when life inside an egg lasts for five years, ten years, twenty-five years, nobody can imagine. When asked about this subject, the shamans who have assumed the task of spotting eggs under the surface of mass graves in order to crush them cannot help but cringe with horror, and say nothing.

Scenes of violence could occur at any moment, linked to the appearance of groups whose threat was wrongly evaluated, or provoked by sudden, rageful, suicidal, criminal, inexplicable tensions, which could flare up briefly among four or five individuals before being quickly snuffed, once blood was spilled. But, in general, the atmosphere among wanderers, for the last decades, was remarkably peaceful.

One image among others: Kree with her dog atop a crest, standing out against the sky, two black silhouettes against a black background, then everything goes dark in the night and nothing more can be seen.

Nauseating winds for a quarter century, and then only the smell of mud and vegetation struggling to be reborn.

Strange dawns, rains so acidic at times that they attack the eyes and bring tears, electrical phenomena resembling thunderstorms, a permanent humidity, miasmas carried on gusting winds, but, on the whole, acceptable survival conditions for the few organisms that have gotten past the peak of the devastation.

*I*t's the smell that wakes her. Dirty rags, soiled skin. Someone has stopped in front of the door. Not touching the door but stopped just in front. A refugee, a vagabond. A newly arrived wanderer who does not respect the curfew.

Or a dead man, Kree thinks.

She opens her eyes on darkness. She isn't in the habit of getting scared for no reason, but here's her heart beating fit to burst. And goosebumps all down her legs, her arms. A dead man. A dead man prowling around in the building.

She has the impression that she let out a scream just before coming out of sleep, but she isn't sure. She tries to recall the last dream visions that tore apart her head. They're hidden. Nothing remaining but black, a dense, impenetrable black. And that smell of dirty clothes forming the pathway between reality and nightmare, that stagnant wind of unclean skin, of mass grave. If there was a story, or images, they've dissolved at high speed.

Around Kree the night goes on, but the deepest darkness has already passed. Behind the window the sky has started to change color. A good number of the stars have gone out.

The room's angles are becoming discernable. The bare walls. The bare angles.

Nothing out of the ordinary. The door hasn't been forced. The lock and chain are in place. The table, the trunks, the chair haven't moved. Nobody has entered. Obviously. Nobody has entered, nobody has approached her during her sleep.

At the foot of the mattress, Loka yawns, lets out a whine and goes back to sleep. Kree has just risen to a seat. She needs to move, to change position so she can chase away whatever has assailed her, the idea of a living dead man spying from behind the door. She hears the blood tapping dully behind her eardrums, less and less quickly. Her heart is slowing. She listens for what is moving farther away, outside her body. Loka. Loka is breathing loudly. She's always breathed loudly. A powerful black wolf-dog. She has remained lying down. A sign there's nothing to fear.

Much farther down, in the street, three or four men are pulling and pushing a cart, now and then letting out grunts of effort. Reeducateds, no doubt, on provisions or cleaning duty. The rubber-coated wheels crunch gravel and skid. An unhappy voice. An indistinct curse. Then nothing. Then once again the squeak of suspension springs, again sighs that sound like complaints. There's a dip in the middle of the street; on foot you barely notice it, but it's different when you're hauling a cart. The cart moves alongside the building for a minute, then the noise decreases. On the first floor, Brother #9 is seized by a fit of coughing. He has lung cancer, he doesn't have much time left. Brother #9, Kree's only neighbor. Then silence returns.

Five stories up, where Kree lives, not a sound on the whole floor.

She lies down again. She's settled onto her back. Whatever woke her no longer floats anywhere but in her dreams. Male sweat, worn-out cloth, organs open to the sky. Just the kind of stench the dead leave in their wake when they come out of the mass graves. Or else maybe. Maybe it came from that guy, the one Myriam Agazaki gave her address to, that former soldier with the sailor hat. Kree breathes, inhales carefully. Try as she might she can no longer catch the vile stench that pulled her out of sleep.

Now the first thing in her nostrils is dust and rancid blankets, and then Loka's breath, the acrid warmth of Loka's fur.

The dog smell is getting too strong. Kree will have to bring her to the river for a wash.

Dawn approaches. Only a few stars shining beyond the windows. Dark blue above the city. But fewer glistenings, no longer that abundance of icy stones. Less clear darkness.

Kree sniffs and sniffs, trying to revive her memory of the smell. She reconstitutes it mentally without perceiving it again. She imagines someone behind the door, just outside the apartment, a malevolent shadow. But she doesn't believe in it anymore. Her calm has returned. She knows nobody was spying in the hallway. A fear that came from nowhere has disappeared into nowhere.

She thinks of the shady barefoot guy smoking across from Myriam Agazaki's house the other day. A guy her friend thinks is good-looking. The head of a stubborn soldier, a fighter forged in great defeats. A ferocious loser. She imagines him, gives him life. Since Myriam Agazaki was so stupid as to give him the building's address, he might well have managed to work his way up six stories and find her door, stand like a statue before the door waiting for her to open it. Considering the hour, certainly not to take tea with her. No. Maybe not to cause her any harm, but to surprise her and enter her apartment. To have sex with her.

Kree's sense of smell has sharpened over the past few years. She's realized that she trusts her nose just as much as she trusts her eyes or ears to gather information about her surroundings. And even to assess people. Maybe because of the fact that her vision has weakened. Her body is trying to compensate for the weakness. The world of smells has opened up to her, as if she had stumbled into the world of wild animals. Then Loka came into her life. The beautiful black dog, her beloved black dog. Loka came to live with her and, very soon, Kree judged her animal companion was more competent than herself when it came to sniffing out the dangers that surrounded them, and to learning about the individuals they encountered via olfactory means. Kree entrusted Loka with that role. Her own sense of smell, however, had retained the capacities that had appeared before the dog's arrival. And, basically, they made a team. They were accomplices. Facing an unknown something or someone, they sniffed at the same time and almost in the same manner. Then they would exchange a brief glance to verify that their intuitions were in agreement, and if a need arose, they divided up the task and they acted. If it was necessary to fight, for example, which occurred only rarely but did occur, they fought together.

Kree throws off the sheet and gets up. She goes to the window.

Loka rises to her feet and, after a second, she moves toward the apartment door. Kree hears her snuffle a few times and sneeze, muzzle at ground level, then the dog returns near and leans her head against Kree's leg. She's signaling to Kree that there's no nasty scoundrel in the corridor and there never was one. Kree bends toward her, caresses her spine, the dog gives her two licks on the hand and, with this rite accomplished, she goes back to sprawl at the foot of the mattress.

In her place as friend and guardian.

Now Kree faces the window as the grip of worry loosens. She turns her back on the door. With dreary pleasure she reimagines the scene of her fear and she writes a little internal play. The theater set has only one actor, a man or a corpse, motivated by sleazy intentions. He waits in the hallway, he approaches the door, he stands still, and he waits. He holds his breath, he takes care not to betray his presence, but he exhales an odor that denounces him. Sweat-soaked soldier's rags, a cadaver's underpants. An odor that denounces him and wakes her with a start.

Then she lets go of her fantasy. The aggressor, the corpse, the deserter, becomes once again an inoffensive shadow. She doesn't even go back to verify one more time that the chain is in place, the lock is set.

No more anxiety. She hesitates; she could do the same as Loka, lie back down and go back to sleep. And then, no.

She opens the window. It resists, as it often does. She has to force the handle. The wood has swollen in the humidity of evening. The hinges weren't crooked when they were attached, but, between the war and a couple of earthquakes, the frame shifted, so everything is off. Kree doesn't like sleeping in an enclosed space, but she prefers to seal up any openings while she's sleeping, even if her bedroom becomes uncomfortable for lack of air. She makes sure to barricade the door, of course. And everything else. Evacuation routes, the badly covered vents where the warmth of central heat once flowed, back when the climate was harsher, when the buildings were inhabited by fragile, delicate people and not by survivors who are indifferent to everything or almost everything. Obsessed with the intrusion of undesirable pests, she blocks holes, possible entry points.

Pests. Insects. Arthropods of all kinds, spiders, millipedes, centipedes. Birds. When darkness descends on the city, the pests come to life. They take advantage of the humans' silence and inactivity, the creeping things, the bats, the vultures. All these creatures like nothing better than to take possession of rooms they consider available for their convenience. They're hard to chase away, and even when they have no intention of setting up camp, they foul the ground and the walls with their excretions, their feathers, their webs and sloughed-off skins.

She sets her elbows against the windowsill and leans out. A warm humidity falls across her face, a heavy veil of city smells. Burnt fuel oil, dust from demolished areas, dust from crumbling cement, earth dust from the countryside, dust descended from sawdust, pollens, faraway dying forests, animal sweat, human sweat, butane, excrement. Wood, smoke from campfires, grilled meat. The air is soft. In the city, as elsewhere, the temperature is pleasant. A permanent warmth with variations in moisture according to the season, a few drier weeks before and after winter. Down below, the streets form a patchwork against a black background. The buildings are all alike, mostly one-story houses. Kree's building is an exception, along with the four or five other towers punctuating the landscape here and there, which are too dilapidated to be occupied. From the height of the sixth floor, Kree enjoys an exceptional view. She overlooks everything.

After the last exodus the city was rebuilt under the direction of the terrible mendicants, and a good tenth of the buildings have been spruced up and rehabilitated, which does not prevent the whole from maintaining a uniform ugliness. A few spots, here and there, to which a name can be attached. The shopping center in Central, the Aniya Viett sector, the House of Mendicants, the Mariya Kahn sector, the Mariya Kahn dormitory, the river.

The sky is just about to brighten. Kree doesn't move, she waits. She watches as the final stars disappear. From time to time she closes her eyes, she enjoys taking her time to absorb the silence. She has always loved the dawn. The best moment to take stock or to die.

And then.

Then, the day comes. Three vultures take off from the nearest tower, the Stern Tower, sailing toward the river, disappearing. She ends her contemplation. She leaves her spot at the window. She rolls the mattress against the wall, she folds half of the covers, which have been adequately aired during her long pause before the void, and she puts them away in one of the trunks. She does not forget to slip in, here and there, the perfumed stones Myriam Agazaki has given her, which Myriam says are better than soap chips for absorbing moisture and fighting the lingering odors of sleep, the lingering odors of private dirtiness, intimate salts, and sebum.

Loka trots from one room to another, tail beating against her flanks, impatient to go out.

Kree hesitates at first before opening the door to the outside. Just at the moment that she's pulling the lock and the chain, she thinks back to her dream, the stranger who might be standing sentinel in the hallway, spying, and even though she's entirely convinced that this is nothing but her imagination, she lays her hand on a bladed weapon that always hangs suspended at the entry. A long, slim machete, finely curved like a samurai sword. She unhooks it. And finally she opens up, for the sake of the dog and her swollen bladder. Everything is ink black beyond the threshold. Kree does not edge her head into the doorframe. She knows there's no risk that she'll be confronted by an aggressive bandit, wearing a sailor hat or not, but she remains on her toes. She adopts a low defensive position, the door won't get in her way, at the least attack she will swing, cutting an arc that starts at the adversary's groin and terminates under the ear, a fatal slash. And then nothing happens, there's nobody there for her to cut. Loka slides past the length of her right leg, leaps down the stairs, and takes off. A second after the dog's departure, Kree's already slammed the door. Once again she closes, locks, and chains it. Loka's outing will take a while. A half hour, an hour. Time for Kree to wash up and do some housekeeping.

She grabs the broom and right away she has to tangle with a massive spider, enormous. A makhagamba. Big abdomen, big head, thick claws. Anchored on the bottom of the brush, near the handle. One might wonder by what path the spider could have entered, and when. In any case, she's there. Horribly tarantular. With several pairs of indecipherable eyes shining amid her fur. Determined not to capitulate, to occupy that which she considers her own territory. The spider refuses to move, she is sure of herself, her claws have contracted slightly, gripping her perch with the violence of one who knows she is within her rights. Kree holds the broom outside the window and shakes it. The spider hangs on. At every shake she emits a puff of stubborn, shadowy and suicidal terror, but she hangs on. Kree scrapes the brush against the windowsill, as if a chunk of tar were stuck to it. She tries to trap the spider between the cement and the wooden handle. Suddenly the creature lets go. She is not seen again.

Kree murmurs a prayer. She doesn't care about wishing the makhagamba safe travels in the spider bardo, and she isn't thinking of asking the gods to pardon her for disrespecting one of their creations. She doesn't have the same religious sentiment as Myriam Agazaki, she feels no remorse when she snuffs out an existence. In reality, she is praying for herself. She'd prefer for the horrible thing to drop to the ground floor like a rock and not, instead, to choose to cling to the building's façade a few centimeters below, with the intention of hobbling back into the apartment and taking her revenge. This is what Kree's prayer asks for. She does not know whom or what superior forces she's addressing, but she asks.

Just in case, she closes the window.

She goes to wash up. Her hands are trembling. She has fought men and women and wild dogs, she has fought heavy and malodorous rapists to the death, she has fought soldiers. She has beaten them, or else she would not be here to say so. This doesn't mean that she's sure, after combat, of remaining always the supreme mistress of her nerves. One is never all that proud when stepping away from the aggressor one has maimed without pity, and sometimes decapitated for good measure. Most of the time, on the contrary, the feeling is emptiness and shame. But what Kree knows for sure and certain, at least, is that after an altercation with a spider her hands always tremble and her temples throb. She has already thought about this issue and discussed it with Myriam Agazaki. Why this exaggerated emotion, why this froth of anxiety. There's no doubt about the outcome, the adversary is tiny, and yet she spends ten times more energy than needed, as if the beast before her were monstrous in size, as if she might lose. Myriam Agazaki has her theory. The fight is to the death against death, she claims. Each time you find yourself again and again settling scores what are a half-million years old. If Myriam Agazaki is to be believed, in the Paleozoic era a competition began between the spiders and the rest of the world. A competition to the death against death between incompatible forms of existence. And, again according to Myriam Agazaki, the struggle will never come to an end. Or rather, it will.

The struggle will end with the total defeat of the rest of the world. When nothing else can remain standing, she says sometimes, when no one is left to say anything, not a single animal left to eat the rest of the plants, the spiders will have won the war, and then the spiders will dance.

This morning, the water pressure is strong enough and the temperature is pleasant. The tanks on the roof are full, they were fed by the previous week's rain and, since then, showered with sunlight for hours and hours. There are times when the faucet barely condescends to spit out a thin trickle. Times when drought threatens. But now the flow is continuous. Even if the clouds balk at caving in, if they pass on high without letting loose a downpour, the reserves are not quickly exhausted. And then, in the building, there aren't many residents to be satisfied. Only two. Kree, on the sixth floor, and Brother #9, on the first.

She crouches in the shower stall and soaps herself in strategic locations. Her feet, her hands, whose palms preserve the memory of grappling with the makhagamba. Armpits, between the legs. She isn't obsessed with the constant renewal of acidity and grime in the folds and cracks, but she thinks about them. It's something that bothers her whenever she thinks about it. And she thinks about it often. She started to attach importance to this when she switched from childhood to adolescence, when, although for a long time she had been a little girl, she found herself changed from one day to the next, changed into a woman, adult and alone in the world. It disturbed her to bleed between her thighs in a regular and irrepressible manner, and from that point on she began to hate, not really her body, but that which worked constantly against the hygiene of her body. The incessant excretion of ferments, impurities, and filth. That nauseating animality that reminds us of the slightest negligence. A humiliating degradation at every moment. She never forgets it. While she washes, for example, she never fails to ruminate on the topic. Or in her mental monologues, when she argues over the subject of sex, on the question of having or not having sex, on her memories of the times when she's had sex.

She washes and rinses with care. The faucet flows generously, the water is delicious, from time to time the froth of warm pearlescence that escapes from the shower head seems burning hot, just as long ago in normal houses or in the sanitary barracks in camps.

She's thinking about nothing.

She's thinking about the deserter who might have come prowling around her place.

She thinks about the needles that pierce her head, which started to blur her vision again a week ago, bringing on the sudden rains of blood. It hasn't even been very long since she went to see Myriam Agazaki about the pins. She'll have to return to get a few more of them pulled out.

She thinks about Loka, who has started to smell bad and whom she must absolutely take to the riverside for a bath.

She lets her thoughts come and go in contact with the water.

She thinks about her life: how many years left.

Or maybe how many months, how many days.

*M*orning. Bright morning.

Kree has gotten dressed after her shower. Again she opens the windows of her little apartment, bedroom and kitchen. She opens them wide. The damp heat brushes her face as it enters, then continues on its way inside. Just as at dawn, the wave of moisture is infused with residues of smoke and gusts from the city.

The sky is very bright. Barely visible in the distance, a handful of vultures form vast circles in the direction of the river. They must be soaring over the Mariya Kahn dormitory. There was a death among the refugees, and they've placed the dead man on the dormitory's terrace, so that his flesh will be shared between the birds, the scavengers. A sky burial. A ritual that the terrible mendicants tolerate, even if they disapprove and encourage putting cadavers in the earth. For a brief second, Kree is visited by the absurd idea that she has been through several types of funerals, and that maybe, somewhere in that series, she, too, was once torn to pieces by vultures. Ah well I don't know what I would like that. The idea disappears after an instant. It melts in the light of the sky. It is no longer there.

In the west, a few clouds. Over there is the Ölguz Kunguryang sector, which often serves as a passageway between nowhere and the city. Nobody lives there, except refugees who wait for one or two nights to get registered and then reeducated. Besides those fear-crushed shadows, the west also carries promises of rain, but this morning the clouds are thready, without density. They'll disperse as soon as the sun starts blazing. The day will be pleasant.

If what a blood rain doesn't darken it, Kree thinks.

She leans over to inspect the façade, then she pulls back. She doesn't want to get the makhagamba stuck in her hair, nor one of the makhagamba's companions hanging above the window either. She has to squint against the already blinding sky. No trace of the spider. She must have fallen vertically and crashed fifteen meters farther down. Or maybe not. Kree's gaze did not follow the spider's black fall. Who knows if the makhagamba didn't quickly catch hold of the wall, or if she took advantage of some protuberance in the masonry, a gutter? And then scrambled nightmarishly back up, full of fury against her fate and the human who tried to murder her?

Kree passes a hand over her head. Her body under shelter, separated from the windowsill by a secure anti-makhagamba distance, she gazes at the now brilliantly sunlit city. Now the houses are gray and white. You might almost think you were looking out over a metropolis that had not suffered through a war. The city was low, there had been no spectacular collapses. Rubble, ghosts of cars and trucks scattered around everywhere, but it was relatively rare that a street was impassable. Kree squints, she tries as always to reconstitute the city's geography. She goes over the most recognizable buildings, the ones around Central, and farther to the northeast the ancient gathering antennae for wanderers, the wounded, the traumatized, for survivors, for the destitute, the unemployed, the insane. The remains of the things trying to exist in the emergency, at one time. Everything blurs together. Between the brilliant sky and her terrible vision, anyway, she can't distinguish much.

Loka scratches at the door, and when Kree doesn't open it immediately, she yelps, once, twice. Kree cuts her reverie short. She unlocks the door, unhooks the machete suspended on the wall, and she ventures out into the hallway, letting the door gape open behind her. So she'll have room to fall back in case of a problem. Loka throws herself against Kree's legs, barks, runs into the apartment, then turns around and comes back. The hallway is bright with light from her apartment and from a translucent trapdoor that allows access to the terrace. The ladder has not moved. In the dust, prints left by Kree and the dog, none that are strange. Kree goes to check the apartments next door, which she has closed up so she won't have any neighbors. The boards nailed across the frames haven't been pulled down.

Loka sniffs at the entry to the stairs, in front of the ladder, in the corners. In front of the closed doors of the neighboring apartments. She seeks out Kree's eyes to convey the results of her investigation. Nothing suspicious on this floor.

Kree shrugs, she goes back over the threshold of her apartment, she retakes possession of the space. She pours some water in Loka's bowl and shares a piece of soaked pemmican with the dog.

It's a basic recipe that always reminds her of the man who taught it to her, a Bachbak soldier who followed her for a few days in a column of refugees, who claimed he wanted to give her security and protection. She was barely a teenager. They went off to camp in a shack a little apart from the group. When she crushes the bits of dried meat and mixes them with some ground grain meal, when she pours water over the paste, always she sees before her this soldier, commenting on the ratio to follow, and, with that, she sees the image of this solder who was determined, a little later, to rape her. She sees again the man's frenetic agitation, his pants down, his penis purple in the shadows, his mad eyes, his hoarse words, and then his throat opened up, his blood spurting forth as if chasing Kree's blade, then the sound of him falling to the ground. Not her first murder, but still, a moment in her life that her memory does not relinquish.

Kree prepares her Bachbak-style pemmican a day in advance, with crumbled meat, fat, and cornmeal. In the morning, she adds a bit more water and eats it cold.

"Okay, let's go," she says to Loka once their bowls are empty.

She often talks to Loka. Sometimes she makes whole speeches. When she tries to dissuade Loka from venturing down to the riverbanks where some shoeless, poorly reeducated bums catch dogs and eat them, for example. She addresses Loka as she would a person. Loka gives her opinion; she comes in at the end of the sentence. A little whine, a bark, a head tilt. And always a spark of intelligence in her gaze. Her bright brown eyes shining.

The intelligence of her gaze, Kree thinks, as she padlocks the door.

She enters the staircase without taking any particular precautions, since the dog is going ahead and does not stop, does not growl, does not signal the slightest dangerous oddity. The stairs turn like a snail shell around the elevator shaft. All the doors opening on this shaft were cemented shut when the deserted building was rehabilitated by a group of pioneers. Before the arrival of the terrible mendicants.

The pioneers. From very far away and no one knows where. From nowhere, no doubt. Wishing to create an example of a utopian commune here. An impenetrable citadel within which they would realize the seed of egalitarian society. A magnificent plan. Constructing communism in a modest corner of the ruined world. Welcoming recruits and teaching them.

Swiftly they began fighting amongst themselves. With ferocity, over personal problems, linked to food and women. Within a few months, the utopian commune had become a hell of blood, brawls, and fatal ambushes. The collective project produced nothing positive, with the exception of the security of the lugubrious pit of the elevator and the light that pierced up to the third floor inside the shaft, which were inarguable improvements to the space, made in the first enthusiastic weeks of occupation. Above the third floor, the work was interrupted and never finished. Everything remained dark. Once the building was abandoned, no squatters turned up to take ownership. Such elevated shelters did not suit the urban culture of survivors. They sought low, isolated structures, easy to abandon in case of fire or aggression. From the beginning the pioneers had gone against custom by choosing a six-story tower for their utopian commune. Also against custom, unfortunately, was their hope to work together despite reality, misery, promiscuity, as well as, most of all, their idea they could avoid or overcome the insatiable human desire to make things worse. Their commune did not last; they killed each other and their confrontations made most of the building's apartments unusable. One more reason Kree isn't likely to be bothered by neighbors. Nobody is trying to live next to or below her apartment.

She has no neighbors, and she isn't complaining about it. As for Brother #9, who lives almost at street level, let's just say he doesn't count. He often stands next to the door, as if watching the comings and goings, when she's the only person passing by him. They exchange polite greetings, and often he asks, with an informer's curiosity, about her plans for the day. Kree responds in the appropriate manner. He doesn't count.

Kree calls Loka so she won't jump on Brother #9 or dash off into the street like a mad thing, but the dog doesn't obey. Kree continues to descend. Already Loka is going wild on the rubble of the entry hallway. Kree can hear her running off into the street and disappearing. On the building's threshold, Kree stands still. After the shadowy descent, the shock of daylight is suddenly too strong. A pain deep in her ocular spheres. A piercing pain. Now, without any warning, she can't see anything. Then a crimson curtain sways before her, a curtain of blood replaces the streetscape. Vertical stripes, red dashes falling to the ground. In silence, although sometimes the din of a deluge rushes over the wine-dark image. Today, only the red downpour, without the sound. No hammering. She closes her eyes. She counts slowly to ten. Sometimes the rain lasts only a fraction of a second, other times it goes on for an hour. The curtain that empurples everything, fogs everything, the hail, the streams. But this morning she counts to ten, to twenty, and there is no sound around her; she counts to thirty and the colors begin to fade. The rain of blood flows back into a private reservoir of hallucinations, below awareness, in the hermetic territories where she is lost. She counts slowly, thirty-one, thirty-two, thirty-three, to forty.

Then she starts again, from one to fifty, more and more slowly. Pain and color vanish abruptly.

Loka has returned to twist around her legs. A conspiratorial whine and, again, the dog runs to the intersection. She turns her head toward Kree. She's waiting. She's asking if she should go right or left.

From the entry to the building, Brother #9 makes a sign with his hand. Kree waves her hand to greet him in turn.

She sets off. She takes a right.

Before going to work, she'll have time to get some food at the cooperative near Central.

Her service as housekeeper begins at seven o'clock.

She'll make a detour through Central and the cooperative. And then she'll arrive at the House of Mendicants. Brother #15 will tell her the schedule for the day, she'll take up a broom with no spider on it, and she'll begin cleaning the courtyard.

And then, a normal day on the horizon.

Work until the early afternoon.

Then a walk with Loka to the Aniya Viett sector. Maybe some tea with Myriam Agazaki. The blood rains are coming back. It's time to make an appointment for yet another session of needle extraction.

*T*he cooperative has taken over the area of Central's former commercial gallery. Its purpose is to provide food for those interested in food or who need it in order to continue living, which is not at all the case for everyone. Basic food products are available in trays and containers. All night, teams of reeducateds sort through it. Surveillance patrols lend a hand as well. The food is crude, with little variety. Vegetables and fruits come from the gardens in the Jan Oltchum sector. Dried meat is prepared in the Baherdjee combine. You can take some at your discretion, although not in excess, of course. Canteens have priority, but after distribution to the collectives, individuals are allowed to glean as they wish from whatever's left. There are always two or three terrible mendicants there to prevent abuse, spot the sneaks, and begin elimination procedures against them. Their system has never failed so far, and no one dreams of questioning it. The products never run out. Dishonest gluttons and thieves disappear and do not reappear. The terrible mendicants take care of it. It's the basis on which both our present and our future is constructed.

After making her selections, Kree goes to the House of Mendicants. She carries a bag full of provisions over her shoulder, she has taken some for herself and some for Myriam Agazaki. Basic ingredients. Flour, strongly scented pieces of meat, dried beef, maybe, or lizard. A small armful of greens.

Brother #15 is sitting on a stool, before the front desk. They exchange casual greetings. They know each other by heart. Kree has been doing the housekeeping here for years.

Look, thinks Kree. A weird look what he's got this morning.

Is he angry with me or what? she thinks.

Bah. I've got nothing to fear from him.

Nor from the others, she thinks.

The terrible mendicants are like all administrators and directors since the dawn of time, they are privately rejected by the population that they administer. All things considered, though, they aren't so terrible as all that. That adjective was attributed to them when they first took power in the city, and to get started, they established rules and put an end to disorder. It is true that, during that time, it was better not to go against them. But today, once you've understood and you share their vision of the world, there isn't really much to fear from them. Kree has little trouble molding herself in their image, she doesn't have to do any mental contortions to adapt to their language. All in all, the terrible mendicants' ideology is basically very close to her own. She adopts their vocabulary with sincerity, she repeats their magic words. With sincerity, and, at the same time, without belief, because she doesn't believe in anything. She entrusts herself to fate as if she were walking in the world after death, she feels that she is floating without memories in an existence that does not end, that will not end, she moves forward in that existence from day to day. So, to her, being a passive sympathizer to the terrible mendicants seems like an excellent thing, or at least, the only thing.

"Kree Toronto," Brother #15 says, "just in time. Just when we were looking for a representative from the working class. We have a reeducation meeting on the schedule that will end with maybe a self-criticism or an execution order."

"An execution order?"

"A request that the masses they want to be done with an agent of the enemy."

"That's got nothing to do with me, and anyway there aren't any more enemies," Kree objects.

"There will be enemies for another thousand years," #15 says.

"And then, I don't have time," Kree goes on.

"It's a solemn meeting. We cannot do it without a representative person what represents the poor or the assimilated peasants," #15 says.

As always when a terrible mendicant pronounces a sacred political phrase, his voice hardens. He's stiffened in his seat. Suddenly his gaze is directed toward past struggles and the coming of the classless society. The left corner of his lips trembles slightly in a dominating smile.

"I don't belong to the peasants, and I live somewhere other than a dormitory," Kree retorts.

"And so?"

"And so I'm more one of the semi-poor people."

"Bah," #15 puffs, to sweep away the objection.

Really, she has no desire to represent the masses in a public gathering. She is a sympathizer, she approves of some eliminations, but when she can, she manages to escape the most boring political tasks. Not always. When she can.

"People know you, Kree Toronto," #15 continues. "You're not just anyone in the city. You're one of the first to arrive. From the beginning you have never behaved in a reactionary manner. We've never gotten any complaints against you. Nobody has ever said anything about your dog."

"What is there to say," Kree grumbles.

"And then, you are a role model for our children."

"What children?" Kree says, startled. "There have been zero children around here for years."

Brother #15's lips contract into a sort of pout, his expression becomes simultaneously more severe and wearier. He's beginning to tire of Kree's arguments.

"Children or no, you are a role model, Kree Toronto. I'm telling you that you must come. We need your presence as a delegate of the workers and the peasants. I'm telling you that you must attend the self-criticism. It's so everything will be done according to the rules."

"I don't have time," Kree digs in. "And you didn't tell me who it is what has to do their self-criticism."

"That's not your business. We're not asking your opinion on that."

"And why what you don't do the execution without a trial? Self-criticisms they're useless if you've just offed the critic."

Brother #15's gaze hits Kree like a bullet. In his beggar's uniform, he looks very much like an immovable stone.

"Self-criticisms they are not useless. They are useful in educating the masses," he intones heavily.

Kree gives in with a half-submissive, half-idiotic look.

"They are not done so that the enemy will get pardoned," #15 clarifies.

"Oh well, okay," Kree says docilely. "I didn't know that."

"That's how it is," Brother #15 concludes.

"But we don't pardon," Kree remarks.

"We never pardon a class enemy," snaps #15.

They remain silent for a handful of seconds.

"It's in the early afternoon?" Kree asks.

"Yes, fourteen hundred hours."

Kree accepts, she nods her head yes.

"Okay, and now?" she asks. "What am I doing this morning?" #15 gives her a light schedule. Quick cleaning in the offices. No mopping, so she can go faster. A message to bring to Brother #27.

"Don't forget the meeting at fourteen hundred hours."

"No," says Kree.

She opens the door to the service closet. She leaves her bag with the packets of more-or-less dried meat, more-or-less lizard. She's even managed to rustle up a gingerroot and a box of vegetables by digging deep in the container. The vegetables don't have a name. They have small, thick yellow leaves: strange. She'll ask Myriam Agazaki to identify them if she thinks of it.

She pushes the dried-out mop aside with her foot and takes a broom. She looks at it. There's no spider on it.

*B*rother #27 occupies a lodging on the ground floor of a small two-story house where nobody else lives. It's on the border between Central and the Mariya Kahn sector, at the start of a very long street that stretches all the way to the river. Kree knows the house; she's passed by it often, sometimes accompanied by Loka, sometimes not. #27's house is marked by an unvarnished, blackened wood façade, which the owner has augmented with black and red fabric streamers and clusters of bells, as if it were a religious building, although no doubt #27's idea is only to show new arrivals that the place is inhabited and there is no use in trying to requisition it. But it's true that it feels as if you were approaching a modest sanctuary. That impression is further strengthened by a vertical banner hanging behind the window, dark red, with calligraphic characters belonging to an unknown alphabet—known, perhaps, only to the communists and wizards of the old times.

The message. What Brother #15 charged Kree with carrying to Brother #27. She pinches it between her index finger and thumb. She'd like to get rid of it as quickly as possible. It's a folded piece of paper, and she is not so indiscreet that she would read it on the way, nor does she have any desire to do so. A gray paper, smelling of coconut oil, just like the back offices of the House of Mendicants where they rarely ask Kree to sweep, as if their territory were more sacred than elsewhere, as if the delegates of the martyred peoples and their rags weren't really welcome there. When #15 gave her the paper, he had such a severe and solemn air that she took it without a word, as if it were an object to be handled with caution, a dangerous package rather than a letter.

She knocks on the door of the little house and Brother #27 opens up with a wide smile, pronouncing a phrase of warm salutation. His hands are busy with a broad macramé panel, which he has just been finishing when Kree arrives. His smile chills when she holds out what she has brought. A shadow passes abruptly over his face, just as severe and solemn as the one fixed on #15's physiognomy a little earlier. Then he sits down again, with a good-natured invitation to come in and drink some tea. He shows her his incomplete panel of woven strings and explains that it's a demon-ward meant to keep counterrevolutionaries in retreat.

"And it's also to scare Brother #8."

"Bah," Kree comments.

Lifting her eyebrows, she asks him why he brought up Brother #8, a terrible mendicant who isn't often in the city, who lives nobody knows where, as if he were following the rules of clandestinity, and appears only on meeting days. Facing her, #27 stifles a laugh; he even makes a vague gesture corresponding to repentance, as if he wished she would disregard his previous words, and he doesn't explain. He leads her into the room and shows her to a chair. She sits.

#27's home is just as spartan as Kree's, nothing but a gas burner, three chairs, a trunk, and a bed with slats and no mattress, although the walls aren't quite so bare. Magical objects instead of the machete and weaponry. Amulets, belts in brown leather stretched over bits of iron, tufts of red fur, the shriveled paws of small animals. All decorations belonging more to the world of witchcraft than the world of egalitarianists. That said, #27 never professes anything departing from official orthodoxy, and, if he stands out among the Brothers, his shamanic performances are in no way the reason. From a sartorial perspective, he blends in with the others. Like all those who hold power in the city, he wears a miserable, black, anonymous uniform, going either barefoot or in canvas shoes. Of course, he is fatter, even a bit pudgy, with furry arms and hands, traits that distinguish him, physically speaking, but most of all it's his manner of addressing anyone and everyone that sets him apart. Rather than taking a sententious tone, he hammers out the sacred phrases with humor sparkling in his eyes. He doesn't frighten his listeners; he puts them at ease. No doubt his belief in the terrible mendicants' ideology is sincere, hard as iron, yet one might imagine he hopes the masses or, shall we say, the representatives of the working, peasant, and martyred masses, such as Kree, would adhere to that ideology with a sort of insouciant joy.

After sitting down, Kree gets back up and remains standing while #27 heats water. He jokes around; he drives the conversation without demonstrating any interest in the letter from the House of Mendicants. He hasn't unfolded it, he's thrown it on the bed next to his macramé demon-ward and, when it slips between two slats, he watches it fall to the floor and makes no move to pick it up.

They speak of one thing and another. The weather. The increase in spider attacks. The color and smell of the river next to the Mariya Kahn dormitory. He teases her by seeming to doubt Loka's existence, pretending he's never seen Loka next to Kree, pretending he doesn't believe she has a dog. He criticizes the tea he's just served her; he considers it insipid, and when she returns to the question of Loka, he makes ironic reflections about Brother #1 and Brother #2, whose existence he also contests. His words are ambiguous to the point that Kree wonders if he's not taking advantage of the chance to compare #1 and #2 with dogs. She does not dare comment about this to him. He asks her about Myriam Agazaki; he knows the ties of friendship that the two women maintain. He has learned, who knows how, about the shaking tent Myriam Agazaki has installed in her courtyard. He asks questions about the shaking tent, he'd like her to tell him if it works, if she knows the installer. Kree keeps things vague, suddenly putting up her guard. She has a feeling that #27 is trying to worm information out of her. Even if she likes the terrible mendicants well enough, her personal ethics forbid her to act as a snitch. Or even simply an informant, which often comes to the same thing. If the mendicants in power want information, they can talk to someone else.

Brother #27 perceives her reticence and he does not take offense, and, as the conversation peters out, he moves to pick up the letter that Kree brought him from under the bed. He's still smiling, and then he isn't. He peruses the sheet of paper. Kree sees him lose his debonaire attitude, let out a long sigh. He studies what he has just read a little longer, as if verifying the meaning of an unclear phrasing, then once again he tosses the letter onto the leather bed frame. This time it does not fall to the ground. He turns his round bon vivant's head toward Kree, all his air of mischief vanished. His gaze crosses Kree's, but goes beyond her, somewhere far away where she isn't there.

For a half minute, Kree concentrates on sipping the last drops of her tea. The silence between them is unpleasant. Now she's in a hurry to leave the room.

She rises, goes to return her tea cup to the sink.

"Bad news?" she says casually.

"Oh no," Brother #27 says. "Just an invitation to a ceremony."

"Is it for right now?" Kree asks.

"Yes. Right now. So that the poor peasants can put me back on the right path."

*A*t fourteen hundred hours she presents herself in the Party Room at the House of Mendicants. The place is familiar, partly because it's the place where large reeducation and self-criticism sessions take place but also because she cleans it regularly with broom, rags, and mop. She cleans the walls only once a year, and even then not all the way to the top. She doesn't use a stepladder to reach the frieze of ridiculous red and black cockades up near the ceiling. She lets it gather dust. Tarnished, worn, the frieze doesn't evoke the eternal revolution so much as it creates an impression of abandonment. The same goes for the three macramé panels hanging above the stage, no doubt the work of Brother #27. Someone once told Kree they represented the fundamental principles, but the explanation was brief and unconvincing. They're sacred panels, yet the design is so abstract that, if not for the red ribbons and streamers stuck to them, nobody would have the slightest idea that they carry any kind of message or tribute to the mendicants' powerful ideology.

Six reeducables are sitting in the first row. Rigid, plunged into minute contemplation of whatever lies before them: a stage of gray planks and, on top of it, a dark wooden table and three empty chairs. A theater scene. The six main spectators have arrived in advance and they're on very good behavior. Scattered around this little group stand the terrible mendicants in traditional garb, the mourning uniform in black cotton borrowed from images of Asia, maybe Cambodia, old photographs taken in the times when Asia and Cambodia still existed; that was a long time ago. They like slipping into the matching unisex uniforms.

It assures them that they have concretely realized the radical fraternal equality that they espouse.

And, all things considered, it is a step in that direction, after all.

Kree remembers. She herself once wanted to adopt those pauper's rags. To blend in with the terrible mendicants. To melt into them. She did not find them at all repellent, very much the opposite. She was in the city when they came to take control, when they were taking the first steps toward extinguishing the nightmare of war and wandering over the infinite destroyed lands. For some time after she arrived, agitated with the euphoria of having survived the massacres, she dreamed of actively working toward what the Brothers sought, the transition to a more just society. She wanted to join completely with those who played a galvanizing role. She didn't mind losing her name; she found the idea appealing, to exist only in the form of a number. With whatever fabric she could find, she set to work constructing a black jacket for herself. Then, after a period of exaltation, she had doubts. She repressed them, then she let them invade her. At her core she felt that it would be hard for her, as it had been hard during all of her preceding existences, to integrate herself into a monastic collectivity that would accept no deviation, no ideological distance, no contradiction. Hard to literally annihilate herself in that collectivity. And, rather swiftly, she realized that she was more interested in dressing up in black than in the Brothers' morality. She'd made her own morality for decades; she could be egalitarian without any need for terrible mendicants. Some of the Brothers' proclamations suddenly started to strike her as debatable, or absurd. Her motivation crumbled away. The desire to be associated with a number was starting to go away. It came back now and then, that desire, when the solitude grew too strong; it still does now and then, but mostly it doesn't haunt her anymore. That was the end of her laborious sewing exercises. The black jacket and pants remained unfinished in a corner, then one day she tore them apart to make dish rags and underpants.

Not far from the reeducables, in the corner between the stage and the wall, Kree recognizes Brother #27. He's standing with his back turned, but he's easy to identify. His heavy body, his hairy neck. Black clothes worn lusterless from frequent washing. He is immobile, a little hunched, and like her he is focused on examining the stage in front of him. His macramé demon-ward is tied around his neck. He had time to finish it, Kree thinks. She wonders what he's doing there, why he stays in that spot, in that inexplicable position. He has always been a bit apart from the other terrible mendicants, and in that spot, he is even more so.

He's not participating in managing the reeducables, Kree thinks. It's more like he's one of them.

She chooses a place near the door. On an empty bench, she leans back against the wall. She sits. She'd rather not get herself noticed. She'll attend the meeting as she's been asked, in the role of representative of the poor and assimilated peasants, but she has no desire to make herself visible. She prefers to remain in back. If there's a vote by raised hands or by acclamation, she will get up; she will show that she is not lukewarm politically and that she approves one hundred percent the building of the transition and its more severe demands. But then, as soon as possible, she'll leave. She doesn't disapprove of anything, not much anyway, but she'll be the first to leave as soon as the audience is invited to disperse. She'll take off without looking over her shoulder, she'll leave them to their final sorcerors' incantations and their secret sayings, which always follow decisions made by the masses in public.

Gradually the room fills. Normal citizens, residents of Central that Kree recognizes, from the Jan Oltchum sector, the Ölguz Kunguryang sector, women and men dressed in whatever they could find, the recently reeducated, unknown people from the Mariya Kahn dormitory. A hundred or so people in all. Self-criticism meetings always attract people. Myriam Agazaki hasn't come. She hates this kind of spectacle.

Brother #8 and Brother #12 enter one after the other. With their carefully shaven skulls, they look like two monks disguised as Khmer Rouge, or the opposite: two genocidists trying to pass themselves off as monks. All signs indicate that they'll play the starring roles in the meeting to come. The roles of hosts and supreme judges. They stand very close to the first row. They do not even glance at the six reeducables. They turn toward the audience to assess the numbers. A good crowd. The masses are there. They approach Brother #27, speak to him without looking at him; he doesn't look at them either. They order him to take off his demon-ward, which he does quickly, without arguing. It vanishes into a small bag, which he sets down nearby, then he pushes it farther away; he wants everyone to understand he's separated himself from it.

There's no one sitting next to Kree. She leans on the divider, and she starts thinking about Loka. She imagines the dog at this moment: digging among the ruins in search of rats or forgotten scraps, strolling freely through the city. Like a mother worrying about her child, Kree tries to persuade herself that Loka avoids the areas where some refugees trap dogs to eat them in a stew or to use their skins, to make clothing out of them. Loka is smart, she has a map of the dangerous areas in her head, she knows she must not make incursions without her mistress into the Wastes or near the Mariya Kahn dormitory. She can transform into a she-wolf if anyone gives her trouble. But she might not be big enough to defend herself against hunters, seasoned trappers, the starving. Every evening, Kree returns to her sixth floor with the same anxious question: will she or will she not find Loka before the door, safe and sound, wagging her tail and blinking her amber eyes?

As she's dreaming and imagining Loka returning to the house, lying in front of the apartment doorway, Loka and her magnificent eyes, Kree hears someone saying her name. Brother #15. He approaches swiftly and plants himself in front of her. He looks as though he's terribly irritated. He repeats something, something that was said on stage when she wasn't paying attention. In the audience, several of the tattered paupers have turned around and are staring at her reproachfully. #15 touches her arm, he shakes her, at the same time addressing her in a curt voice. Brother #8 and Brother #12 are waiting for her. They've just taken their place behind the table that occupies center stage. They've invited her to join them. A representative of the martyred people must sit in between the two of them, before the poor and semi-poor urban masses. And that representative is Kree. The aforementioned representative gets up. Without wasting time on excuses or guilty looks she obeys Brother #15's order. She walks up the side aisle with a firm step and, in the silence and the creaking of the stage boards, she sits down facing the audience in her turn.

The smell of wood, dust, sawdust, too, for longhorn beetles have been digging out their tunnels here and there. Trace odors from the mop that she passed over the stage four days before, when she hadn't the slightest idea that the Brothers would call on her to put on a show there soon.

As if she were presiding over the meeting with Brother #8 on one side and Brother #12 on the other, now she looms over the room. An ideal position for examining the reeducables and terrible mendicants in the front row. Despite the blurry image transmitted by her defective eyes, she recognizes the guy that Myriam Agazaki is trying to marry her off to, the shady-looking deserter that she suspected of prowling the hallway of the sixth floor in the night. Well, there he is, she thinks. He isn't wearing his sailor cap, and there are pale lines clearly visible on his bronze-colored head. Scars due to kicks with a broken boot, saber cuts, or torture. She directs her nostrils toward him, but she can't manage to distinguish his smell among all the others. The odors of collective habitation waft from the reeducables' skins, smells of unfinished showers, soap without lather, damp rags. A pathetic cleanliness. All have made an effort to present themselves with the least neglected appearance possible.

And other, nearer smells. Just next to her, Brother #8 and Brother #12 are emitting strong gusts. A powerful remnant of coconut oil clings to the fabric. They must have participated in a late meeting last night, at the House of Mendicants. In the back offices. The lamp smoke is encrusted in the fibers of their black cotton uniforms. On the collar, the sleeves of their mourning overalls. On their naked scalps.

By way of introduction, Brother #12 explains Kree's presence on the stage. He says she was chosen as a representative of the struggling proletarians and the peasants and the assimilated urban groups. In a vibrant voice he assures everyone that there is no known blot on her revolutionary record, and through her they will listen attentively to the perspective of the masses and the marginalized classes. Unsure how to respond to this avalanche of magic words, Kree acquiesces quickly by nodding her head and, when he turns toward her, she mutters two syllables of approval. They ask no more of her.

Then Brother #12 forgets Kree and begins a longer speech. He talks about egalitarianism, the transition to the future, the even more radiant times to come afterward, about real egalitarianism, the final preparatory stage of egalitarianism, egalitarianism in its higher stage. He insists on discipline, on the love of work well done, the meaning of sacrifice for the collective well-being; he encourages the refusal of despair even when it's evident that nothing's moving forward. He demands effort on the part of those men and women who haven't yet sincerely joined the society under construction, those men and women who remain attached to the ghosts of the past, he stigmatizes those men and women who would turn back the march of history.

He says "those men and women," yet there are only men among the reeducables, and for a second Kree wonders if this precaution isn't directed at her. But only for a second. If there were the slightest doubt about her ideologically, they wouldn't have chosen her to carry the banner of the working classes.

Brother #12 gives way to Brother #8, on Kree's left.

Brother #8 repeats, in overall theme, Brother #12's speech. But he expands on the question of religious deviationism, the temptation that some men and women experience to consider the world from a less materialist angle than is proper, then he goes on to the current resurgence of superstitions, the recent usage of lucky charms and demon-wards among the population, including by certain individuals who have fraudulently inserted themselves into its first ranks. He fulminates against the practice of witchcraft, which carries the seeds for the fall of egalitarianism. Kree isn't quite sure, but she gets the feeling Brother #27's magical decorations are what he's railing about. Brother #27 doesn't seem completely relaxed. His eyes aren't lifted frankly toward the speaker, his gaze flits around, lands now on Brother #12's feet, his canvas shoes, now on tiny details that he seems to have noticed on the boards, maybe the longhorn beetles annoyed by their voices, or bits of wood.

Next comes a moment of reeducational recitation. #8 and #12 take turns speaking. They reel off very short fragments from the dogma, phrases that they invite the reeducables to repeat after them. The reeducables obey. They reproduce the dogma diligently, in a contrite and humble manner. When the text takes on more inspired notes, at the end of the slogan, they raise their tone to indicate how much fervor they're experiencing. The exercise goes on forever. In a struggle against boredom, perhaps, a few anonymous people in the room take upon themselves a choral function, beginning to mutter in time with the reeducables without being asked. Kree doesn't open her mouth; she lets her mind wander, all the while maintaining a stiff mask. In her role as spokesperson for the repressed classes, such a sullen mask is proper, full of intransigence and bitterness. In the first row,

Brother #27 moves his lips; he, too, accompanies the reeducables' recitation, and, in the midst of all the noise, Kree can clearly recognize his voice. He isn't acting like the anonymous audience members, like the free listeners, he isn't participating spontaneously in the liturgy, he is in fact obeying the order given from the stage and he's speaking loudly. He's obeying the terrible mendicants who want to correct his errors in judgment and his deviations. He's being reeducated.

Well, yeah, obviously, Kree thinks. That's what the message she brought him this morning must have contained: a summons to a reeducation meeting. With, perhaps, a self-criticism and a pronouncement of execution to top off the show.

Brother #27. His plump wrestler's silhouette, his solid muscle that looks deceptively like solid fat. His hairy face, his hands furry as a great ape's. Kree isolates his voice effortlessly, more assured than the voices of the other reeducables. She tries to read his expression, a veil of unorthodox humor, but her vision is too poor to catch it at a distance. She doesn't catch anything. The phrases Brother #27 is repeating are ones he's known by heart for many years. He does not distort them. He makes sure to pronounce them in a distinct and forceful manner. He rocks gently back and forth, he avoids looking around, and he addresses the words to himself rather than to his peers as they watch him from the stage or to the divinities who created egalitarianism.

After they've gone through the dogma slogan by slogan, Brother #8 and Brother #12 end the litany, and silence falls. Then #8 begins speaking again. A scolding tone. He recalls that, even among the best, there is a great temptation to wander toward unacceptable shamanic practices. Some can be tolerated, others are clearly seeking alliance with enemy forces, uncontrollable forces, demons, ambiguous divinities, suspicious divinities. One of the greatest threats to menace the survivors or assimilated is the lack of vigilance, that they will allow themselves to be seduced by dreams and nothingness. His speech complete, he turns toward Kree. He asks her if the poor peasants and the mothers of children agree with what he has just said. Kree quickly and solemnly agrees. #8 then declares that they must eliminate those men and women who draw the community in a direction counter to history. As he speaks of both men and women at once, again Kree thinks that maybe he's accusing her indirectly of having allowed the egalitarianist ideology and hope to rot within her. She swallows her saliva. #8 once again interrupts himself, looks at her, seeks her approval. She raises her gaze to the sky, as if she's thinking intensely, then, with theatrical intensity, again she nods her head in affirmation. Satisfied, but without flaunting his satisfaction, #8 speaks of the unanimous agreement of the popular masses. He explains that this agreement was necessary. Unanimity is always required before a decision of elimination can be pronounced. He goes on to say that the eliminated are not always called to a public self-criticism, because they may counter the procedure and take advantage of it to diseducate the masses. He turns one final time toward Kree so she can confirm that the vanguard and the godless and masterless proletarians accept this exceptional disposition. At this second, Kree perceives distinctly a movement from Brother #27, who lifts his gaze toward the tribunal and then lowers it, and there, perhaps, the hint of a smile. Again she nods in agreement, in a serious yet demonstrative manner. No sound comes out of her throat. Above her, #8 makes a small series of hand gestures to show that they are closing a file, regarding which there is nothing more to be said. One might really think he was manipulating a stack of papers, putting it back in order and closing up the stiff folder that contained it. He sits up straight in his chair again, for he's gotten a little hunched, and he gives way to Brother #12.

#12 distributes the tasks in the collective interest that they must accomplish in the days to come, until the next evaluation meeting, which he hopes will be positive, for everyone's sake. He names the reeducables and the exemplary citizens who will act as their tutors. Doumfaf Moroudji, Sariyan Lov, Leonor Morskoï, Trystal Daadour, Abayïl Whitewater. Kree hears these names and she knows that she'll forget them, but she focuses her attention on the man with the sailor hat and the scarred head, the wanderer who might have prowled around her building in the night. And thus she learns two things at the same time: this man's name is Griz Uttikuma, and Brother #12 wants to assign her, Kree, to oversee him and to monitor his progress in egalitarianist consciousness.

Griz Uttikuma will do roadwork.

She exchanges a look with him.

Prior to this, she hasn't watched the reeducables from the height of the stage, so as to avoid adding to their troubles, she's avoided meeting their gaze. They keep their eyes lowered as a sign of docility anyway, and it would have been impossible to communicate with them, even in a furtive manner. Now that the hour of reeducation is coming to an end and the atmosphere has not been weighed down by a standard self-criticism, everyone returns to their normal attitudes. Everyone among the active participants as well as the audience. Theatrical necessities are no longer required. Kree seeks the gaze of Griz Uttikuma and, with contact established, he does not turn away. He is just in front of her, below but very close. She can see him well.

They meet calmly and in silence, as if they were suddenly outside the House of Mendicants and away from the swelling noise that marks the end of the meeting and the departure of the spectators. Kree has a silent exchange with Griz Uttikuma, not really by telepathy, but almost. Immediately, she senses their relations will be peaceful. In an instant her distrust falls away, her precaution against him, against his suspicious appearance, his supposed nocturnal incursions in her building. Griz Uttikuma's eyes are the color of dark ashes and they express a nonchalant fatalism. And perhaps the desire to share it with Kree, this nonchalance. He is proposing a nonaggression pact with her, within the context of his reeducation, first, but his proposal is also more general, less defined. Kree responds with a nod; she lets him know that she agrees. She does not waver from her severe rigidity as representative of the peasants and poor urban masses. But she signals to Griz Uttikuma that she agrees. Everything will go forward without trouble, with a good understanding. The man sustains her gaze for two or three seconds, then he lowers his eyes.

Then, bravely, he looks at her again.

Then he turns away to join his comrades in misery, who are leaving the room in single file.

*T*hey meet again three days later at the appointed hour, in Drödzaki Street, where one end is blocked with rubble and the other obstructed by the wreckage of a truck. Partly obstructed. The crumpled chassis sits on rims without tires, scaly with rust, shedding flakes of rust year after year. Wanderers may have occupied the cabin, forty or fifty years prior, and everything that might have once existed inside has disappeared. The doors are gone. The hood is torn off the front, which looks like a dragon's gullet, stripped of its motor, the batteries burst and melted into a formless mass, yawning open with a black tongue. Maybe a military vehicle, but it's hard to tell. Not much can be recognized amidst the scrap metal. The dragon is hunched at a slant, watching over the passage. It discourages intruders from wandering into its territory.

A street one might hesitate to go down. There's the dragon, first of all, but nobody would have any desire to go farther. The rutted street. Patches of tar, piles of dirt, gravel, holes. On the left and on the right, gray houses stuck close together, one after another. No façades, a series of back walls, what used to be called a back alley in English, back before English became a dead language. Sometimes, down at the bottom of the decrepit walls, a backdoor, a hidden, shameful door. And on the first and second floors, miserly, narrow windows here and there, probably for ventilation in bathrooms and closets.

An incongruous cicada stridulates hysterically somewhere within this gray passageway.

The sun beats heavily on the city. Its heat is almost hellish, humid, more humid than usual. Kree's temples are dripping. She wipes the drops off with the back of her sleeve and they reappear. More spring forth in her armpits, on her back, her belly.

At some point, someone set up a square plywood sign near the truck. WORK. Someone took the trouble to write that in white paint, with a hard-to-read symbol that might be interpreted as forbidding passage. Probably a terrible mendicant painted it with a zealous brush. Forbidden to nonauthorized persons. Recalling it, Kree shrugs. She goes around the ruin of the truck and she plunges into the street.

The cicada's deafening cry fills the space. When Kree comes to the singer's level, it falls silent. It must be hidden in a tuft of grass overflowing from a gutter. It falls silent, back to a burning silence of sinister walls and sweat.

For a long time, the street with its two ends blocked has been a long rectangle without any clear purpose, an urban space with no reason for its existence. Something about the atmosphere suggests, also, that it bears more relation to a cemetery than to a passageway. Something in the odor that hovers within the leprous ugliness of the walls.

A cemetery. A cemetery atmosphere. The smell. The ugliness. Kree doesn't ask any questions about them. This isn't the first time she's been here. She knows very well where it comes from.

She's been released from her morning's work at the House of Mendicants, since Brother #15 named her head of the team. She's carrying a shovel over one shoulder. It's not for repairing the road. She's already performed this same task several times, here, in the same conditions, with requisitioneds or reeducables. It's almost always the same thing. A burial. Make a hole. Place the cadaver of the executed in the earth. Fill the hole back up. Spread tar over the hole. A task in service of the collective, a duty to be accomplished in the name of the popular masses. A task like any other. Not glorious, not exciting. Just like any other job.

In the middle of the road, sitting on a pile of dirt next to a wheelbarrow full of tar, Griz Uttikuma is smoking calmly. Wearing his habitual sailor's cap on his head. Kree comes up; ever since the meeting at the House of Mendicants she's known that she would meet him again at some work site or other, him as a road worker and her as supervisor and reeducation agent. She skirts a pothole, then she gives him a long, untroubled look. His hard features, the creases on his forehead, on his cheeks. His hooked nose with its broken bridge. His eyes a piercing gray. A manner like he fears nothing. Like he's lived through too much to feel any fear. He doesn't move, he doesn't get up. Kree comes closer, she leans her shovel against the wheelbarrow. The handles are burning, the powerful emanations of tar coming from underneath the oily drop cloth, protection meant to keep the mix at the right temperature.

"I can give you my name again," the man says. "Griz Uttikuma."

"I know," she says. "And I'm Kree. Kree Toronto."

In the ashes of his gaze, fine black lines. Kree has never been at such a short distance from him, has never looked deep into his eyes like this. During their last encounter, she was on a stage, and he was lower, humbled, in the first row. They had exchanged a sign of understanding, but they were too far away from each other, and she hadn't really been able to examine his iris in detail. She is doing it now.

Slowly she examines his iris in detail.

She allows a second to pass like this, then two, three, four. She savors the vertiginous gray with its brutal confidence. She can justify this, if necessary, by her poor vision. Then she realizes that she's staring him down as if she wanted to make him surrender, as if she wanted him to admit his inferiority in the hierarchy, and she lowers her gaze. That isn't what she wants. Soon she tries a smirk to put an end to what he might have interpreted as the arrogance of a camp guardian. But already he's lowered his head. Like an animal that is not obliged to submit but isn't seeking conflict, he recognizes her authority. He pivots to the hole that he's dug.

"I came early with the tar," he explains. "Brother #8 he came by with Lov and the tools. He ordered me to do this, to dig there. Here. There was a hard crust I went after with a pickaxe, but after that it was practically no problem doing it with the spade. It went quick with the spade."

"I know," Kree says. "The soil is good, not rocky. That's why what the terrible mendicants they chose this spot."

Griz shrugs his shoulders.

"Looks like a grave," he says. "Is it for me, or what?"

"It's not for you," Kree reassures him. "There's never any executions here."

"Bah." Griz allows himself to doubt.

"No, never," Kree affirms.

The cicada takes up its strident song again. Very loud, though not so loud it prevents them from talking.

She sits next to him on the pile of dirt, her head turned toward the entry to the dead-end street. Beyond the truck, about thirty meters away, the blinding white of the avenue contrasts with the darkness hanging over the work site. Cruelly the sun floods the world. The light forces Kree to grimace, she looks between her lashes. Everything is empty. Nobody shows up.

"Who is it we're waiting for?" Griz asks, from a meter away.

Kree responds with a gesture. She doesn't know. Her arm lifts, stops midway, then falls again.

"They'll come," she promises.

"If this drags out," Griz grumbles, "that tar it'll get cold."

They remain for a minute without saying anything. They listen to the cicada. The odor of tar dominates at first, although the earth beneath Kree's bottom is full of smells, too. Caved-in cellars, animal rot, mouse urine. They breathe in all these smells in great gulps, and they do not speak. Kree would like to question this Griz Uttikuma, to know more about him. Not really about what happened before he arrived in the city. More about his current life, his way of taking things in the here and now. About his present. About the rest, his biography, the horrors he's survived, Kree has no wish to hear. She never will learn anything about that.

*N*obody ever reveals anything about their past. Whether re-educable or reeducated, near the terrible mendicants or at a distance, nobody ever ventures to speak of those things out loud. They know, they've already been told, the subject is taboo, something to keep wrapped in lies so the dirty and monstrous years do not spread anew within awareness, do not crash in again like dirty, monstrous waves. When it is absolutely necessary to pour out what one has lived through long ago, when it is necessary to answer questions during self-criticism and adjustment sessions, only sad inventions may pass their lips.

Kree or Griz, Myriam or Gomchen, one or the other. Or yet others. Even in private our confessions are nothing but fictions and confabulations. We keep the essential parts of our past silent, and when we're forced to come back to them, to plunge ourselves back in by referring to them, strange mirages arise, strange tricks. Through allusions or in details, we recount a life other than our own. We invent a hell different from the one we have miraculously escaped. Hideous tales, imaginary horrors, baroque nightmares. In reality, we have known worse. We soak against our will in these stories, so that nothing or almost nothing unbearable will again start to burn inside us and destroy us. It is a feint in self-defense. It is ourselves we are deceiving.

*B*etween two small windows, Kree notices a black line. Her poor vision doesn't tell her much. At first she thinks it's a large crack due to a seismic shake, then she gets the sense that the line is moving, changing its level and form. Now the line lowers on the wall about a quarter meter, now it disappears and even gets interrupted. She tries to see better but, despite her ocular and facial gymnastics, the line remains blurry.

"What is that, over there?" she asks, lifting her hand.

"Where's that?" Griz asks.

She points more clearly to the line that intrigues her.

"There. Between the windows. I've got bad eyes," she explains.

"A colony of spiders," Griz assesses. "Blue massaquayas. They're moving to a new spot. They're not venomous."

Kree stops looking in that direction. Blurry as it is, the sight disgusts her.

"I wouldn't advise them to come anywhere near here," she says.

"They're not venomous, but they know how to fight," Griz adds.

"So do I," Kree clarifies.

At this moment, three men appear at the entry to the dead-end street. Dressed in black with a straw hat and a wide black-and-white checked bandana tied around his neck, Brother #8 leads the way. Behind him, the two reeducables: Whitewater and Morskoï. They're bustling around a wheelbarrow, which contains an enormous plastic bag. It's not easy work. The bag is hanging overboard, it's slipping; Whitewater has to hold it in place while Morskoï, in charge of the wheelbarrow handles, attempts unsuccessfully to drive in a straight line and reduce the wobbling. Tensed arms, pained grimaces of concentration. Two men in their fifties without much talent for burial work, but putting their backs into it, sparing no effort. Neither is wearing a head covering and their bald, tanned scalps are gleaming with sweat. Streaming, even. Brother #8 seems unaffected by the heat. He swings a small jerrycan at the end of one arm. He doesn't turn back toward the reeducables; he doesn't offer any encouragement, any comment on transportational techniques. He ignores them. When they reach the ruined truck, Morskoï and Whitewater stop before the gullet of the dragon. They stand still next to their wheelbarrow and they wait for orders.

#8 alone moves in Kree's direction and toward the hole that Griz Uttikuma has dug.

Kree and Griz leave the dirt pile they've been sitting on. They get up. Brother #8 comes up to them, he inspects the hole that Griz has dug. He circles around. He observes the pile of yellowish dirt. He expresses nothing, no judgment, neither satisfaction nor reproach. After a few seconds, he addresses Kree:

"Kree Toronto, this isn't your first time. You know how this goes. At the end, pack the tar down well. So there isn't any hump."

Kree nods. She knows how all this goes.

"After that, your job here will be done. Whitewater and Morskoï they'll bring back the wheelbarrow and the tools to the House. Uttikuma he can go back to his dormitory."

"Understood," Griz says.

A submission that may not be entirely sincere. Brother #8 throws him an icy glance.

"Someone will come get you tomorrow at dawn. You are at the service of the cooperative."

The terrible mendicant waits for Whitewater and Morskoï to approach, then he gives them a signal. They mumble a few phrases regarding the virtues of collective effort, regarding work well done, work in the service of the people, regarding the people, regarding the never completed battle against counterrevolutionary individualism and its countless manifestations. Then he points out the jerrycan.

"There's not much, it's heating oil. At the end, don't forget, you have to give them a good cleaning, the tools and the wheelbarrow used to transport the tar."

Then he leaves.

Whitewater and his associate Morskoï have abandoned the wheelbarrow a little beyond the truck carcass. They had approached to listen to Brother #8 speak. Now that #8 has dictated his instructions, turned his back on everyone, and gone away, they, too, lean over the hole to evaluate its dimensions. They wipe off the sweat flowing down their faces, and they let out a syllable of approval. The hole is deep, it should work. Then they return to the wheelbarrow.

Whitewater grasps the handles and gives it a bump with his torso, a first propulsion. He's unable to restrain a wheeze. The wheelbarrow lifts up and, again, just as when they arrived, lists to one side and wavers. The thick plastic bag starts to slip again; Morskoï tries to push it back in place but does not succeed. Whitewater sets the wheelbarrow back down. They haven't managed half a meter. They're really not experts in corpse transportation. They get moving again. They zigzag a few meters. Morskoï warns Whitewater about a depression in the dirt just before him. Whitewater's mistake is that he doesn't go far enough around. A hole of small size, the mud at its base cracked and dry, but the edges are crumbly. Now, there, the wheel gets too close. It pulverizes the tiny earthen rampart bordering the tiny crater; it slides a fatal ten or so centimeters and suddenly stops short. A new wheeze bursts forth from Whitewater's lips. A whimper of disappointment. The wheelbarrow leans portside like a rowboat about to capsize. During the seconds that follow, Morskoï struggles against the bag as it threatens to fall from the skiff.

Whitewater attempts to stabilize the whole, to return the vehicle to horizontality. His arm gets twisted in the effort and he lets out a howl of pain. Now a howl instead of a whimper. Finally he manages to counteract the skiff's toppling motion. Now he can offer assistance to Morskoï. Between the two of them, they manage to pummel and push the black bag and ensure its balance for the final few meters left in their path and, when they're almost certain that the transport will now occur without any further accident, Whitewater grasps the handles anew. This time he grits his teeth and emits no sound. He unblocks the wheel and, in a single burst of rage, throws himself forward. There are five meters still to cross. He's flushed with the energy of despair. Only three more meters, only two. He's coming around the pile of dirt, he's avoiding Kree and Griz, he bumps the jerrycan and the wheelbarrow full of tar, he pays no further attention to Morskoï's potential interventions, whatever Morskoï might or might not do to prevent his cargo from tumbling out of the skiff before arriving in safe harbor.

"Careful!" Morskoï bellows.

"I'm gonna make it!" bellows Whitewater in return.

Full of rage, paying no more attention to the equilibrium of his burden, he rushes straight toward the ditch that Griz has dug.

"Wait! Stop!" Kree yells.

Whitewater has completely lost control over his speed and direction.

One second stretches measurelessly, yells merge and blur together, then silence in the lungs, in the throats. The disaster has taken place. Whitewater has failed to stop in time, and at the moment when he might have tried to do so, the wheel plunged into the unknown. The wheelbarrow pitched over before reaching the hole. It has violently escaped its conductor, not without attempting to brutalize his armpits and jaw with a terrible blow of the handle as it passes. Miraculously, Whitewater escapes mutilation. The plastic bag is hurled from the skiff and tumbles haphazardly into the hole. The wheelbarrow falls immediately after it, as if in spite, as if disappointed that it failed to deliver its uppercut, failed to crack Whitewater's skull. It gets stuck at a slant between the walls of the hole, in an odd yet logical manner, since the hole is neither wide enough nor deep enough to engulf it.

Now, the four people assemble around the scene of the accident, sponging their foreheads, scalps, and eyelids, breathing hard. All are nodding in a pensive manner. They're keeping their thoughts to themselves, but at first glance one might think they all approve of what has happened. Morskoï whistles between his teeth, expressing something like relief, or in any case expressing no objection. Work in service of the people might be accomplished with a bit more skill, but this doesn't seem to bother him. Whitewater, for his part, hasn't raised his hands to his head, so as to at least feign some consternation at this chaotic ending. On the contrary, Kree can see a feeling of triumph shading across his sweat-slicked face. The shadow disappears, but it was there.

"That thing almost smacked me in the snout," Whitewater mutters.

Obviously the two men still have some progress to make before they can call themselves reeducated and feel proud of it.

Despite her role as intermediary between the reeducables and the Brothers, Kree has no intention of holding forth with any moralistic speeches. Brother #8 has disappeared and, here, she doesn't feel like the representative of the poor and the assimilated peasants. She doesn't feel invested with the slightest ideological responsibility. In silence, she helps Griz disengage the hapless wheelbarrow. They park it off to one side.

Once the wheelbarrow problem is solved, Kree returns to lean over the hole. The plastic bag was damaged and torn in its fall. Part of its contents have become visible. The cadaver to be buried isn't occupying the space in the traditional manner. The body, rather than reclining on its back, looks like it's trying to crouch in a corner, but since it hasn't quite succeeded, now it's in the process of figuring out how to stand back up, whatever the cost. One can make out the shoulders straining against the black plastic, the knees pushing. A mummy that wants to be finished with an uncomfortable situation.

Through the tear an arm and part of a black cotton jacket are recognizable. A furry arm, a hand covered in hair.

So that's really it, they executed Brother #27, Kree thinks.

They killed him down by the river, or probably in one of the back offices of the House of Mendicants, among the shadows and close smells of smoke and coconut oil. She can picture the scene in her mind without difficulty. The killers in their pathetic uniforms, Brother #27 not moving, waiting and maintaining his dignity.

Several memories. Brother #27. Three days earlier, he was chewing and regurgitating the magic words they were throwing at him in the tribunal, like food for animals being fattened. Obvious precepts, pompous and idiotic. His impassivity while his peers humiliated him in public. When she thinks back on it, deep down, he didn't believe the things coming out of his mouth. He was pretending. Another memory: the demon-ward made of string, an object that he'd had enough time to complete, but it wasn't sufficient to protect him. Another memory: the austere room with its shamanic decorations, the traps for malevolent forces, the dream catchers. The warm welcome, the tea. Ambiguous jokes about Brother #1, sarcasm directed casually against Brother #2. The letter that he tosses on the bed, that falls down to the bare floor, that he doesn't pick up. And then his poorly hidden bitterness when finally he took notice of the message that it was her mission to bring him, that message of death.

Griz has asked her a question. She hasn't answered. He repeats it.

"Should we put him the way he's supposed to be?"

"Not worth the effort," Kree says.

He's better this way, she thinks.

"Fine," says Whitewater.

If what he wakes up and wants to get out, he'll have less work to do than if what he was lying down, Kree thinks then.

Next, they fill up the hole, all four of them. They help each other with their hands, with the shovel and spade, or with bits of wood that fall in. At the end, Morskoï and Whitewater work on leveling out the soil by stamping on it. They follow a rhythm. Maybe the dance steps of Indians on the plains. A hunting dance, a war dance, not a dance for calling the dead, anyway. Who knows where these two men come from. Who knows what people in the process of dying off they lived with in their previous lives. And, besides, it's possible they do not follow any sorceror's rhythm. Maybe they're simply dancing a spontaneous dance of despair. In her role as worksite supervisor, she puts an end to it.

"That's enough," she declares. "Let's put the tar down now."

She lifts the protective sheet that was keeping the tar hot under cover, and she begins to throw shovelfuls over the fresh earth. It's a tiring operation. The tar is heavy, and since it's already cooled down a bit, it's not very malleable. Griz spreads out the very black and smoking clumps. In the absence of a rake, he does his best with the spade. They're all trying not to touch the burning paste directly. They succeed, but at the cost of wavering or capricious movements giving their collective the look of a disorganized ballet. Whitewater and Morskoï use the scraps from a gutter. They spare no effort. Kree turns the wheelbarrow over to evacuate the final black clumps. There's pain in her hands, in her guts, in all her joints.

A heat that vibrates among them, under them, invisible fumes that seize them by the throat. The vapors of petrol and asphalt. They're everywhere in the air. They're intoxicating.

To pack down the tar, Whitewater goes to pull the bottom part of a door off a ruined house deep in the dead end. He needs help from Morskoï. They carry this panel back and place it over the tar, then they climb on top and take up their dance again. They stamp their feet in rhythm. Yes, maybe they are, in fact, performing a sorceror's dance for the dead, for rest, or to encourage the dead not to be afraid, no matter what happens. To offer some commonsense instructions: continue elsewhere without the burdens of memory, regrets, or mementos of defeat. When they've finished tamping down one side, they move the wooden rectangle so that the oily surface will be perfectly level. They don't stop until all unevenness is gone.

"Well, there's no more bumps," Whitewater concludes.

"Is that good?" Griz asks, turning toward Kree.

"Yeah, sure," Kree approves.

Next everyone cleans the tools with the heating oil: the shovel, the spade, the inside of the wheelbarrow that was used to transport tar, the soles of their shoes.

Griz goes to rest the half-door against the wall of the ruined house.

Kree gathers herself on top of the remade street. A meter below, Brother #27 is snoozing in an impossible position, no doubt having accepted his fate, or perhaps unhappy because he doesn't understand what's happened to him. What he did to find himself there, in a torn plastic bag under a heavy layer of earth and tar. Maybe his memory is playing tricks on him and already the final moments of his previous existence are no more than a meaningless dream. In this moment, who knows, he might imagine that he was killed by some monsters bursting out of the black space. Maybe he's forgotten the details of his execution, the final minutes, the final seconds. Kree doesn't dig into the question, she simply wants to say a prayer. She hesitates. No doubt Myriam Agazaki would know better than she does how to attend to Brother #27 in his tomb, what phrases to pronounce, what soothing, consoling spells. Myriam Agazaki has much more knowledge than Kree in this area.

And so now Kree stands at the edge of the hot tar. She concentrates and in silence she says a prayer, the first one that comes to mind. A prayer asking forgiveness, as if she were directly or indirectly responsible for Brother #27's death. A prayer after killing. Very similar to the one that Myriam Agazaki says when she has to prevent a spider from causing harm. The words don't correspond to this situation and Kree knows it. But if Brother #27 is listening, he will receive the message with kindness. She thinks about him very hard; she wishes him the best. Then she lets the others know her moment of mystical solitude is finished.

Morskoï has gathered the tools and the empty jerrycan, and he's thrown them into the wheelbarrow that once contained the shrouded body. He's entirely soaked, and the sweat has not stopped emitting from his exhausted face, from his scalp wounded by the blows of sun and insect bites.

"Morskoï, what's your name, your first name?" Kree asks.

A grimace. The question irritates him.

"Leonor," he answers finally.

"That's more of a girl's name," Kree remarks.

"They made a mistake when they signed me up and it stayed that way," Morskoï tells them.

He'll have to get used to explaining himself on this point, but he's a little annoyed.

"It's not very important," Kree consoles him.

"For me, at this point, no. It's not important at all."

A silence. All four standing, one next to the other, in the heat of the road, two steps from the rectangle of tar still radiating additional heat.

They set out toward the opening of Drödzaki Street, toward the dragon in its terminal stage. Both Morskoï and Whitewater have an empty or mostly empty wheelbarrow to push, now light. Kree takes care to walk as far as possible from the line of spiders, who have continued moving from one house to the other. She makes sure not to look closely at them. She doesn't want that obscenity of transhumance engraved in her memory.

"What are those bugs?" Whitewater asks.

"Blue massaquayas," Kree says. "Not poisonous, but they know how to fight."

While Whitewater and Morskoï move away with calm steps, two workers pushing their wheelbarrows with their labor complete, Kree asks Griz where he's found a place to stay in tent campsite or in a dormitory, or if he's squatting in a house. She wants to know which way he's going to go now.

They've left the shadow-filled road of the worksite, and they've stopped in the sunshine, Griz and Kree, with the rusting dragon that guards the grounds behind them. Rather than separating on a brief goodbye, they follow the two reeducateds with their gaze, as if they were in charge of watching them. Once Whitewater and Morskoï have turned a corner and disappeared behind a wall, Griz takes out a cigarette and lights it, without offering her one, as if he knows she doesn't smoke.

"Mariya Kahn dormitory?" she suggests.

He doesn't answer her question until he's already taken a drag.

"No," he says, "another one. Near the ford. The Holsch dormitory, it's called."

Kree asks other questions. They begin discussing. She's conscious she's keeping Griz back. She wonders what her relationship is to this man. Or rather if they're going to have a relationship after this, after this foul funeral episode, the cleaning oil and the blue massaquayas who know how to fight. If they'll see each other in some context other than reeducation and forced labor in the service of the people.

A semblance of conversation ties into the Holsch dormitory, the lodging conditions in the various sectors of the city. Griz explains that, once his reeducation is complete, he'll look for an individual space somewhere near Central. The dormitory is fine, it's got the correct sanitary fixtures, the occupants near his bed are refugees, not too noisy. Despite all that, he's in a hurry to move into some nook where he'll have complete independence.

"Even if there's a lot more spiders in the city than on the port," he considers it wise to clarify.

"There aren't any spiders in your dormitory?" Kree asks.

"The syndicate uses disinfectant," Griz explains. "They don't enjoy that. And then, in my opinion, on the port they seem less numerous. That's how it is."

They start talking about spiders: gray mygals, massaquayas, makhagambas, tataguamas, tchakagagnas, spotted tarantulas. All those creatures that make Kree nauseous and that are part of our daily life, just as the terrible mendicants are. Kree offers Myriam Agazaki's theory on the rift between the spiders and all the other living species on Earth, as old as time, and, rather than continuing in that vein, the conversation turns to Myriam Agazaki, her abilities as a healer.

"She told me I was going to die, and she gave me your address," Griz announces calmly.

Kree swallows.

"Bah," she reacts.

She frowns. She looks off in the distance. Uninhabited houses, roofs in poor condition, terraces tufted with growing brush. She can't make anything out. Everything is blurry.

"I wonder why what she said that," Kree answers finally.

"Why she said I was going to die?" Griz returns immediately.

"No, the address. Why what she said the address where I live."

Griz shakes his head. He doesn't seem to see any problem there.

Kree decides this is the right moment to bring up the subject that's been bothering her for several days. She's waited long enough. Now's the time.

"I don't know if it's true one of these nights you came exploring my building," she says in a cold voice. "You climbed up to the sixth floor. You stood in the hallway a minute. Did I dream it or what?"

"Bah," Griz says elusively. "Maybe you were dreaming."

"An hour before dawn," Kree specifies. "You came up to my door."

Griz pulls his cigarette out from between his lips and lets a little smoke escape. He doesn't show any intention to comment.

"You came up to my place that night or you didn't come?" Kree attacks.

Griz frowns.

"I went up, then I went back down," he says finally.

"Why?" Kree asks.

"Why did I go down?"

A tone carrying as much irony as carelessness.

At the same time, Kree has to acknowledge that it's all the same to her: this Griz Uttikuma strolled up to her place, the stroll took place at night, and he strolled back down without insisting. He is in reeducation, but he doesn't look like he belongs to the enemy class, and besides, if that were the case, the mendicants would have taken him aside and eliminated him as soon as he arrived. Suddenly she's finding excuses for everything he says, everything he does. Suddenly she accepts him as a normal guy with whom she can quite easily begin a normal relationship, as a comrade or even a friend.

She stares at Griz point-blank, without blinking. Again she stares at him with an intense nonchalance, even a provocative ambiguity. She's aware that she's breaking boundaries. She moves toward him and without considering the consequences. But something pushes her to leave all caution aside. At the heart of this rough, bony face, with its dark, tanned, and crevassed skin, shine eyes of an extraordinary gray. Maybe one day she'd like to lose herself in them. One day, or soon. Or maybe right away. Myriam Agazaki was right: he's a good-looking man, this

Griz Uttikuma. She wishes Loka were here. The dog would have come up to his legs, she would have smelled him, she would have evaluated him objectively, animally, and she would have given her opinion.

Griz meets her eyes without turning his away. In truth, she cannot decipher anything in them. As if he expressed no feeling at all. It's the gaze of a man who knows how to handle himself in the face of aggression. A fighter's gaze. He doesn't give Kree any indication of what's going through his mind, what he's planning to do or say in the next few seconds. Kree plunges into him, then she reemerges. She doesn't let herself drown there, at least not today. She has almost let down her guard and now she takes herself in hand again. The instant of turmoil will last only a fraction of a second. She possesses some aptitude in combat, too, some of the skills of a killer. Anything that might have been legible in her pupils, in her irises, some weakness, an expectation, she allows to fade. They go on looking at each other, only a slim distance between them, but there is no more exchange.

A silence.

"On that topic," Kree says. "Since that night you came just in front of my door. I don't know what Myriam Agazaki she would have told you about me. But something what she might not have told you, I'm telling you. I hate anyone having sex with me. If what you ever come to my place and that's your intention, I'm warning you: I'll kill you."

Griz shrugs. He keeps on holding Kree's gaze, but without the slightest hint of defiance. He has something to say, but he isn't in a hurry.

"I don't have sex with anyone," he says when he decides to speak.

"Ah," Kree reacts.

"I've taken a vow of abstinence," he declares.

"Ah, so that's it," Kree marvels. "You're a monk?"

"No. I could have been, at one time in my life, long ago. But no."

A handful of seconds later, Griz returns to the question of abstinence.

"It's to be faithful to Smoura Tigrit," he explains.

"Your woman?" Kree asks.

"No," Griz replies. "An egg."

Kree flinches. She cannot avoid a clenching of her eyelids, an almost panicky flutter of eyelashes. She questions the peaceful gray of his eyes. Under the surface, nothing seems to have changed. On the surface, even less. He's crazy, this guy, she thinks. He's insane.

She falls back a few centimeters, as if shifting her balance on her legs. She swallows a little. She has to camouflage her uneasiness. To continue the conversation as if everything being said was entirely normal.

"We all do that," she comments.

"Do what?" he asks, then finally he looks away.

Kree doesn't know how to go on.

"We're all faithful," she says.

He lets out a long sigh.

"Yes," he says. "It's either loyalty or betrayal."

Smoura Tigrit, Kree thinks. An egg. Staying faithful to an egg. Taking a vow of abstinence to stay faithful to an egg. We all do that.

*B*ut Kree Toronto and Griz Uttikuma got together at her place fairly regularly after that. One day he brought some disinfectant in a plastic canteen that he'd found in his dormitory, and together they doused all the areas surrounding the windows and the bottom of the door. The consequence of this operation, whether logical or illogical, was that no makhagamba ever again returned to haunt Kree's wee hours.

Griz chatted with her about one thing and another, although, of course, never about the past. When it came to opening up the chapters of their previous existences, both of them remained evasive. They claimed to have completely forgotten, to have buried away the details of those hideous events, and, in fact, even the idea of unearthing them was repellent. The present was sufficient, with its highs and lows and improbable tomorrows. Griz never complained about the terrible mendicants. He accepted reeducation as an ordeal necessary for his integration in the city and he never missed a single session. As far as he knew, his reeducation was moving smoothly toward its completion. After that, he planned to work with Gomchen, with whom he got along well, expanding the Tibetan's business by adding to telephonics a line of shaking tents. "Shaking tents, that's the future," he claimed, with an emphatic tone that made it impossible to tell whether he was joking or serious.

The Brothers had not assigned the task of overseeing him during his work praxis to Kree again, and he got a variety of people as contacts, men and woman who spent a day or an afternoon accompanying him and taking him under their wings, but he hadn't made friends with any of them. He saw Kree as having a special status. He did not take it too far. He went to her apartment; he helped her out a bit from time to time. He climbed up onto her building's rooftop terrace to exterminate the spiders. He cemented a broken step in the darkness of the fourth-floor staircase. He was trying, so far without success, to dig up some glasses for her that would suit her weak vision. He never ventured into subjects that were ambiguous or obscene.

Sometimes Kree wondered whether, all things considered, they shouldn't lie down one alongside the other, take off their clothes and have sex, but since she didn't really want to and he didn't suggest it, they never did so. She spoke to Myriam Agazaki about it. Myriam Agazaki did not encourage chastity. Glowing from her Tibetan, she advised Kree to try the experiment, at least once. Kree objected that Griz Uttikuma had made a vow of abstinence so as to remain faithful to Smoura Tigrit, the egg called Smoura Tigrit. The conversation wandered then, over nightmares brought on by the war, over the birds, the floating worlds, magical worlds, parallel worlds. Myriam Agazaki lamented the insane visions that came upon men traumatized by the horrors of the front and the black space in general. Apocalyptic visions of flames, cadavers, an infinite march through infinite landscapes of ash. Not all had lived through abominations connected to eggs, to imprisonment in an egg or undying love consecrated to an egg. In this, Gomchen and Griz were a bit different, and their nightmares did not connect to anything with real consistency out of Kree's memory or Myriam Agazaki's memory. "I like them very much," Myriam Agazaki would say, "they're our comrades in disaster, but there's something in their heads what sure isn't working right. They've accumulated some bad muck what rots their lives. It messes up their common sense."

Kree liked Griz Uttikuma very much, and when he had finished his reeducation, she had him come over even more often.

She appreciated his solidity, his lack of sexual aggression, the consideration he showed for her. She had nothing to reproach him with, except for his neglectful attitude regarding Loka. He acted as though the dog did not exist. Even when Loka came to rub against his legs or gave his hand a lick, he did not react in any way. No pat on the back, no pets, not even a furtive one, not the slightest glance. He ignored her. The dog did not take offense, but Kree had ended up feeling a certain resentment. Loka was an important part of her life, and she didn't understand why Griz refused to take any notice of her.

A friction persisted between them on this topic. It was natural that things about their past existences remained unsaid, but less natural when it came to things about the present. One day, as she was dividing a piece of soaked pemmican in three equal portions, one for herself, one for him, and one for the dog, Kree even asked Griz about his relations with dogs, and, in addition, what he thought of Loka. Griz, ordinarily very sure of himself in his answers as well as in his silences, suddenly hesitated for a long time.

"Loka, yeah . . . Her, it's something else."

He bent his head without saying anything. His gaze wavered. Then he continued:

"But dogs, you know, I don't like to touch them. The memories are too bad. One night someone sent dogs after me. Four of them. I killed all four. Even when the dogs they're big, even when they're fierce, I can do that. As long as they don't get to your throat you can do that. But that means cracking their joints and you feel sorry for them. The dog's suffering is horrible and you feel sorry for them. In my hands the feeling is still there, what I'm dismembering them. Dogs when they come near me, always I feel like I'm tearing them apart."

Kree didn't want to know anything more. She, too, knew the technique for taking down a fighting dog at close quarters. Take advantage of the moment when the dog has immobilized its jaws in empty space to grab it by the paws and violently wrench them. A very short time. She had done it, too.

Griz was not talkative when the topic was Smoura Tigrit, either. Kree sometimes tried to imagine Griz's relationship with an egg, and the vow of abstinence he had made in the presence or in memory of this egg, but nothing came to mind, no image, and, after a half minute of wandering, she gave up on the subject, considering it too freighted with madness, too worrisome and sickening. It was one of the numerous rifts between the two of them that she had given up on crossing.

But sometimes she returned to Smoura Tigrit and spoke of her as if Smoura Tigrit were a missing woman. He did not unburden himself, but a few phrases escaped him, always the same ones as the conversations flowed by, as the weeks flowed by. Their dialogue was strange, but in the end they did not always avoid it, in the end they trusted each other enough to approach the topic and make Smoura Tigrit a topic of conversation that did not upset them, perhaps because Griz's lies were perfectly established and perhaps because Kree, who held no illusions as to their veracity, made no effort whatsoever to dismantle them.

A conversation similar to this one:

"So you, you lived in an egg, too?" she would ask, gently, as if she attached no importance to the question.

"I'm not the first," he would say discreetly. "And not the last either."

"For a long time?"

"You don't count the time. You suffocate."

"You remember everything?"

"When? When you're in the egg, or afterward, when you've gotten out?"

"Both."

"Inside the egg you suffocate. You think you're going to die. You think you can't get out. You don't think you're going to be reborn. You think about your whole life beforehand, you remember that. Your entire awful life beforehand, up until your death. You might not have any air but memories you've got."

"And then, when you get out?"

"When you get out, right away you're plunged into the terrible life of the world. The outside world. You don't have time anymore to remember what it was like, life before the outside."

"But you remember the egg, you remember Smoura Tigrit."

"Yeah, sure, I wasn't able to forget it."

That sort of exchange. In the afternoon, the morning, the night. Griz might come at any time. Kree was always happy to welcome him.

Or this dialogue, about Smoura Tigrit:

"One day Smoura Tigrit she came into my egg. We were both suffocating, the two of us. We shared the air between the two of us. We were squeezed together."

"Did she talk?"

"Not much. She spoke so I would swear a promise. After the promise we had memories what they were the same. We were too much together to tell the difference. I promised fidelity and abstinence. She left first, before me. She left under the rain."

"Under the rain?"

"Yeah, under the rain, in the mud."

"What was she like?"

"The mud?"

"No. What was she like, Smoura Tigrit."

"I don't remember. But I promised. I remember the promise."

"And now where is she? Are you going to look for her?"

"I promised I would find her. I don't know where she is now. I know she is far away, I know she is close. I'm waiting. She might be looking, too. One day we'll find each other. I get dizzy sometimes. Myriam Agazaki she predicted not too long until I die.

Maybe I'm dying one more time again soon and over there I find
her. I'm dying soon and I'm looking for her until I find her."

"And then?"

"Then what?"

"Then."

"Then, nothing."

*F*irst the absolute blackness, forced stillness, total inertia for a time impossible to measure, a time you are incapable of naming.; long ago the monks would say a snap of the fingers or forty-nine days to measure the duration of their famous bardo, their famous floating world, but in reality it's hellishly longer, insanely longer. From all around you come sounds that are sometimes indistinct, unintelligible, at other times the opposite, so clear that you can name their origin. The impermeable calcareous crust that protects you is thick and you should be deaf to everything rustling outside, but nevertheless sound filters in and helps you to construct the world that awaits you, to construct the first images of what will be your present, one day or another, after your shell has been broken. The first images of the beyond. You hear this sound and, whether you want to or not, you listen. There is nothing to do other than listen to what exists outside. Other than reconstitute the beyond according to its sordid music. You identify, you name, you imagine. Movements, slow, tiny, rhythmless, the degradation of bodies in the process of rotting, the laborious disaster of flesh and fabric in rags as they gradually come to mix and blend, compressed, crumpled, muddied. The uninterrupted plink-plink of dripping. The mud drips, above it's nighttime, most of the time it's night and it's raining. All these sounds are the sounds of the pit. Of the great mass graves in general but, here, of the one into which you have fallen. You are inside the pit, at the bottom or almost the bottom, difficultly conscious, your ear pressed against the inside of an egg. Comatose when it all begins, but then difficultly conscious, most often lost in an opaque dream. Nothing harmonious around you, except sometimes the dripping. Nothing human. Only the repulsive echoes of decomposition, only the promiscuity of cadavers thrown by the thousands one on top of the other, only the monstrous superposition of the dead, the layers and layers of bones and clothing and flesh. The whispering of the dead who whisper without knowing it. Above the rain falls without end. On the surface of the container that hides you droplets plink constantly, at disconcerting, variable intervals. On the other side of the shell, in the hermetic space of the egg, your thoughts struggle to take form. Slowly and interminably you imagine the tricklings of black, blackish tints on black materials that flow with slowness, sticky, sometimes downward, sometimes upward, without any logic. Long ago the monks claimed that low and high were the same thing, and about this they were right. For once they were right. You rest upright in a world where dimensions are muddled. This lasts a lot longer than forty-nine days. About this number they were mistaken. Maybe forty-nine months or forty-nine years. Neither high nor low exists. You have trouble finding words, then you stop searching for them and resign yourself merely to listening. You listen. The pit murmurs and sometimes you understand its language, sometimes you don't understand anything, sometimes you try to act as if you didn't hear anything, sometimes it's like you're imprisoned in a hideous slumber in which there is no language and no absence of language. Sometimes instead your mind sharpens and you go inside yourself, you swim, you dive into yourself to the point of imagining what came before, you dive to great depths. You go far, as far as before yourself. And then you see again or you think you see again the scenes of general killing, images of extermination and images of the end.

A long time ago you were thirty-two or thirty-five years old, you were in the prime of your life and you knew your name and even a bit about your past. What you'd been told about your past or what you understood of it. Thirty-two or thirty-five years of life, a third of a century of disorder and violence, in places devastated by the war, by the ancient nameless wars and by the new ones grafted onto the old, three long decades passed in the company of what remained of human shadows. You were one of them, one of those shadows. In the aggressive night that screamed or stilled all around you, the survivors that you knew had assumed as their sacred task the cleansing of the wreckage. Relieving the wreckage of its dead. To avoid promiscuity with the cadavers, perhaps also to respect old traditions of religion and sanitation. And you, first as a child and then an adult, you were with them. Surviving soldiers and volunteers dig immense pits in which they throw the countless corpses, and you, you're with them, doing this work. The exhausted shadows who bury roughly nine-tenths of the members of the species, or rather nine hundred ninety-nine thousandths. You participate in the effort, you belong to a generation that lives among the dead and you have been raised in something that might be called communist morality, although this morality is mostly based on the fatalism of defeat, a morose contemplation of the wreckage of the human race and no more hope of any kind. Then new episodes of the conflict arise, and during a raid by mercenaries, the oldest of whom must have been about fifteen, a machete demolished your skull. The child who brandished it thrashed the weapon several times, laughing, and your life was interrupted, and there you were in your turn, tossed into the pit. You are maybe thirty-two, maybe thirty-five years old. And, even as day after day bodies fall from above and crush you, you have the confused feeling that once again you exist, but the feeling is like a weak signal coming from far away and, for months, you remain terribly passive, almost no different than the bodies piled in the pit, the strata of bodies that bar your route toward the surface or, at least, complicate your path for a very, very long time. And yet already there is an envelope separating you from the rest of the naked or raggedly dressed flesh, a very thin envelope at first, then it gets stronger. You are incarcerated on the inside of an egg, isolated from the others, an egg in your size where all movement is fettered, impossible, even unthinkable. You try to reassemble memories of myths or stories that might allow you to understand what is happening to you, for your memory was emptied the moment the machete struck home in your skull and, since then, it doesn't help you at all. You don't know what belief you can cling to that will make your fate make sense. The theories of rebirth peddled by some monks in your group don't apply. You are deceased, you aren't walking toward reincarnation, you're not assailed by any visions of wandering divinities, whether peaceful or furious. You're on the inside of an egg, relegated to the very bottom of a giant pit, a situation explainable only by magic, a disgusting magic that horrifies you, but, at the same time, you accept that fate has given you this, this exceptional prospect of lasting still and perhaps getting out. It is dark and it is raining and you are very far from the surface of the world, but you understand and you accept that this is the way it is, that fate has given you this, being surrounded by a shell like a bird's embryo, surviving in the dark, surviving still a little longer in the dark in the midst of the dead, surviving and waiting.

Months later. Or maybe years. Now Griz Uttikuma knows his name. He doesn't know how he learned it, but he knows it. Once and for all he's accepted that he must wait, that he is on the inside of an egg and that an infinite number of dead surround him. He knows he is slowly moving upward toward the surface. Up there storms and fog are frequent; it is dark, it is dusk, and it is hot and humid. Up there sometimes soldiers pass by, seeking who knows what form of combat or victory, then calm is reestablished, a semblance of community life. Long and large, very long and very large, the pit dominates the landscape, and in reality, the pit itself constitutes the landscape. There is nothing but the pit in the midst of the nocturnal plain. The pit is fed regularly, and over the course of years, it has never been completely full. The task of removing the dead from the ruins is the work of a generation. There is always room for new corpses. Those men and women who have dragged the bodies there end up joining them, thus adding a fresh new layer to the whole. Other pit-diggers have taken their place, selflessly pursuing their work, the work of an entire lifetime, but they have become rare. In the permanent night there are no longer many people to fill the pit by throwing in bodies or going there to lie down in their turn. The mud spreads constantly above them, as if nature, rain, the waters of the ravine, and the soil of the small surrounding hills have taken on the task of bringing the construction to an end. Now nobody stops before the pit to recite a prayer to the dead or to think about the monstrous accumulations of the disappeared. The survivors, solitary or gathered in hordes, move past, avoiding the path to the pits, and prefer to extend their journeys by several dozens of kilometers to go around them. Scavengers and raptors are unusual. There are few wild dogs and few birds in the world these days, and it is true that when the pit began to fill they often gathered around the dead, but then, after one or two years, they became rare. On the path to extinction as well. They end up abandoning the pits entirely. The only people still interested in the pits are fanatics, monks who consider it a limitless abomination that hypothetically some eggs might emerge out of the depths. The end of humanity leaves them stone-faced, and yet the idea that the pits produce revenants drives them mad. They were alerted by prophecies, they were attentive to the rumors, the legends, and they've proclaimed themselves guardians of the original orthodoxy, they wait for eggs to appear on the surface of the pits in order to crush them and kill, as quickly as possible, their occupants, whether male or female. Their numbers are very small, they camp out and waste away in the area, ferocious and sectarian, never leaving their post, likely subsisting on worms, ferns, and rainwater. Griz Uttikuma hears them fairly often, walking the length of the pit. The steps of skinny, exhausted men. They can barely stay upright on their legs yet they make the rounds. Some years they disappear. Because of bad weather, perhaps, or because anemia has finally laid them low, or because they got tired of the constant fruitless watching, since no egg ever breaks through the surface of the mud. But others come after them. At least, this is what Griz Uttikuma has deduced from the sounds that come to him. He also goes through long periods of absence, which must be taken into account, periods when whatever is happening up there escapes him. He can feel that he is inexorably rising but he does not know where he is, at what level of the pit, does not know how much time has gone by while he was thinking of nothing. He does not know if his immobile body is developing, what his organic status is; he does not know what he looks like nor does he know whether he has broken with his previous existence or if something of himself, in spite of everything, persists, the imprints of memories carved into him from one time to another, coming from elsewhere, coming from before who knows what, belonging to who knows who. He wonders if he is visited by dreams or if he is a real visitor of reality. The question doesn't worry him, but he is incapable of answering.

One day he has the feeling that somewhere nearby a second egg has formed, and, six or seven weeks later, he feels a very soft contact between the two of them. The exchange endures, intermittently at first, then continuously. It is Smoura Tigrit. She knows her name. She is proud of her name; according to her it is a name of Ybür origin, and the number of Ybür survivors is tiny. Griz Uttikuma objects that the numbers of survivors from other peoples are just as tiny, no matter which people. This dark observation makes them laugh. Their friendship grows, built on this sort of black humor. They are very close. They do not feel the need to communicate all the time. They are unable to determine how much physical distance separates them; sometimes they theorize that they are in telepathic communication and the pits where they reside might be very far apart from each other, and sometimes instead they see reality from a different perspective, they think they live and speak to each other from within the same single egg. They imagine that they are pressed against each other, though they cannot verify this through fleshly sensations, for they are still far from possessing the nerve endings that would tell them this, and further still from being able to move even a tenth of a millimeter. When you're inside an egg you're not aware of very much, whether or not you have the curiosity to wonder about your place in the nothingness or the world. It is like being at the heart of an inert dream, a dream you will not remember; you are strictly inactive, only by some miracle do you know your own name, and you are suffocating. Smoura Tigrit and Griz Uttikuma might be imprisoned within the same shell, in a state of semi-fusion, but they might also be separated by a few meters or a few hundred meters. What is certain, and this they know, is that they are together. They are very, very close, and they are suffocating together.


You are extremely close and that's what counts. You make promises to each other. You promise that you will not separate in the life to come, when you will both be unburied. You swear your loyalty, your assistance, and your love. You make this vow to each other, in case something separates you—an evil power, a terrible renewal of the black war, death—that you will never give up searching for each other and you will do everything you can to end that search with success, meaning by finding each other.

So you already have plans for the future, and even if these plans take into account the horror and darkness that dominate the outside world, they are illuminated by the violent brilliance of love. There are weeks when, having pronounced your magnificent vows anew, you both remain silent for an immeasurable gulf of time. You listen together to the trickling among the bodies, the crumbling of bones and skulls, the work of ants and scavengers, and you listen, too, to the steps of the monks who walk the length of the pit waiting for you to rise from the surface so they can crush the shell that shelters you and kill you.

You hear the rain beating and beating against the surface of the pit. It's very close now. You can easily picture the earth that drinks and filters the water in the night, you can imagine the cadavers above who serve as a roof to the rest, who lie on the mud surface, almost directly exposed to the sky, to the shadow of clouds. Perhaps not whole or identifiable bodies, because it's been a long time already since they were thrown there; the part of the pit where you are has been neglected for one or two years. The vision does not lack for detail, with the final debris of flesh and brownish garments attached to the bones, and here and there dirty heaps and little inexplicable monstrosities, clumps that look like shoulders, like knees. You project yourself in this image, you see yourself already standing up in the free air, in the center of the horribly brownish plain under the rainy night sky, under the clouds that sweep across the scene, standing in the absolute dark gloom of the grounds. You have not yet come out of the egg, but everything indicates you are now in the top of the pit, just below the surface, barely separated from the surface by a final layer of clay and human debris. Everything points to it, the intense outside noises, with a clarity that you have never known up to this point. If all goes well, in less than an hour you might have broken your shell, you might be balancing on your legs, making the movements of life, breathing with full lungs, with the dizziness of standing in mud, feeling the cold drops hitting your face, and feeling the weight of darkness and wind on your skin. And, as you are gathering the words to inform Smoura Tigrit of this news, you realize she is no longer answering.

Smoura Tigrit is no longer answering and you call her, and between two calls you hear the monks who are running, trampling down the walkway and charging into the territory of the pit, taking care not to get swallowed up among the dead. It is a soil on which they have never set foot, which disgusts them. You hear them and you make the images to see them, there are three at first and then a fourth one joins, all in shredded robes, in rags, all rendered skeletal from fasting and despair, from years of waiting in vain, from madness. You can sense their rage, their ferocious haste, their obsession—to fight the abomination, to prevent the abomination from reaching the world, their world, the world of survivors, eliminating what has come from the depths, the appearance of which their prophets have announced, killing, in the name of what remains of the human race, the scandalous being that the pit has brought forth. You hear them moving a little away and you realize they are rushing in the direction of Smoura Tigrit. She must have broken through the last layer of soaked earth and suddenly revealed her presence. You call and call to Smoura Tigrit and she does not answer. There is no more communication between you, or she does not have time to respond. Now she is practically within range of your voice but there are still obstacles between you and her, your shouts cannot yet crack your shell and cross the awful world that comes after the pits, your shouts cannot yet ring out beneath the soot-colored sky, you have yet to pierce the final stratum of gangrenous soil, your own shell has yet to break. The monks zig and zag, growling their prayers, they do not move very quickly, they are afraid. For the first time they dig into the surface of the pit; they fear feeling the earth suddenly giving way beneath their feet, opening to suck them into the depths. They zig and zag. They growl. They skid in the mud. Their path wanders, but in the end, they throw themselves on Smoura Tigrit. They are drunk with that will to murder the other that inhabits the human race, whether on the path to extinction or not, a visceral hatred full of fear of the other. In tatters, eaten away by hunger and disease, half dead, intelligence utterly replaced by religious delirium, the four monks defend human blood, the integrity of the blood of the human species. You hear them shrieking in terror, shrieking with savagery, shrieking with triumph as they break the shell of Smoura Tigrit. You hear them setting upon her, one of them has an iron club and he bludgeons her several times. And then, as they fall silent, you perceive that you, in your turn, have emerged, the rain is pattering directly on the egg, and now a few movements are all you need make to reach the world.

Griz Uttikuma leans his weight violently against the inside of the shell, he can feel it cracking and splitting, he continues to apply pressure; a crack stripes the space around him and suddenly it is possible to move his arms, he bangs powerfully against the walls that imprison him. The shell bursts in the area by his belly and, almost at the same second, it crumples against his left shoulder and around his head. He enlarges the breach with blows from his knee and slides outside. Now he is standing next to the egg-shell debris, finally he has arrived in the darkened world. The rainy night, black as pitch, is there to receive him. The monks approach. He waits for them. He knows what to do. Elsewhere, before, he learned how. The skills have not been lost, nor the reflexes. He feels it, he feels he is completely capable of fighting. In the shadows, in the midst of gusting winds, he sees the defenders of the human race coming. Only one of them is armed with a club, the others have nothing. They possess nothing but their criminal ardor. Years of sterile surveillance, the monotony of the pit where nothing ever changes, and suddenly two eggs appear a few minutes apart. They have nothing to fight with, they have foreseen nothing and, caught in a panic, blinded by rain and their irrational fears, they have forgotten their weapons in their encampment. They run as fast as their skinny limbs allow, their soaked robes so reminiscent of the shrouds enveloping the cadavers that they're trampling, that they're stumbling over. They wobble in the mud, often they lose their balance and put a hand to earth to right themselves, the last one ends up dropping his iron pipe. They bark out magic spells, let out growls; these are no longer monks, these are dogs. Dogs. They have transformed into canines of good size, scrawny and no doubt lacking power, but powerfully nasty. They run towards Griz Uttikuma across the surface of the pit, their speed impeded by the dead, by the bones and rags, by the soaked ground, now on two feet, now on three, now four, like drugged animals dancing with fury and murder. Griz Uttikuma is ready. For a very long time his body has held the necessary knowledge and skill. They are going to rush him, to claw him and bite him. They will attack with their paws first and then their jaws. Since they cannot all reach his throat at the same time, he has practically nothing to fear. He will defeat them one after the other. He moves lightly aside; the first one's jaws close on empty space and he takes advantage of the microsecond of its confusion to grab its forelegs and pull them hard enough to break the joints at the level of the shoulder blades. The second dog leaps and meets the same fate. The third has fallen before the attack; he reaches out with his arms and grabs its leg. Griz Uttikuma crouches and kills it with a terrible forearm blow between the muzzle and the eyes. The fourth one is on him, it is digging its sharp claws into his head, digging furrows down to the bone, trying to bite his nose and catch his lips. Griz Uttikuma shakes himself to get rid of it, gets his bloodied head free, strikes its throat, succeeds in pushing it off. In the moment when the dog is regaining its balance, he grasps its forelegs and twists them. The joints crack. Almost immediately the monk gives up on attacking again. He is the last one, he is broken and he is screaming. He has fallen next to his peers, who drag themselves all around, groaning. Griz Uttikuma kills them one after the other. He crouches and then stands again. He crouches again and stands again. Now he's put an end to the painful crawling, the screams of suffering in the mud, among the shell fragments. The dogs are dead. He has heaped debris and rags on the bodies, and more than anything he feels the nauseating sensation in his hands of having dismembered living beings before putting them to death. The first monk is still moving, despite having received the fatal blow. He looks like he's still breathing. Griz Uttikuma goes back to him and kills him with his feet, this time for good.

A hundred meters farther in the mud. The storm has calmed, the wind is no longer blowing. The landscape is almost invisible, drowned in shadow. You are standing on the land of the dead, on top of the immense pit, no longer giving the slightest glance to the dogs you have just torn apart, that are lying behind you in improbable and hideous positions. It is the first hour of your existence. You are immobile in the night before the remains, before that which was Smoura Tigrit. There isn't a single living being within dozens of kilometers. You refuse to contemplate the footprints and the marks from the killing, the splashes and residue that cover the scene of the crime. You do not accept seeing the crushed face of Smoura Tigrit, the wreckage of her body. Smoura Tigrit is beautiful, radiantly beautiful, without equal. Like you, she is naked. She is incredibly beautiful, she is covered in a gray-blue down of which the thought alone brings tears of love. She is naked and the monks have killed her, and, if one existence is not enough for you to find her, there will be others to follow, and as you promised each other, in the end, you will be together. At the end of time or even before, you will be reunited. You murmur this in the midst of your prayers. It is the first hour of your existence and already you are thinking about the last one, the hour when you will find each other again.

# VI

*S*he was sleeping. A light sleep as always, as she had retained from her previous existences, during her wandering or during the war, a watchful sleep. And so this sound, a second before opening her eyes. Maybe another person would not have awakened. But she did.

A muted crash in the hallway. A brief bang. A mass, of which she formed an imprecise image, a large sack or a large animal. Then nothing more, not the slightest response to the initial shock, not a rustle. Kree was sitting up in her bed, interrogating the silence. She held her breath in order to hear better.

Nothing. All was quiet.

Swiftly she recalled a similar awakening. Weeks, months earlier? She had thought there was a hostile vagabond spying from behind her door. And later, the idea had dissolved in the night. Then one day Griz Uttikuma admitted that he had indeed climbed to the sixth floor and stopped in front of her door. Nothing, all was quiet, but in reality there was someone in the hallway.

She set to work examining the air with a widening of her nostrils. She stayed paralyzed on the sweat-damp mattress. No smell had yet seeped underneath the door. If Loka had been there, she would have lowered her head down to the floor to investigate what was beyond the threshold, she would have sniffed; Kree would have heard her snuffling, maybe sneezing once or twice.

Loka. If she had been there.

Without moving, Kree tried to determine where Loka was.

"Loka," she called very softly.

Loka did not react. She was nowhere. The evening before, though. The dog had disappeared into the apartment, as always simultaneously excited and exhausted from gamboling around all day long. She had drunk and eaten and she had laid down at the foot of the mattress. At no point had Kree opened the door to let her out again. Kree had smoothed the dog's back before lying down to sleep herself. The dog had turned her magnificent gaze on Kree, and she had let out a little yip of friendship. Her behavior was normal as could be. And, in the course of the night, she had disappeared.

Something is really wrong, Kree thought. This is too impossible.

She was avoiding making any sound as she breathed, she went on listening. Went on looking for Loka. Maybe what I'm having a nightmare, she thought. A strange crash out there, my dog she's gone walking through walls. Who knows, maybe I'm stuck in some kind of dream.

But no, she thought then. I'm not anywhere but the real. I'm in some sort of fucked-up real.

Nothing new happened for a minute. She was sitting upright in the shadows. And nothing. In the stifling heat of the closed room. Nothing moved. Even the drop that slid down her back was not cool.

She leaned forward, feeling around on the creaky floor. There had been a sand-filled wind two days earlier and she had not bothered to sweep. The tiny grains rolled beneath her hand. With her fingertips she recognized the iron plate and the glasses set on top of it. Before she went to sleep these days, next to her bedside she left the glasses that Griz Uttikuma had managed to find for her. He had methodically explored the backrooms in the former shopping mall, the stockrooms and shadowy hallways where nobody had ventured for half a century. According to him, you could find anything in there. He had dug around in the repulsive humidity, swallowing the unbreathable air and constantly annoying the creatures that had taken possession of the space. Venomous salamanders, blind rodents, woodlice, tataguamas, and enormous tchakagnagnas. And, one day, he stumbled across a carton where an optician had stacked his treasures. Kree had tried on thirty or so pairs before finally she found the lenses that worked for her. They were large and thick. When she put on her glasses now, she looked like an old Marxist-Leninist woman from the mythical times of the worldwide revolution, one of the ones who sacrificed themselves day and night to keep society from veering too quickly toward the worst. Immediately she took on the strange mien of a sixty-year-old Party elderwoman and she did not care. What mattered, to Kree, was not her appearance. What mattered was that she could see better.

As she did every time, every morning, when she felt the frames settle into place on her nose and ears, she gave a tender thought to Griz Uttikuma. Without falling for him as Myriam Agazaki had managed to fall for her Tibetan, Kree had come to think of him as a companion who was important in her life. A solid companion in disaster. Someone with whom she did not have sex, but perhaps, if all went well, someone who would not go away from her during the time to come, who would remain close to her for a long time, and share with her the monotony of everyday life in the city of the terrible mendicants. Who would follow her day after day on the path of deterioration and, near the end, who would help her confront the final hard blows and the walk toward death. If all went well, if fate or the Brothers did not, in one manner or another, oppose their companionship.

She stood up. The night was starry, the moon on the horizon nearly round. She could move around the studio as if there were full daylight. She made the rounds for her own peace of mind, to assure herself once and for all that Loka had not wedged herself into some improbable hiding place. The rounds, though detailed, were complete in twenty seconds. There was no secret den underneath any of the few poor furnishings.

The dog's smell. That, too, had dissolved into nothingness. Gone out through the walls. The not entirely pleasant smell of her fur, her dirty claws, her backside, her drool, her breath. Kree stood still, inhaling small breaths in order to capture any trace. She captured nothing. No floating impression. She went to the door, putting her nose close to the crack and sniffing again. Nothing there either.

Maybe what I lost my sense of smell at the same time Loka she disappeared? Kree wondered.

She returned to the room, stopped in front of the window. Gray lines and blotches wavered across the city, pale marks punctuating a chaos of coal. Across the rooftops dark shadows alternated with milky lunar light. The labyrinth was more legible than before. Now that she possessed excellent corrective lenses, Kree could make out details, and even guess, within a few buildings, where her friends lived. Myriam Agazaki's street, Gomchen's shop, the Holsch dormitory where Griz Uttikuma had lived while he was still in reeducation, his new place on the border of Central and Mariya Kahn.

At this moment, her friends were sleeping. It was far too early for her to go and tell them about Loka's disappearance.

No movement in the streets. No figures moving, no light. The city was sleeping, its few inhabitants remained hidden and, beyond, the world was neither inhabited nor asleep. Beyond, the world was dead.

For a moment, Kree plunged into a contemplation of the difference between life and death, between an inhabited world and a dead one. She sought arguments that might establish a real separation, she sought images, details. She found no difference in the nature of the two worlds. Neither in the settings, nor in the passage of time, nor in the burdens or voids of memory.

She remained pressed against the window. The steam from her lips had gradually blurred the image of the sky, the night, the city inhabited by survivors, asleep or already dead.

In recent days, even as her existence was passing by without trouble, without any great cause for anxiety, she had begun to feel a sort of progressive inertia taking hold of her. Her way of being in the world was changing, and she was aware of it. She felt much less desire to hang on at any cost, she had no interest in fighting for who knows what faraway collective, or personal goal. Indifference was taking hold of her. If one imagined that she had a light inside her, now that light was wavering and, physically, in every way, she felt her capacity for endurance diminishing. Her killer warrior's reflexes, inherited from her previous existence, were never put to use in the small, calm city of the terrible mendicants, and when she dreamed some nights that she found herself in a close-combat situation, the confrontation always ended with her at a disadvantage. Dreams of defeat, dreams in which she had already given up on surviving. Deep down, something within her was warning that soon she would enter the decline of a new bardo, a world after her death where she would be forever old and forever vanquished.

Maybe it was true that she had begun to grow old, to set out on the final march toward death. Has to start one of these days, she thought.

She wiped the steam off the window. The night went on, the hour of the wolf had not yet come.

And next? she thought. She meant: after old age, after death.

"Bah, next, it'll go on like it did before," she muttered.

Then she was quiet.

She remained still, facing the sky, very dark in the west, dotted with a hundred thousand gems farther south, creamy blue around the moon, on the horizon. She was waiting for dawn before she went to see what had collapsed in the hallway.

Behind her, the smells of sleep, dirty laundry, heavy breath, dirty human breath. Nothing that recalled the presence of a dog.

Outside, down below, an urban mess that had survived cataclysms, its few inhabitants crushed under the Brothers' vigilance.

And elsewhere, who knows where, maybe already in the black world of dogs after death, in the dog bardo, Loka. Wandering, always with her magnificent eyes.

She made up some images of Loka wandering through deserted streets, under the horribly dark sky. The dog was moving; she had survived, she did not seem entirely unhappy in this new world. New but, fundamentally, exactly the same as the one that came before.

"In this black world of after you're dead," she muttered.

*O*nce night had given way to day, she washed and got dressed, and without any tidying up or airing out the room, she unlocked the door and went out in the hallway. She was armed with a machete to cut any aggressive intruder to pieces. She had not heard anything in the hallway for hours, but she was still wary.

The voluminous mass that had collapsed on the sixth floor that night was easy to recognize.

Brother #27.

The terrible mendicant was slumped over, his back partly leaning against the wall, legs stretched out, arms completely limp, as if dislocated. Kree let her useless weapon hang down next to her thigh. Her sense of smell had diminished, it was less sensitive than Loka's now, but it still worked, and she could not help but grimace. Brother #27 was emitting powerful, earthy gusts of tar and rotted meat.

The terrible mendicant had not changed much since Kree had last seen him, back in Drödzaki Street fifty-some days before. She had buried him without joy, convinced that he would never return to the surface, and though she had recited a silent prayer that all would go well for him in the times to come, she had never imagined he could regain consciousness, leave his personal bardo, tear apart his black plastic shroud, and escape his dirt prison.

She approached him. She did not know how best to behave. She considered him for a long moment without speaking, letting herself grow accustomed to his bad smell.

"So, in the end, you managed to get out of there," she said after a minute.

#27 was illuminated by two sources of light: the apartment, whose door Kree had left open, and the plexiglass skylight. He was rigorously still. His time under the tar had turned his black cotton coverall brown, bits of dirt remained stuck to his face and the hair on his arms, and the nails on his large, hairy hands had a rusty color. His eyelids showed no pulse, his stare was fixed and empty.

Since there was nothing else to do at the moment, she murmured a few benign phrases over him, as if the two of them were continuing a briefly interrupted conversation. She asked him if the blue massaquayas in Drödzaki Street had finished their transhumance from one window to another. Brother #27 showed no intention of answering. She waved the blade of her machete in front of his face to get a reaction. He did not bat an eyelash.

"Don't be afraid," she said. "You're not alone. We'll take care of you."

Then she went inside and returned the blade she hadn't needed to its hook.

It was very early. The day was just beginning.

She would not go to the House of Mendicants; she would go see Griz Uttikuma and explain the situation as concisely as possible: Brother #27, after leaving his tomb, had made his way through the night, dragged himself up to the sixth floor, and collapsed in front of her door. He needed some help. She did, too.

She made a final tour of the apartment, with the very slim hope of discovering that her dog had mysteriously reappeared in some corner, and then she left. Just at the instant that she was closing the door, turning her head toward the slouched body of Brother #27, something fled before her eyes and two enormous carmine drops splattered before her feet. A third drop followed. On the wall next to her several splashes were spreading simultaneously. Without warning, a downpour followed, a downpour of blood. It took barely two seconds to fill the small space of the hallway. A red cascade, a violent stench of slaughter. Since there was no way for her to take shelter, all Kree could do was fall back until she felt the cold ladder to the terrace against her shoulder. The drops and blotches fell as if shot from a great height, ceaselessly splattering and bouncing off the rungs, blinding her. It was a tempestuous, tropical rain, much more forceful than the brief showers and red clouds she'd experienced over the past few years. From the very first splashes, continuous dashes striped the space in front of her. Everything was groaning and beating mercilessly against the cement, with horrible fluctuations of color, bursts of wine, bordeaux, sometimes dark, sometimes an intense vermillion, the color of madder, raspberry, vibrant rose, beef blood, purple, crimson, raspberry red again. Mad curtains danced around her, threatened her, stuck to her, and slapped her. She had taken off her glasses, she closed her eyes, opened them again, but the ferocity of colors did not diminish. The red splashes and spatters all over her, on the ladder next to her, on her hands. A heavy layer of blood covered the floor, hiding everything beneath its surface. The hideous surge shifted, swelled within the hallway; a current had formed, close to throwing itself into the dark gulf of the stairwell. The noise was deafening. The ceiling was invisible, she could see nothing above, everything was streaming, everything was dizzyingly red. Against the wall #27 looked very much like a miserable wreck—a pile of rags wallowing in a pattering pond. His black Khmer cowboy outfit was torn at the shoulder, the knees, above the chest, and in many places the bloody shower streamed directly down his hairy skin. The features of his rounded head were obscured, and through the tears, his own and Kree's, it was impossible to make out his glassy eyes.

And. Very suddenly. Suddenly all was calm and quiet. The hallway had resumed its usual appearance. The cement was dry, gray, with no trace of a drop remaining. The air held no stench of slaughter or killing, only the smell of Brother #27 once again wafting aloft, a mix of gasoline, old clothing, and death.

Stunned, exhausted as if she'd had an attack of malarial fever or epilepsy, Kree remained leaning against the ladder. She was having trouble controlling the trembling that had overtaken her hands. Her mind spinning, she stared at the inanimate mass of Brother #27 without quite recalling what it was. Five minutes went by, maybe only four, and her intelligence returned. She moved toward the terrible mendicant to say a few more words. She apologized for the blood rain, hoped he had not been frightened during the downpour. She assured him that he was safe here. She advised him not to move; she advised him to wait until she came back with Griz Uttikuma. Then she turned her back on him.

Then she started down the stairs.

She was still a little confused.

She said: "Okay, Loka, let's go."

*S*and had accumulated in the building's entryway. She examined the ground. There were many footprints. None of them matched a dog's paws. Loka had not come through here in a long time. Other marks in the direction of the staircase. Long and blurred. They might have been produced by Brother #27's clumsy progression. The hesitant walk of a dead man.

Her head was still bent toward the ground when Brother #9 greeted her.

"Kree Toronto," Brother #9 said, "did you happen to hear any noise last night?"

"No," Kree lied.

#9 coughed. An awful, cavernous cough. He cleared his throat and continued:

"Someone dragging something heavy, a sack or I don't know what. Was that you?"

"Oh, no," Kree said.

"I opened the door to look. But I didn't see anything. So it wasn't you?"

"No," Kree reaffirmed.

Their eyes met. Brother #9 was an ageless man, with a cancer victim's grayish yellow face, a face that looked placid at first glance and, as soon as you examined him a little longer, seemed to hide a sort of malice, in any case a total absence of compassion. Aside from his black attire, like a Khmer peasant in mourning, he often topped his head with a straw hat. Among the terrible mendicants, people said, he was dogmatic and pitiless, like in the early days of the new power's establishment, and Kree always had the impression that he watched her and made reports about her when the terrible mendicants gathered behind closed doors, when they were governing the present and the future from the back offices of the House of Mendicants. During public meetings, #9 did not comment. He remained in a corner, as if hidden, and sometimes he took notes without allowing the slightest emotion to show. Kree exchanged greetings and casual conversation with him, but she did not speak to him willingly.

"Maybe someone was coming to see you," Brother #9 suggested.

"Oh no, I didn't see anyone," Kree said. "And actually I've looked everywhere around the stairways and the floors. Because my Loka she's disappeared."

"Your Loka?"

"My dog, Loka. Morning and evening what she runs up and down in the building. She goes through the entryway. She goes with me."

"You have never had a dog, Kree."

"Large and black with intelligent eyes. There's no mistaking her."

"You have never had a dog. These are nothing but lies in your head."

"What do you mean, lies?"

The terrible mendicant considered her with an unchanging expression, that is, without any discernible expression. The yellowish physiognomy of an impassible dissimulator. He lifted a hand and brought together the index finger, middle finger, and ring finger, the gesture of a priest or an orator, when he was neither of those things.

"These are only memories and illusions," he said. "Under your head it's broken. It makes up stories what you think are true. You have never had a dog. The people here they have never seen your dog."

"My Loka," Kree corrected.

"Never," #9 insisted.

She had not lost her calm, but she wanted to spit in #9's face. Or break his nose with a machete blow to the bridge, well aimed and fatal. She wanted to and she could have done it. But since she did not want a conflict to break out between them, and she didn't want the terrible mendicant, on the suspicion of something abnormal or out of a simple, bitter desire to hurt her, to climb up to the sixth floor and discover Brother #27 there, she lowered her gaze.

"Well, I believed that for a long time," she sighed.

#9 nodded his head with a satisfied air. Now his face showed some expression—the pleasure of having talked some reason into an idiotic representative of the people and the assimilated masses.

*L*ater, Kree and Griz Uttikuma arrived in the hallway of the sixth floor.

Griz bent over Brother #27, grabbed his elbow and shook him. He was impressed by neither the lamentable posture of the dead man nor his general appearance.

"#27," Griz shouted in his ear. "Don't be afraid of what's happening. You've gone through a bad time, but now it's going to be all right. You've done the hardest part."

"You got out of the bardo," Kree added. "That's the hardest part."

Griz went on shaking #27's arm without getting any reaction. After Kree's intervention, he let go of the terrible mendicant and stood back up.

"How do you mean we can get out of this mess?" he said, turning toward her.

"I don't know," Kree said.

"He's still right in the middle of it," Griz agreed.

"Like us," Kree said.

"Yes, like us," Griz Uttikuma confirmed. "He hasn't gotten out. Not us either. You don't get out of that."

For a moment they remained contemplative. They considered Brother #27 without giving way to speculation. They were standing very near to him and breathing what the terrible mendicant exhaled, a vile amalgamation—soaked coverall, flesh at the last degree of exhaustion, disused lungs, hair long drenched in sweat, skin in the process of wilting, stained underwear, unnameable humors, loose bowels.

Less than an hour earlier, they had developed a plan of action. First off, there was no question of going to the House of Mendicants to tell them about Brother #27's escape. Since they had been in charge of his burial, they would be accused of negligence and, immediately afterward, of active complicity. With the prospect of a severe, months-long reeducation regimen for Kree—as a representative who had betrayed her class—and a sentence of execution for Griz—as a disloyal reeducated. So they would take care of Brother #27 without collaborating with the authorities and, on the contrary, they would keep the terrible mendicants out of it completely. They would hoist Brother #27 onto the terrace on top of the building, a place where nobody ever set foot. They would set his corpse out in the open air, so that it could be pecked by birds of prey. They would give him a sky burial.

"Okay?" Griz Uttikuma yelled in the terrible mendicant's ear.

He had just finished informing #27 about the different stages of the plan, the arrival of the vultures and the dispersal of his body under the clouds.

Against all expectation, Brother #27 reanimated awkwardly, coughed and mumbled a few thick sounds that, by way of deduction, one might interpret as a positive response. His breath was repugnant. Kree backed off a half a meter.

"Don't tire yourself out talking," she recommended.

Brother #27 emitted an attempt at lowing, which must have meant something, but neither Griz nor Kree understood.

"Okay," Griz said. "Enough talk. We're going to bring you up to the terrace."

Brother #27 acquiesced, then fell silent.

Grabbing him under the armpits from either side, they helped him stand up and walk to the ladder. Entirely focused on maintaining his balance, the terrible mendicant did not say a word. His lungs were working in an incoherent manner, in fits and starts, stirred more by the general movement of his body than by the traditional respiratory accordion of living things. He seemed like he was out of breath or gasping, but not breathing. Griz Uttikuma and Kree did not have to drag him like an obese cadaver, however, for he made an effort and moved himself in a rudimentary fashion, just on the edge of falling, with slow, very slow legs, with strange hesitations at the point of pushing his feet forward, but without collapsing. Held firmly vertical, his arms and shoulders imprisoned by his two accompanists, he advanced. When he came up against the ladder, he gripped it with both hands. He managed not to stumble backward and did not sit down.

Griz Uttikuma climbed up to the trap door, unlocked it, slid the plexiglass cover to one side, then put his upper body through the opening.

"There's a bunch of spiders," he remarked, addressing Kree.

"Bah," Kree reacted.

"Makhagambas," Griz Uttikuma specified.

"I'll bring him up with you, I'll help get him through, but I won't stay up there," Kree promised.

Brother #27 opened his mouth. His lips twisted. He wanted, perhaps, to express an opinion on the creatures that inhabited the terrace, or perhaps he was working on a joke regarding Kree's arachnophobia. Or perhaps he wanted to recount an anecdote about Brother #1, who, so the legend claimed, had eaten spiders to survive in the jungle, which caused great harm to his common sense later on when his comrades charged him with the task of developing a political program. After a dozen incomprehensible syllables, #27 followed his speech with a mephitic sigh, then he began a new series of clicks and long vowels.

Kree patted him on the shoulder.

"Spiders, that's all there is in life," she philosophized, for the sake of saying something.

Contrary to their fears, the climb up to the terrace was accomplished without any great difficulty. #27 scaled the ladder without complaint, even with a relative ease. He paused a few times, lifting one foot fastidiously after the other, clinging to the rungs and flattening himself against them as if he were terrorized by the idea of a backward tumble, but, all in all, he made upward progress, and Griz and Kree's assistance was unnecessary. In his manner, he made progress. Getting through the narrow square of the trapdoor was more difficult. There was no longer anything to grab onto and he hesitated, perhaps frightened by the idea of open air and sunlight. Griz was holding him around the torso, Kree was holding his calves in place on the second-to-last rung. She could feel him wavering. His legs now stiffened, now began to tremble, and he stopped moving them. Griz did his best to pull #27 up and stabilize him. None of them wasted their energy on talking. Breaths, nonbreaths, grunts of effort, puffs, and panting mixed together for two minutes. Or maybe three, and no doubt more. In the end, #27 succeeded in getting past the trap door and standing up beyond it. With Griz guiding him, he passed out of the blinding patch of sky and disappeared. Kree lifted her eyes to the gray cutout, a dazzling empty square. She could hear the two men's slow progression above her head. With an effort to overcome her horror of spiders, she scaled the final few rungs and went through the trap door in her turn. She had said she would not set foot on the terrace, but in the end, she decided against that. She could not leave Griz all alone in taking charge of the tasks involved in a sky burial rite, and she had not separated from Brother #27 properly. In the end she hoisted herself up onto the burning cement, made sure that no makhagambas were in her path, and joined the two men or equivalents who were limping along a bit farther on. The makhagambas were far away, near the cisterns, and they weren't moving. With an effort, one could forget about them.

Then Brother #27 slumped near the little wall that separated the terrace from the abyss. They dragged him a meter farther and undressed him. The terrible mendicant had returned to his comatose inertia. He let them go to work without helping to make their task any easier. After they got his clothing off, they threw it over the side. They watched it fall into a vacant lot behind the building. They stayed there a moment, leaning over, considering these ruins of dirty fabric, then they went back to Brother #27.

"We have to make some cuts so the birds they'll get to work," said Griz Uttikuma.

Once naked, the terrible mendicant was harder to recognize. A mass of cadaverous meat with all dignity and personality gone. A plump corpse with hairy chest and limbs, downy in places.

"I have knives," Kree said. "I'll go down and come back up."

Brother #27's corpse did not bother her, but the makhagambas, immobile and numerous in the shadow of the nearest cistern, as if gathering for a collective attack, set her very ill at ease. Try as she might, she could not manage to forget their presence. Their indecipherable stare, which she had never met but which she knew was borne in four pairs of black marbles, their catatonic vigilance barely disturbed by the tiny ruminations of their mandibles, their patient preoccupation with establishing their supremacy over the end of the world, the vile surface of their bodies.

"I'll be back," she said again.

Griz approved with a nod and did not speak. He glanced at her briefly and nodded one more time. She met his gray eyes and she read there, as she often did, friendship, an inexplicable nostalgia, and a great determination.

She made a few steps on the ground where designs, crescents and curves, had formed in the sand, toward the trapdoor, and as she began descending the ladder, she observed carefully the places where the spiders were lying in ambush, so that, on her return, she could check whether or not they had begun to move around. They always watched from the area by the cisterns, in groups of five or six. For now they remained far enough from Brother #27's body and from Griz. His back was turned to her as he stood immobile before the naked corpse. Kree thought that he was praying silently, and no doubt that was in fact what he was doing.

She opened the trunk in her room. Inside several weapons were mixed with her clothing. Without hesitation, she chose the knife she would use to make slashes in the cadaver. A dagger from the naval infantry, with a heavy cutting blade that she'd sharpened one recent evening to stave off boredom when she could not sleep. She remembered clearly where it had come from. She had found it the day that she had moved into the building, in a hiding place in one of the apartments on the fourth floor that she was exploring with the idea of condemning them soon. The dagger had belonged to one of those unfortunate pioneers who had tried to construct an egalitarianist commune in the tower and succeeded only in killing each other. She had taken ownership of the dagger as a relic from the past, and sometimes she trained with it in her studio, but she had never carried it with her in the street. Knife fights never occurred; they would make no sense whatsoever in the society governed by the terrible mendicants. The Brothers had put a stop to criminal discord among the masses. Now they had a monopoly on violence, and they had established peaceful relations among the individuals whom they led toward the future. It would have been ridiculous to walk around with a knife in her pocket. Kree weighed the dagger in her hand, returned it to its sheath, closed the trunk, and left her room.

When she climbed back up the ladder, she first made sure that no makhagamba, or equivalent creature, had squatted at the edge of the trapdoor in her absence. The threshold was clear, the area around the trapdoor was clear. Before she had climbed the final rungs, her gaze raked the dirty gray sand surface of the terrace. At the very end there was a cistern, and five meters to the right, the body of Brother #27.

Brother #27 had not been moved by Griz Uttikuma and he

seemed to be sleeping peacefully, his legs spread shamelessly, exposing tired-out flesh and tattered sexual organs to the view of all, like a fat nudist bathing in the sunshine. Above him the sky was a dazzling gray-blue, faintly striped with four or five clouds, outstretched mare's tails that promised no rain.

The wind was very weak, but it carried the smell of Brother #27 to Kree. Augmented by a cocktail of urban dust: silica fallen from the sky, spiders, rusty water.

Kree got back up on the terrace. The sand screeched beneath her feet.

And then, a blow to the heart.

Griz.

She looked all around. With her glasses, nothing could escape her. But Griz.

Griz Uttikuma had disappeared.

A vulture had come to perch on the edge of one of the cisterns. Its wings were half folded, as if it were unsure whether to remain where it had landed.

She made a tour of the terrace, leaning over the half-wall. She was afraid of what she was going to see all the way down there, next to Brother #27's clothing in the vacant lot, or elsewhere, in the street, before the entry to the building. She imagined in advance the broken body of Griz Uttikuma, his arms in a horribly twisted cross, his skull smashed. But no, there was no such thing at the bottom of the building. Griz Uttikuma hadn't fallen into the abyss. He had disappeared. He was no longer there.

Maybe he came down from the terrace what I didn't hear him, she thought, she hoped without really believing it.

Another long look around. Nothing. She gave up on calling him. He had not gone away on his own. He would not come back.

Or maybe he preferred that she take charge of cutting up Brother #27 by herself. He had not said anything to her, he had not explicitly conferred that task upon her, but maybe he wanted her to take care of it and take care of it alone. Maybe because something he had lived through long ago prevented him from manipulating the dead, made the acts involved in the sky burial excessively painful for him. The incisions down to the bone, the active transformation of the corpse into meat and food, the repulsive massacre of the body. Or maybe he judged that Kree, moreso than he, was responsible for Brother #27 and the final throes of his fate. For she'd had a special relationship with him, and really it was she who basically gave her public approval of his elimination in the name of the people.

She speculated for a moment about this, about this task that had fallen to her, for which she could no longer count on her friend's help.

Minutes passed. The grains of sand and cement crackled in the sun. On the cistern, the vulture was making itself comfortable. It had folded its wings, moved neither its head nor its neck; it had found a position of perfect equilibrium. It was waiting.

Under the cistern, the makhagambas were waiting, too.

Kree let another minute flow by, then she turned back to Brother #27. Old phrases came into her mind, and she improvised.

"Brother," Kree said. "Do not fear. Everything is peaceful around you. Finally you will go to your end. Soon you will be in flight above the earth. Far from the demons and everything."

Once again Brother #27 seem deaf and inert. His eyes were closed. Nothing quivered in his dead flesh.

"I will help you," Kree said. "I will prepare your passage. Don't pay attention to the cuts what maybe might seem strange. It is only one more illusion. It is necessary and it is nothing. The birds they know what to do next. They know how for your passage."

#27 made a brief sign of acquiescence, a very slight displacement of jaw and chin.

"Then it will be over for good," Kree added.

She crouched down and proceeded to the ritual cutting. She settled for letting her knife pass back and forth three times across the inside of Brother #27's thighs, seven times across his belly, three times across his arms, in the fold of the elbow and under the shoulder. Seventeen times, and seventeen more for the rest. The blade cut better than a razor, it sank in deeply and encountered no resistance, even as she sliced through tendons and ran into bones. She did not attack the terrible mendicant's face. From time to time, she spoke to him, and she addressed herself as well, calling on both of them to face fate with tranquility, exhorting both of them to accept the instant and not to take things as tragedies.

The vulture had begun to observe what was happening five meters away, then, at one moment, it turned its back, as if this operation did not concern it in the least. Very high in the sky, one of its comrades had begun to trace circles. It was barely discernible against the dazzling gray.

Not the smallest drop of blood had disgorged from Brother #27's flesh.

Kree wiped her blade anyway, rubbing it on a tiny sand dune. She was crouching. All around her she could smell the very strong odor of the terrible mendicant's exposed limbs. Soon that vile stench would dominate the terrace without mercy, mixed with the gusts of feathers, of sweating crops and vultures' beaks working to accomplish their sacred task. For several days. And then, nothing. Then, once again, nothing but the smell of spiders, hot cement and uninhabited sky.

She rose and stood upright before Brother #27. Her naval dagger was heavy in her right hand. She slid it into its sheath, but rather than putting it on her belt or in a pocket, she set it next to the dead man.

"Here," she said clearly. "In case this goes badly."

She knew that she should pray, accompany the deceased in the beginning of a second or third voyage, maybe an umpteenth voyage. The crossings of floating worlds came one after another, and she had no desire at all to reflect on what that meant, exactly, for #27, for Griz Uttikuma, or for herself. She was not really familiar with sky burials; she only knew the process through secondhand chatter, and even if she had done her best at guessing the preparation of the corpse, she was not sure that she had respected the magical requirements and the ritual. The spirit of it, yes, she had respected that, but the ceremonial details might have gotten messed up. What was important, however, was a prayer.

She did not know the best words for the situation, and she concentrated on what came into her mind, images of scavengers soaring over the city, over the destroyed lands, over the destroyed world and its black landscapes, over the mass graves. The images lacked precision and epic or religious dimension. She made them appear within herself and she tried to join them with something that resembled a silent prayer. When they got too muddled, Kree addressed Brother #27 directly.

"#27," she said, "don't be afraid. Your liberation is coming. It's coming very soon."

She shifted from one foot to the other on the sand of the terrace. She did not know how to end the ceremony. She circled around the slashed body of Brother #27 to make sure all the wounds were large enough, then she made a second circle for no reason other than to pronounce a silent goodbye. The corpse was ready. The terrible mendicant's physiognomy, without a cut anywhere, expressed a sort of impassive camaraderie.

She continued her internal prayer, then she said her goodbye to Brother #27.

"Hang on," she said, as a final word of advice. "You'll get out of this."

Then she went to the trapdoor, made sure no makhagamba had been so bold as to descend the ladder, and after a final look at the terrible mendicant, the cisterns, the spiders and the vulture, she returned to the sixth floor.

*I*n front of the building, Brother #9 stopped her. He was in the middle of a coughing fit that would not let go, and he indicated with his hand that he wanted to ask her something.

"What's going on up there?" he asked, after spitting out a bloody glob.

"Where?"

"Up there, on the roof."

"Oh, nothing," Kree assured him.

Brother #9 looked skeptical. He was panting, he was having trouble catching his breath. He cleared his throat, as if preparing to spit again.

"Oh, I was getting rid of some spiders," Kree explained. "I went up on the terrace and I got rid of some spiders what they were getting in too close to the cisterns."

"I saw shadows what they were moving," the terrible mendicant said. "Were you with someone?"

"No," Kree said.

"Shadows around the shadows of the cisterns."

"Bah," Kree said doubtfully.

"I thought there were a few of you," Brother #9 insisted. "I wondered what you were all doing, messing around together on the roof."

"Oh, no," Kree said. "There was a bird, for a second. But I was all alone."

"You weren't with Griz Uttikuma?"

"Griz Uttikuma, he's disappeared. I haven't seen him today," Kree declared.

"But I thought he went up to your place this morning."

"Oh no."

"I thought so. I'm not mistaken."

"Maybe it was only in your head," Kree said, conscious of her brazenness.

"Bah," Brother #9 said.

"He's disappeared," Kree repeated. "He's not there anymore."

.

*M*yriam Agazaki's hair was even messier than usual, and what was more, her long silvery hair looked dirty. A crooked collar on her floral print dress, which was clean but terribly wrinkled, as if hastily chosen from a pile of ragged old clothes, the bottom hem coming unstitched, a belt made from badly braided scraps of fabric, mostly blue and white, and on her feet, a beggar's broken-down shoes. Her eyes shone with tears, with great purplish circles sagging below; she looked like a witch who'd just learned she'd be burned at the stake. The same disarray, the same terror. She opened the door to Kree, let her hair swing to and fro for two seconds, then swiftly pivoted and walked away, toward the small courtyard.

"Gomchen he's gone," she sobbed, without turning around.

She had not waited for Kree to reveal her own troubles or even say hello.

"When was that?" Kree asked, following close behind.

Myriam Agazaki answered something Kree could not make out. In the little courtyard several cicadas were singing, and their infernal racket reverberated between the walls and into the hall-way.

Kree: not really the look of a witch sentenced to the stake, not really the demeanor of an exhausted shaman; rather, because of her glasses, the look of a middle-aged communist from the time of the world revolution, enlightened and psychorigid, but her face, too, was distorted with anguish, much like her friend's anguish.

In front of the shaking tent, amidst the drone of insects, the two women shared their suffering and their questions without answers. The situation was nightmarish. At almost the same time and in the same inexplicable manner, the men they loved had disappeared. Kree's animal companion had disappeared into thin air, as well.

"Loka, that's not the same thing," Myriam Agazaki said after a moment. "She was never with you. Everyone we acted like she existed. But she didn't exist."

Kree shook her head. With her glasses she could see all the flaws in Myriam Agazaki's face, all the little wrinkles around her mouth, the stained temples, the white hairs growing thicker in her eyebrows. She let her friend's words flow over her, without reaching her. She concentrated on Myriam Agazaki's aging face, the physical fatigue they both felt. The claim that Loka did not exist still did not become anything concrete for her.

"Well, in any case, she's not there anymore," she sighed.

"It was only in your head what she existed," Myriam Agazaki insisted.

"You sound like Brother #9," Kree commented.

"#9?"

"The terrible mendicant what he lives in the building below me. You know him. A dirty guy."

"Ah, yes!" Myriam Agazaki said, after searching her memory.

In the middle of the strident insect song, there was a silence of two or three seconds. Then the shrill vibrations began again.

"The terrible mendicants a lot of what they say is stupid," Myriam Agazaki continued. "But there the Brother he wasn't wrong. Loka she was nothing but a dream. Nobody bothered you about it, out of kindness, but she was never real."

"Bah," Kree said, shrugging her shoulders. "And what if Gomchen and Griz they were just a dream, too?"

Myriam Agazaki recoiled.

"Oh no, Gomchen and Griz always what they were real. With their weird stories about birds in their head, and maybe that's why they disappeared so quickly. Maybe their existence from before called them back. But always they were more than just a dream."

They spent a minute without speaking, examining the shaking tent, lifting the edge of some fabric here, a badly affixed square of fur there, as if trying to assure themselves that no crawling creature had found inappropriate refuge within. The stitches of the entryway were unstitched. Kree pulled it open to look in. Against her face she felt the hot gust of confined air, the smell of leather, the wooden framework, feathers.

"If what we used this to find Gomchen and Griz Uttikuma?" Kree suggested.

"It's never worked like it's supposed to," Myriam Agazaki observed.

"We have to try," Kree said. "Even if it doesn't work right, we have to try."

"Gomchen he always said it was junk," Myriam Agazaki said. "He said without a user's manual we'd get nowhere. He put up this tent just on a whim, he told me. He reimbursed me the dollar for the installation."

Again they circled the tent. The courtyard and its walls emitted heat, strong smells of cement, guano, leather, and lizards. The cicadas went on singing endlessly, forcing them to raise their voices as they spoke.

"I'm going to try even if it doesn't work well," Kree said. "It's for traveling to Griz and Gomchen. We have to."

"You have too many pins what will start moving around in your head," Myriam Agazaki objected. "The needles too they travel. You could drown if what you have a blood rain in your head."

"The blood rain, I already had it this morning," Kree said. "It never happens twice in one day."

For a moment they talked it over anxiously, needles, blood rains, the disappearance of those they loved, the black space, travel, shaking tents, birds. Gomchen had disappeared two days before, a total mystery. His telecommunications shop was closed; Myriam Agazaki had gone there several times already. Gomchen had been more somber in recent days. Something was bothering him. Two terrible mendicants had visited him and harassed him about his business, accusing him of fostering the absurd hope among the working classes that electricity might soon be reestablished, and also of propagating counterrevolutionary magical beliefs. They'd asked him about his relationship with Myriam Agazaki, about the objects that Myriam Agazaki stored in her home, the remains of bourgeois technologies of long ago, radios, toasters, shaking tents. A certain Brother #18 had advised him against getting mixed up with a self-proclaimed healer who would rather forage for demonic herbs than attend a public meeting.

"I started having terrible dreams about him again," Myriam Agazaki said again. "He was gliding, soaring over I don't know what piles of dead bodies. I don't know if he was flying or if he was already dead."

Myriam Agazaki recounted other dreams about Gomchen. According to her, Gomchen and Griz Uttikuma had never gotten out of their egg nightmares. Both of them came from the same land of mud and graves.

"And if they've disappeared, it's what they've gone back there," she said in conclusion.

They were both quiet, and stood for a moment, anxious and pensive before the tent.

"I'm going inside," Kree said. "I'm going to find Gomchen with Griz Uttikuma and Loka."

"First I'm going to look at your needles if what they won't come out while you're in the shaking tent," Myriam Agazaki said.

"You think they will?"

"Yes, otherwise in there you could get hit by lightning or too much blood."

"Bah," Kree said waving her hand to show she didn't care.

"First what we look at your needles," Myriam Agazaki insisted. "The needles, a cup of tea with the herbs what they'll lead you on your voyage. And then, the ceremony."

"Then what?" Kree asked.

The cicadas' buzzsaw chorus was so violent, she hadn't heard the end of her friend's sentence.

"The ceremony!" shouted Myriam Agazaki. "What you're going to go searching for dead and missing people!"

*A*fter sharing a small pot of herb-infused tea with Myriam Agazaki, Kree went to settle inside the shaking tent, and to start off, she had trouble finding a position. The cement underneath her buttocks was sandy, and she had to get up and use her hand to clear away the bits and dust she'd been sitting on. Resettling, she sat down again with her legs crossed. She sat up straight. In front of her, Myriam Agazaki was stitching the entry back up with leather laces and thread. The holes had already been pierced and the process went quickly.

Nothing was happening yet, but already she was enclosed in a canvas cell that she could not leave except by setting out in search of her vanished friends, on the improbable roads of the black space.

The temperature inside the tent was less suffocating than she'd feared, even if it was slightly hotter than outside. She'd been afraid she'd be immediately soaked in sweat. Yet some air came through the circular opening that sketched out a large spot of leaden azure over her head. Slightly tipsy from Myriam Agazaki's concoction, whose first effects she was perhaps experiencing, Kree received this warm breath descending from the sky, and she closed her eyes to savor its hints of hot stones, lizards, and guano. She tried to maintain her calm, tried not to think about what might happen during the ceremony, which neither she nor Myriam Agazaki knew much about. Well and maybe what this shaking tent really doesn't work, she thought.

"But yes what it will work," Myriam Agazaki promised immediately.

Serenely responding out loud to a thought that Kree had formulated inside her head.

"So you're listening to me brain to brain?" Kree asked.

"Now we are two," Myriam Agazaki said. "The whole time during the ceremony we'll be two."

Then she went back to work without offering any further explanation.

Calmly, Kree started to look around.

Added to the feathers hung here and there were plumes of down, left behind by birds who had stayed in the tent very briefly before realizing it wasn't a suitable place to rest or nest. There were visible imperfections in the structure: the hoops sagged, the canvas fabric and squares of badly tanned leather were creased and hard, birch branches without a single leaf, clusters of little bells that looked like sick black kidneys. The ground was bare, with a residual scatter of gray crumbs and unreadable marks etched by streams of water, bird shit, and plugs of down feathers along the base.

Kree breathed deeply, getting herself accustomed to the smells. The smells on the inside of the tent.

The only sounds around her now were those made by Myriam Agazaki, in her efforts to close Kree in. The cicadas were quiet.

There was a long pause.

Myriam Agazaki was getting ready for the ceremony.

Kree did not think about anything. She waited.

Then Myriam Agazaki began singing in a monotone, first without hitting her drum, then thumping it with a leather-covered mallet, a piece of hardware that the Tibetan must have graciously provided as a supplement to the wireless telephone, so she would forgive him for burning the user's manual or putting up the tent in an unorthodox manner. The song distorted the phrases that Myriam Agazaki was reciting, elongating the vowels and rendering the few consonants oily and intense. The phrases had meaning, but she who was pronouncing them did not know it. Onto her memory of archaic Ybür Myriam Agazaki grafted magical babblings and the croaks of beasts she had heard in dreams, or in reality, during episodes of war or extermination. If someone had asked her what language she was speaking to call on the spirits, she would not have known what to say, or she would have explained that the language surged up from the depths without being able to specify which depths she meant. The language did not belong to her, and it was of the same basic nature as the mallet thumps on the skin of the moon-drum. She accompanied the beating heart of the world as she ordered the traveler to begin her walk as a dead woman.

Kree sat cross-legged, without a thought or almost, in the center of the narrow space, and straight above her head an imperfect circle opened to the mass of gray-blue sky, still dazzling, still burning, and she listened to the shaman song and she waited, and after only a few minutes, the opening lost its color, the light dimmed, and everything became twilight.

Everything became twilight, and then black.

The temperature changed, the space enlarged. In the increasingly solid darkness, paths opened.

Then Kree got up and began to walk.

*S*uddenly Kree almost fell; it was well past midnight and she had been walking for hours without stopping. Her right foot slipped between two clumps of mud. She wavered, found her balance again, and stopped. The rain was falling harder, the rain was hammering violently against the ground all around her. Kree was dressed like a peasant woman from the rice paddies, barefoot, in dirty black cotton pants that fell to mid-calf, and she was protecting herself against the foul weather beneath a straw cape and a conical hat with a large circumference.

The night was crushing with blackness and she screamed.

The nauseating warmth of the soil. The shadows. The dizzying tumult of water.

The water. The dizzying tumult.

Eight or nine hundred meters away, a point of light attested to a human presence or something of the sort. In the rest of the landscape, there was nothing. Kree stood in the midst of a cultivated expanse bereft of vegetation, a shadowy plain of black furrows. And so that faraway light, strong enough at that distance to pierce through the darkness and the thick curtains of deluge. Kree was going in that direction.

Then she was closer. A low, elongated building. Maybe a warehouse or a workshop. In the middle of nowhere. Surrounded in black, in puddles and stinging rain. The light came from a stretch of glazed windows, not very high up, set underneath the roof.

Kree went closer and stopped wondering about the purpose of this building. She knew what this was. She knew it intimately and without the slightest doubt. A pemmican factory, a slaughterhouse that prepared, smoked, and reduced cadavers in order to make pemmican.

Cadavers of animals. Of dogs reduced to meat.

And she knew just as intimately and without the slightest doubt that this was the place to which Loka had been transported after her disappearance or her death.


Lightning strikes nearby, without thunder, and for a long moment it illuminates the building of exposed cinderblock, and it lights up the entire uniform and roadless countryside beyond, the black infinity of plowed lands, and the thick, twisted and congested clouds in a quarter of the sky above take on a bright blue coloration, a transparent blue, a smoky and then a very dark blue, and then they go out. A long moment, for the phenomenon lasts several seconds, three, maybe four. Which gives Kree time to notice someone in front of a door, under an awning, someone with a cigarette in his mouth. Someone. A man who is smoking and squinting in her direction. He has just seen her come out of nothingness, he is wondering what's the meaning of this destitute figure, this peasant woman hidden under her hat and rain clothes, he is wondering what she wants and what she's going to say or what she's going to do.

Darkness returns. The rain has marked an instant of hesitation under the lightning, but then it comes back stronger. Without any change in pace, Kree crosses the last few meters that separate her from the man with the cigarette. He's a foreman, he's wearing a black rubber apron over his chest and belly, he is immobile, corpulent, and calm. He is not afraid of her.

Kree stands up at her full height, dripping. Her large headcovering hides her face. The light from the factory windows is not enough to make her fully visible. She uses this to her advantage. Now she knows where she is, what she must accomplish here. Certainty anchors deep within her, she has not come here by chance. She has come to avenge Loka. And, for the time being, there are basic rules to observe, so that the action may take place without any obstacles. Do not frighten the person you are going to kill. Do not reveal your intentions. Leave the future victim his absence of concern.

"Any chance you're hiring?" she asks.

The man looks at her. He does not like the way her face remains in shadow; no doubt he'd rather meet her gaze, decode what she has behind her eyes. Nothing but her voice and movements are available for him to judge by. He is fifty-some years old. He is sheltered from the rain and she is not. He is head of the factory, thinks he has a little power over things around him. He has no idea who this woman is, but the fact that she remains out in the pouring rain as she speaks comforts him in his belief that she is his inferior. Down and out, wandering, unemployed, dripping, not daring to slip under the awning without his permission. An inferior.

"It's no work for pussies," he offers reluctantly.

"I've done it before," Kree assures him.

"Bah," the other says.

"I know how to cut meat," Kree says. "Except dogs. No dogs. Dogs, I don't like it."

"Here we do a lot of dogs," the foreman remarks.

"Oh," Kree says. "What kind of dogs?"

"Whatever dogs come through."

"And female wolf-dogs who are very black and intelligent, with magnificent eyes?"

"If what they come through, we do them, too," the man says.

Kree pretends to think about it.

She pretends to think about the man's response, the dark things it contains that he doesn't say. Then suddenly she throws off the panels of her straw cape, and she has closed her hand over a long piece of steel that she's been hiding underneath, a piece of slightly curved sheet metal, slightly larger than a saber but with the same shape. She's been sharpening its cutting edge for days. That's what her memory tells her. Her mind is not burdened with memories, all she remembers is that Loka has disappeared, she has lost Loka and she has spent hours and hours refining this piece of metal, making it into an instrument of death as effective as a katana. A makeshift weapon but a fearsome one. She springs it forth from the protective sheath that she has cobbled together with wood and rags. And now, without wasting even a tenth of a second, the blade goes to work. Holding her breath for later, without a care for the curtain of rain falling before her, she splits the rubber apron with one slanted blow, from bottom to top, from the left hip to the right shoulder, a deep, decisive cut, which takes the man by surprise and immediately renders him helpless. Then she repositions herself on one side of the man's head, she slips under the awning, and from there, she draws a whistling half circle. The man doesn't have time to react. He still has his cigarette butt between his lips, his eyes wide open. She decapitates him.

Then she gathered herself underneath the awning for a short, static moment, the cascade falling from the roof behind her and doubling the cascade falling from the sky. She did not say any prayer, but she remained immobile. Then she decided to be done with this sequence. She stepped over the foreman and opened the factory door.

The odor assailed her. Kitchen smoke, fresh meat, smoked meat, the flesh of slaughtered and skinned dogs and animals.

There were three people on the night shift, a man and two women, who looked absorbed in their work, so intoxicated with their work that they attached no importance to the entrance of a creature from the night who was now replacing their foreman. Kree approached the table and examined them.

The two women's heads were entirely covered in long, shiny black fur that hid their eyes and mouths, in contrast to the human normality of their facial features. One was young and rather plump, with a prominent belly, perhaps due to pregnancy, which she protected behind a semi-rigid apron that shone like a scarab's shell; the other was neither old nor young, and terribly dressed, the upper half of her torso wrapped in shredded webs of clothing that hung from her shoulders and fell in a tangle to the ground. The hands of both women were busy at work on the carcasses, using small knives or their fingers to pull off the last fragments of flesh. Whatever they detached from the bones they threw into a zinc container that they shared in common. Since each of them had four forelimbs rather than two, the work progressed very quickly.

The male worker had two extra arms as well. Three quarters of his face had been burned in a fire and the rest of his fur was permanently singed, giving him the hideous appearance of a monster escaped from an oven.

Kree gave the three of them names: Roach Girl, Raggy, and Char.

On top of the grills smoking behind them, bits of meat were slowly stiffening. The small number of coals burning below ensured they would dry out without roasting. The coals smoked. All along the walls, here, there, and everywhere, hung carcasses or parts of carcasses. From time to time, Char went to unhook one and deposit it in front of himself or one of his comrades in dismantlement. Once the bones had been carefully scraped clean, they were tossed onto a careless heap on the other side of the table, the half of the workroom where Kree was standing. The floor was covered in clavicles, ribs of various sizes, knuckles, and tibias. Kree wasn't sure if she recognized the animals whose hindquarters had ended up on the worktable. She didn't think that there were either dogs or wolves on it, at least not this evening.

The foreman might have been making a dark joke to test her out, or maybe the most recent shipments had been particularly poor in canids.

Kree stood fixed in front of Roach Girl, Raggy, and Char. The three workers paid no attention to her. She kept her distance from the bones they tossed, but not too far away from the central lighting, a few gas lamps that hung on chains from the ceiling, rather low over the table. She said nothing and considered. Whereas she had cut off the foreman's head without hesitation, obeying an order for vengeance that left no place for indecision or doubt, now she did not quite know how to pursue her nocturnal path. Suddenly she felt no certainty about anything. It was difficult to see any justification for her criminal intrusion into this pemmican slaughterhouse where she had never before set foot, of which she had never heard a word spoken. She searched for an image of Loka, for the dog had disappeared from her memories. The dog was gone, nothing but an inaccessible shadow, without physical or affective content. Kree's memory presented her with nothing but vague landscapes without personal history, without stories and without dreams. Everything had escaped her, all the threads that might have tied her to an earlier existence. Again, she thought, aware that something was being repeated but unable to say exactly what. An echo of awareness coming from nowhere. She delved a little longer into the foggy echoes inside her head, now without any objective and without much urgency.

Well, at least they haven't taken the present from me, she thought.

The present. The smoke-filled workshop, the roar of rain on the rooftop, the sounds of butchery, the four-handed women, Roach Girl and Raggy, the man who'd gotten out of a fire or a furnace, Char.

Well yeah, all this, she thought.

She had just decided to be content with the little she had, even if it was extremely disturbing not to know who she was, nor why, after stumbling through the muddy night, she had entered this place with the intention of exterminating everyone working there. Amnesia had pillaged her memories and, at the same time, had attacked the reasons for her vengeance and destroyed them.

She had not dropped her makeshift saber. The point was dripping a little. The foreman's blood and fat were stuck to the blade and had stopped moving down the long cutting edge. Before pushing on the door, she'd shaken her blade above the headless cadaver, as samurais once did after they'd finished off their adversaries. Without changing her position, without moving toward the cutting table, now she broke her inertia and passed a rag over the blade, enveloping it once again in the fabric that served as its sheath, and she slid it onto her belt.

A few minutes passed.

The rain battered against the building and its drumming became a continuous bass, and standing out over it were the quick cuts, wrestings, and tearings from the skeletons, the banging of bones thrown onto the tile, and the total mutism of the workers.

A continuous bass. A drum. A thousand drums. A thousand moon-drums. Kree let the sounds invade her and replace all thought. The ceaseless broken rhythm followed a sort of order. In the heart of the racket, in the heart of this swirl of tumult and silence, she could make out the regular hammering that helped her stand upright, that encouraged her to pursue the path, or at least to continue having a semblance of existence.

She remained a moment as if asleep, inhabited by an inchoate thought, then she awoke.

Char was giving her a measuring look and, next to him, Roach Girl and Raggy were no longer leaning over the fragments of bodies. They were standing up straight, and as each of them wiped her four hands on her filthy rags, they examined Kree with a questioning manner.

The gas lamps cast sufficient light over the workspace, the table and the trays, the ovens for drying, the floor littered with bones. The flames were static, undisturbed by any air current, and the shadows did not dance. The atmosphere was heavy with smells, smokes, and sounds, but at the same time there was nothing hostile or dangerous developing in the room and, actually, the scene in progress was peaceable. Four creatures out of the night stared calmly at each other, under a near-normal light that protected them from the fury of the shadows outside.

Kree regathered her thoughts. During the minutes that had just passed, she had been mentally passive, and now she felt that she knew what she had to do. And, first of all, what she had to say.

"Listen," she began. "I did not come to hurt you. We are alike. We are alike in the night at the bottom of everything. We were born together into the same horrors. I am here together with you."

Across from her and closest to her, Raggy was clearly making an effort to read her lips. The other two had no reaction at all. They stared at her with their mouths slightly open, like idiots or dead people.

"I did not come into this slaughterhouse to do them harm," Kree repeated. "Char he's come out of the fire. Raggy and Roach Girl like him they have two more arms than me, but fine, all of us we come from the same nightmare world. Together we are the same family of nightmare and misery. We are all together brothers and sisters in disaster. Too bad if we have to kill some humans or birds or even dogs. It's so we can continue. It's so the way before us it continues.

"I am not going to attack you," she went on.

To expand on her speech, she embarked on a more political discourse, with magic words that arose within her from some cerebral hiding place over which she had no control. Ideological tirades came pouring into her mouth and she made them sound out beyond her lips. She pronounced them with an air of conviction, but, deep down, she did not care. What mattered was the attention of her listening audience. She had set out to talk about the proletariat and the masses, stupefied by ungratifying tasks. She denounced the capitulation of the unions and the Party, the historical aberration represented by the terrible mendicants, or their equivalents in the few sectors where survivors still lived. Then she interrupted herself, actually rather quickly, and right in the middle of a sentence. She could see that her audience was having trouble following her. Suddenly the thought occurred to her that the three creatures facing her either didn't understand human language or they were deaf and mute.

She fell silent.

She considered them for a handful of seconds without reopening her mouth. Their eyes hidden under glistening fur, their gazes in which nothing shone, two arms dangling down to the hips and two shorter ones with hands that clenched the empty space at about belly level. An immense lassitude emanated from their stillness.

Well, maybe what they really need is instead what I make motions and motions, she thought.

She made a sign asking them to be patient. She concentrated a few seconds, and in the paradoxical silence, in the roar of the rain, surrounded by the continuous hammerings and batterings, she set herself to moving her body, to fashioning simple ideas with her hands.


She tried to exhort them to abandon their work, to leave with her in the night, to go somewhere far from the factory, somewhere else. To drop everything once and for all, their despicable life, their nightmare existence. She had little idea what destination they would seek together, and she was perhaps still hesitant to burden herself with these three in her nocturnal wanderings.

But she was prepared to lead them, toward nothing, toward a new stage on the road of disaster, a new variation, feeling herself guided toward it by something resembling instinct, or a waking dream, or external instructions.

Just as she was about to perform once again her miming motions, thinking her message had not succeeded in getting through, Roach Girl tossed her rubber apron against the wall and went searching in a corner where she had stored a waterproof canvas cape. The others did the same. Char threw his apron among the bones in front of the table. His raincoat was not made of canvas, but looked like the one Kree wore, that ample straw cape that she had not taken off when she had entered the building. Raggy put on a black overcoat with an unstitched collar hanging down onto her chest. Roach Girl pulled on her cape and hood, all of them got dressed, laced up whatever could be laced, with bamboo or straw hats to protect their heads.

Before they left, Char took care to put out the lamps, one by one. Raggy and Kree helped him. Roach Girl did not participate in the extinction of the flames. She stamped with impatience near a small door, which faced the one behind which the foreman lay at rest. She had demonstrated her intention of pouring gas on the ground, and Char, in the name of who knows what principle, prevented her from doing it. She regretted not setting fire to the factory before leaving, and though it was difficult to make out her features under the cape, in the middle of the fur covering her face and the growing twilight, it was obvious that she felt stymied and was sulking.

Out in the night and the mud, they began walking in single file without exchanging a word. Kree had taken the lead, and she did not turn back to verify whether her companions were moving at her pace or letting the distance grow. The dark was ferocious, the rain frenetic. Under Kree's bare feet, spattering puddles, muddy streams, a splashing, oily earth that hissed, that made her slip, a warm, almost hot earth. Despite all of it, Kree advanced at a steady pace. She did not ask herself any questions; she moved as if shadows had always composed the familiar backdrop of her existence, as if all her life she had known nothing but the black space, the water beating all around her, the absence of shelter, the absence of goal.

Nothing in the night indicated that day would come, that the illumination was going to change from one moment to another, and after four or five hours of uninterrupted walking, they called a halt. Roach Girl, Raggy, and Char would not allow her to shake them off: on the contrary. Raggy stuck to Kree so closely that, when Kree stopped, Raggy almost ran into her. The others were close on her heels. All three stopped at the same time and stayed close to each other. Kree soon joined them. She had no reason not to attach herself to this small, devastated group who had found solidarity in the nocturnal walk and the deluge. Their multiplied hands were almost invisible in the dark, their impossible faces disappeared under their waterproof clothes and hats, and, anyway, Kree didn't really care about the physical details that made her different.

She threw out two sentences that nobody answered, a question to which nobody responded. Raggy and Roach Girl seemed exclusively interested in contemplating their feet, which were buried in clay. Char directed his gaze toward his right, as if he were analyzing something on the horizon, even though nobody could see more than two meters in the total shadow and rain.

They remained thus one against the other, in a compact, companionable formation. They were four travelers halting together. They rested. None seemed like they were out of breath or suffering any aches and pains, but they rested. The pause lasted until Char pointed one of his hands toward the distances that he alone could make out. It was a suggestion. Raggy threw a glance in that direction and gave a slight shrug. Roach Girl didn't bother to look. With an opinionated air, she went on observing the bottoms of her legs, which were sunken in the mire. Kree examined the darkness, squinted, pushed her head forward. She could not make out anything beyond Char's fingers, his hairy paw, sculpted in soot.

Okay, Loka, let's go, she thought.

The name had come to her mind entirely by chance. It didn't have any significance for her and for a second she wondered why she had let out those two syllables. Lo-ka. No, really, that meant nothing to her.

She detached her feet from the mud. They had been buried up to the ankles. She set off in the direction Char had indicated, again took the lead of the small troop. She could make out the sounds of suction and plunging into the earth that told her the three others were coming along behind her. Then the roar of the rain took over, the incessant cascades and drums welled up in her ears, and in the world in general there was no longer anything else.


They walk and walk, all four of them in single file, for hours. The time is unmeasured, but the hours go by. Feet sink, stick, and stumble in the rain-stippled clay. Neither Kree nor her comrades complain. They do not grunt when they have to pull themselves out of the muck; they move stubbornly forward in the dark without thinking of anything but their physical efforts, if that. As for Kree, she thinks of nothing at all.

The rain around them marks no pause, it does not alter its rhythm, it makes music on the swamped earth, it makes music on their hats of hardened leaves and cord, on Roach Girl's waxed canvas hat, on Kree's straw cape, it makes a dark music, magical music, ritual music. None of the four listen. They hear it, they submit to it, and they walk and walk.

No end to the night. No respite in the rain.

No rest in the drum and the gush.

And yet, without any sign in advance, the hammering around them suddenly diminishes and stops. The dark around them loses its opacity, and a weak, glaucous illumination brightens the countryside. Maybe in the black space this is called morning. Everything remains terribly dark, even though now it's possible to see a little farther. The gaze reaches distances that previously seemed impossible to attain, fifty meters, a hundred meters.

And a hundred meters away, in fact, there's a chain-link fence cutting the landscape in two, from horizon to horizon, if one can call them horizons. Kree and the others head in that direction, toward a breach that seems to serve as a door. In reality, if a door really was once clipped out of the metal trellis, someone has taken care to replace the chain-link panel and reattached it with knotted threads, or braided grass, or leather. They stop in front of it and Kree draws her makeshift sword and cuts the ties one after another. Then she pulls away the iron rectangle and tosses it aside, into the mud. Then she passes through the cut. Raggy, Char, and Roach Girl cross through in their turn. The passage is narrow, but they manage not to get scratched on the barbed points along its edges.

The downpour has decreased to a fine hot mist. The soil has lost the look of a cultivated field; now it is grassy and firm. Kree hears her companions' footsteps behind her, she does not turn back to encourage them to continue following, and she does not turn back to measure the distance now separating her from the rain, from the bare earth and the chain-link fence they have crossed through. The immediate past is very near and, at the same time, getting so far away that it might have never existed. All four of them move forward. Kree is no doubt the first to distinguish in the darkness a second fence barring their path. They reach it, and at first they do not find an opening. The barbed wires are heavy with ivy, with vines. Roach Girl clings to the fence and shakes it. She shakes it furiously. Her action loosens something in the vegetation, something that looks like a vertical opening. Kree crouches and starts cutting through the knotty stems, the fat leaves. Underneath there is, in fact, a hatch. The edges have been stitched back onto the mesh with cloth ribbons. She cuts through the ribbons patiently, her blade blunted and chipped from grating against the iron wires. Little by little the opening is made. She pulls on the panel of mesh and the opening is complete. She gets rid of the cut out panel and her saber at the same time. To the left and to the right the fence is lost in the night, and before them, some thirty meters away, is another enclosure. All four of them slip between the spiny, vegetal, and metallic hanks of wire. In the weak light, the plants have no color. Everything is shades of black.

They reach the third fence. By hand they untie the knots and ligatures that surround the third door. They all work on it. It is a final narrow passage. Next, they walk for a moment and they arrive within sight of an elongated, single-story building, which resembles the pemmican factory that they left in the night at the beginning of their voyage together. Which resembles it furiously.

Stunned, they regroup, shoulder to shoulder, heads low, as if to consider collectively and gather courage, members of a team on a suicide mission organizing themselves one last time before action and combat, but they say nothing, in part because Char, Roach Girl, and Raggy are mute, and in part because there is nothing to say.

Then Kree lifts her head and moves toward the building. Nobody stands guard before the door. There is nobody for her to decapitate before entering. In any case, she no longer has the blade that would allow her to do so. She turns the handle and pushes the door. She enters. Her comrades in disaster follow her.

The workshop is easy to recognize, although the lighting is much weaker. The fixtures are the same, the hooks, the hanging carcasses, the small vats, the long work table, the floor scattered with bones of all sizes. The light has changed. It is meager, dispersed by only two lanterns positioned over the work area, in the midst of the meat scraps and debris. What burns in these lamps is not gas. It is coconut oil. The smell hangs persistently and strikes Kree right away. Its perfumed smoke is familiar to her. Always she has associated it with the terrible mendicants, with their nighttime gatherings in the back offices, this odor that impregnates their traditional bat-colored vestments, the day after they make their decisions on executions and interrogations. Without warning, part of her memory gets back on track. The terrible mendicants.

The smell is there, the coconut oil whose emanations accompany secret ceremonies. And the Brothers, too, are there.

Seven. There are seven. Neither men nor women, terrible mendicants. Sitting around the table in black coveralls. Hands on the table in front of them, skinny fingers casting arachnoid shadows, still and curled among the bits of meat. They are not picking flesh from the partial carcasses within their reach, they are not at work making pemmican. They are speaking among themselves. Or rather, no. They have just interrupted the debates that were underway. They fall silent and look at the intruders.

They look with closed, unhappy, untrusting faces, where fear is legible here and there. Kree and her comrades carry with them the black shadows of the black space, they are dressed as wanderers at the final degree of devastation, and they do not look friendly. What is this demonic band of paupers, murmurs one of the Brothers between his teeth, his voice very low, but everyone hears him. Another pulls a macramé demon-ward out from under his shirt, a ridiculous and unfinished demon-ward, and he waves it near a lantern. The oily smoke spreads with even greater power, but the demon-ward has no effect on the visitors, and the terrible mendicant shrugs, then puts it back against his chest.

Again, after this nightmare sentence and these useless motions of exorcism, everything is still.

The time of observation and uncertainty lengthens. A half-minute scene of catatonia, then forty-nine seconds, then a minute. Then, with authority, Raggy and Roach Girl go to take their places among the terrible mendicants. They take off their coats, still heavy with rain, they let the coats slide to their feet, and they sit. As if the stools had been reserved for them. Now they are sitting at the work table, as if determined to participate actively in the meeting. The oil lamps shed a weak light over them. Indescribable physiognomies with shining black pelts, and now they extract from their ragged jackets the four arms and hands that each have hitherto kept hidden, and they show their intention to get to work. Raggy and Roach Girl start fiddling with the strips and shreds of meat that the Brothers have neglected to move aside.

Aside from the small rustlings of meat and a few fizzling wicks, silence reigns. Char and Kree remain standing a few meters from the table, in the scent of coconut oil and in shadow. They hold themselves back, Kree because she does not want to compromise herself before the terrible mendicants, Char for hidden reasons or perhaps for no reason, perhaps simply because he is exhausted after the walk and his body is no longer responding to the slightest incitement. Kree does not make a move and within her she can feel a wave of rage rising. The terrible mendicants disgust her. She does not remember where her hatred comes from. It seems to her as if once she was among them, as if she got mixed up with them in the course of her successive travels, but here, she realizes that she cannot stand them, that everything they represent inspires her with repulsion and fear. She can no longer tolerate their power over her, over the survivors that surround them, over the dead. She does not compare them to the makhagamba spiders, she is not sick to her stomach thinking of them, but she does not want anything to do with them. And suddenly she tells herself, if she had not thrown away her happenstance saber, despite the knicks in its blade she would go after them and she would attack them. She would try to decapitate them one after the other, all seven of them. And who knows if she would not ask Raggy and Roach Girl to lean over their carcasses, to pull out whatever they could use to make pemmican, to make food to distribute to the working classes, supposing that the working classes still exist outside these walls.

While these criminal fantasies swirl inside Kree's head, the terrible mendicants return to the normal agenda for their meeting. They take no notice of the presence of Roach Girl and Raggy among them, as if these two were nothing but impalpable visions, as if they could do no harm, as if they had for a moment slid into their fantasies only to then evaporate into nothingness. The terrible mendicants do not see how Roach Girl and Raggy circle first to one side and then another, how with their numerous agile fingers they cut a notch from the throat, the cheeks, the rib cage. The terrible mendicants do not feel how they pull a rib from here, a vertebra from there, and there a cube of flesh; the terrible mendicants feel nothing, they act as if Roach Girl and Raggy did not exist. The terrible mendicants do not want to admit that they are being devoured. They pretend not to notice that Char is approaching the table in his turn and plunging his claws into their bellies or severing their arteries at the level of the thigh or the shoulder. The meeting is continuing as if nothing were happening. They discuss important issues, speak rapid phrases, do not want to waste their time on details. They speak of enemies of the working class, traitors to the revolution, witchcraft, witches. They bring up the problem of men, women, and birds who enter into alliances with demonic forces. They agree in principle on a radical cleansing. Names are pronounced. A list is made. Kree doesn't understand everything. The voices of the Brothers, situated just in front of her, seem muffled by an incalculable distance, perhaps because their origin is far away and their communications have gaps, and perhaps, also, because Char, Raggy, and Roach Girl are impeding their speech, digging around in the terrible mendicants' lungs and mouths even as they try to make their interjections. Even though the sounds are distorted, Kree recognizes her own name and the name of Myriam Agazaki. They are accompanied by death sentences.

Several of the terrible mendicants have fallen to the ground. The head of the Brother nearest to Roach Girl rolls on the ground and joins them. The speakers do not bother to react. They refuse to give in to the forces of the night.


At that moment, drums vibrate outside the building. A tom-tom, regular beats on a stretched skin struck by a hand or a mallet covered in leather. A shamanic drum. Kree gets the feeling that she's waking up. She shakes herself like an animal, she gets herself moving. She moves forward, she moves around the worktable, she avoids the pieces of the terrible mendicants, the head of the one Brother, the bones. She goes around Raggy, who goes on working over a carcass. She heads to the back door; she opens it and she goes out. She doesn't give a single backward glance. She leaves the building behind, and she leaves behind those who exist there. She feels that she is more free when she is alone.

She closes the iron door again. The bolt on the iron door clacks into place. Just in case, she slides the bolt on an exterior lock. She doesn't want to be followed.


Outside, the night is dense, shot through with the strong smells of humidity, soaked grass, swamp plants, muck. There must be running water nearby. For a moment Kree doesn't see anything, because there is no light, then a faint illumination springs from the earth and allows her to understand that she has reached a familiar place. The riverbank where she used to bring Loka for a bath two or three times a month. She cannot make out the setting with much detail, but she thinks she is at one end of the Mariya Kahn sector, on the vacant lot that separates the water from the housing and the refugee dormitories.

She stops moving, as if she has arrived at the end of her route. She lets the hours pass. She waits.

She breathes. She takes several deep breaths. She brings the night to enter her, the end of the night maybe, the end of the ceremony. She recalls suddenly that she should find herself on the inside of a shaking tent, in Myriam Agazaki's courtyard.

She remembers that she sat down inside the tent, that it was hot, that above her was the blinding gray sky. She remembers that Myriam Agazaki went to look for materials to give rhythm to her invocations, her prayers, and her dance. She remembers the beat of the drum.

She has the impression that the light has changed. She can make out the stars above her. Already the last ones. The sky is going to brighten. The nocturnal shadows will dissolve.

From the river comes a humid breeze, a warm steam heavy with scents. Green algae, fish, sand. Spongy wood. Moss. Crayfish. Tired grass.

She waits another moment, a few minutes or perhaps a few hours.

"Not to worry," a voice says next to her.

The voice of Myriam Agazaki.

"**M**orning it's on its way," says Myriam Agazaki.

Morning is, in fact, making its appearance on the embankment. There is almost no sound behind them, Myriam Agazaki and Kree, almost no movement in the Mariya Kahn sector. A Prussian blue fog still envelops the world. The temperature is gentle, far from the extremes of broad day, to the point that it even feels a little cool. Now and then the river murmurs, emits a brief lapping sound, then is quiet. The water is low, the river is not large, the place was named the "Mariya Kahn Ford" at the beginning of the terrible mendicants' reign over the city, and a few handfuls of survivors crossed it in order to then disappear into the dormitories, before being interrogated and reeducated. Tortured souls coming from nowhere, coming from the west, the last ones. The flow of refugees has dried up, but the ford is still in use, no longer as a passage but instead as a place where the residents of the nearest dormitory, Holsch, like to wash up, preferring it to collective showers. There isn't any more privacy, but they enjoy wading in the tiny green whirlpools, in the oily green inlets. This is also the place where Kree used to bring Loka so that the dog would rinse off, getting rid of her greasy fur smell and her parasites.

The image of Loka leaving the water, giving herself a joyful shake, a shower of bright rain drops scattering all around her, an image like a final farewell. Kree does not pause over it.

"Bah it's not too hot," she observes.

"It's dawn," says Myriam Agazaki. "The mendicants they said we're waiting for dawn."

"I don't remember when what they said that," Kree confesses.

"You don't remember anything?" asks Myriam Agazaki.

"I'm not sure," Kree says. "I don't remember everything."

Myriam Agazaki tells Kree what has happened. Kree's amnesia doesn't surprise her. Nobody ever comes back intact from their time in a shaking tent. No need for a user's manual to tell her that.

She summarizes.

The Brothers interrupted the ceremony and put a stop to it. They caved in the moon-drum, and they tore apart the tent's opening. Right there they read the writ of accusation. Both Kree and Myriam Agazaki were accused of illicit witchcraft, collaboration with demons, and espionage in service of dark forces. The Brothers were reading a paper that had been approved by the popular masses, a sentence of execution. Kree and Myriam Agazaki were also suspected of constituting a counterrevolutionary group that facilitated Brother #27's escape. The representatives of the poor peasants and the martyred soldiers had decided to eliminate them. The Brothers had brought them to the riverbank. They had ordered them to wait until dawn.

"And after dawn?" Kree asks.

"Bah," says Myriam Agazaki.

Behind their backs, their hands are tied with necklaces of black pearls, which are theoretically magical but produce no effect on them whatsoever. The knots aren't very tight. There is actually nothing holding them back besides these symbolic shackles. The Brothers did not even imagine that they might try to run. Their punishment is to be inflicted in the name of the sovereign people, and of course the two women, whatever their crimes and depravities might be, will obey the collective rules. It is unthinkable that they might rebel, that they might seriously imagine crossing the ford and losing themselves in the uninhabitable lands that surround the city.

Unthinkable.

"We could cross the ford and get out of here," Kree neverthe-less suggests.

"Yeah, we'll do that soon," Myriam Agazaki says. "But first we have to die."

The sky is getting brighter and brighter. The stars have gone out.

"You haven't gotten my needles out yet," Kree observes. "That's going to weigh me down if what I die now."

"Well, no," Myriam Agazaki says. "That can't weigh you down. Your needles in you those are lives and deaths. If what we take one out, another one will grow back. It will go on that way. There's no end to it."

"There's no end," Kree repeats.

"No," Myriam Agazaki confirms. "The lives and the deaths in-side you. That will last as long what that lasts."

"And then?" Kree jokes.

"And then, nothing," Myriam Agazaki starts to giggle.

She's like a little girl who has just said something silly.

"Then, nothing," she says again. "Like now."

*A* door opened in the wall of one of the buildings for refugees, and two figures set out on the path that ran alongside the dormitories and turned in the direction of the ford. Kree had her glasses on her nose, and she recognized them from far away: Leonor Morskoï and Abayïl Whitewater. Each was carrying a shovel on his shoulder. They looked exhausted, and their image did not remotely match that of workers marching enthusiastically toward a field, toward a heroic task, toward the future. But they were marching, anyway.

They crossed a grassy embankment and entered the narrow vacant lot alongside the river. The two women watched them come.

They approached, and when they were a few steps from Kree and Myriam Agazaki, they stopped.

"Morskoï," Kree said, "do you still have your girl's first name?"

"Yes," Morskoï said, without raising his eyes to look at her. "I didn't ask them to change it."

"You're right not to," Kree approved. "Leonor Morskoï, that's a pretty name."

"Yes," Morskoï said. "It sounds good."

They remained silent, all four of them, for a long minute. Kree, dressed in stinking rags like someone who hadn't had time to change clothes after her stay in the land of the dead, Myriam Agazaki with her shamanic gown in gaudy colors, the two men dressed like workers at the beginning of a long day, their overalls washed clean, not yet soiled with dust, grease, or blood.

"What are we waiting for?" asked Myriam Agazaki.

"Dawn," Whitewater explained. "We're waiting for the dawn."

"It's already here," Kree pointed out.

"They said to wait until the dawn it's really bright," said Whitewater.

The two men danced from one foot to the other. The two women remained still. There was no hostility between them, only a certain discomfort, full of things unsaid. They waited together, four shipwrecked comrades, waiting together for the dawn to become fully light.

Then, as the minutes went by, Kree stopped examining the men's discomfiture and turned toward the river. Myriam Agazaki did the same.

The landscape was not one of prodigious beauty. Silt drying on the banks, a few muddy rocks, tufts of bushes here and there, calm waters, it is true, of a dense green, rather pleasant to contemplate. There was nothing remarkable on the other side, a vacant lot with two collapsed hovels, and a yellowish plain farther off, which led to the destroyed lands, invisible from the riverside.

"Do you see, up there?" asked Myriam Agazaki.

The two women raised their heads at the same time, without worrying about the light that surrounded them and indicated that the time had come.

A hundred or so meters above them, three large birds were circling.

"Vultures or eagles," Myriam Agazaki continued.

"No," Kree corrected. "These birds they're bigger."

"Them, too, they're waiting," said Myriam Agazaki.

Kree tried to make out details in the plumage, the colors, the behavior, the way of beating the air to ride the currents, the facial features, after she had disregarded the beaks. Her glasses suited her vision perfectly. She did not perceive everything, since the birds were in ceaseless motion and the angles of the image were changing, but she could see ten times better than she had before, back when she'd had to squint to make images less blurry.

"I recognize them," she said with confidence, maybe lying, maybe mostly to offer a last-minute consolation to Myriam Agazaki and to herself.

"You think so?" Myriam Agazaki was doubtful.

"Gomchen, Griz," Kree announced. "I recognize them. They're up there. They're going to come down. They're going to join us."

Myriam Agazaki sighed and let out a very small, very soft laugh, almost blissful. She was not sure of what Kree was claiming, but she had decided to believe it. Her vision was not as sharp as Kree's, but she stared at the birds, she followed them attentively, and she found a way to forget everything else.

Behind them, Whitewater and Morskoï had unstuck the shovels that had been resting on their shoulders, inert and inoffensive, up until then. Kree smelled the rising scent of their sweat, the odor of their anxiety, their clean clothes already damp with anxiety, the odor of their work tools that were about to become the tools of death.

"And #3?" asked Myriam Agazaki.

"#3?" Kree repeated.

She could not believe that her friend was still thinking about the terrible mendicants.

"The third one," Myriam Agazaki said. "The bird with white all over its breast and underneath the wings."

Kree concentrated on the third raptor. She had not looked well enough up until then, no doubt because she had paid more attention to Griz and Gomchen. The bird's whiteness was phenomenal, and despite the distance she could make out the delicate, caressing feathers. They had a fairylike beauty. She felt a wave of affection growing within her, soon blossoming, making her dream.

"That's Smoura Tigrit," she said. "That could only be Smoura Tigrit."

"Bah," commented Myriam Agazaki.

*O*n this comment, the shovels struck down, and the conversation was interrupted.

*Manuela Draeger* belongs to a community of imaginary authors that includes Lutz Bassmann and Antoine Volodine, among others. Her works that have appeared in English include *Eleven Sooty Dreams* and *In the Time of the Blue Ball.*

*Lia Swope Mitchell* is a writer and translator from Minneapolis. Her translations include Georges Didi-Huberman's *Survival of the Fireflies* (Minnesota, 2018) and Antoine Volodine's *Solo Viola* (Minnesota, 2021), and her original fiction has appeared in *Asimov's, Apex Magazine, Terraform,* and elsewhere.